The Gatekeeper Trilogy

Book Three

BUFFY THE VAMPIRE SLAYER™

SONS of ENTROPY

CHRISTOPHER GOLDEN and NANCY HOLDER

An original novel based on the hit TV series created by Joss Whedon

POCKET BOOKS

New York London Toronto Sydney Tokyo Singapore

This book is a work of fiction. Names, characters, places and incidents are products of the author's imagination or are used fictitiously. Any resemblance to actual events or locales or persons, living or dead, is entirely coincidental.

An *Original* Publication of POCKET BOOKS

POCKET BOOKS, a division of Simon & Schuster Inc.
1230 Avenue of the Americas, New York, NY 10020

For information address Pocket Books, 1230 Avenue of the Americas, New York, NY 10020

ISBN: 0-671-02750-6

First Pocket Books printing May 1999

10 9 8 7 6 5 4 3 2 1

Printed in the U.S.A.

In the crypt, Buffy froze. Her blood turned to ice in her veins. Belphegor was in Sunnydale.

"My dear?"

She didn't know what to say. A hundred smart-ass remarks died on her lips. From the part in her hair to her toenails, she was terrified.

"All will soon be lost, Slayer, and you will die," it said. *"But if you come to me willingly, I will be merciful."*

"That's what they always say, and then they pull the trapdoor lever," she said, fighting to stay calm.

"Mark it well, my dear," Belphegor told her. *"This day is your last."*

There was a terrible ripping noise far beyond the door. Maybe that was the sound of the demon lord ripping free of the breach . . .

And maybe it was the sound that the fissure made as it separated the floor beneath her feet, revealing sulfurous flames.

"Hell is opening," Belphegor thundered. *"Welcome us."*

Buffy the Vampire Slayer™

Child of the Hunt
Return to Chaos
The Gatekeeper Trilogy
  Book 1: Out of the Madhouse
  Book 2: Ghost Roads
  Book 3: Sons of Entropy

The Watcher's Guide: The Official Companion to the Hit Show
The Postcards
The Essential Angel

Available from POCKET BOOKS

Buffy the Vampire Slayer young-adult books

Buffy the Vampire Slayer (movie tie-in)
The Harvest
Halloween Rain
Coyote Moon
Night of the Living Rerun
The Angel Chronicles, Vol. 1
Blooded
The Angel Chronicles, Vol. 2
The Xander Years, Vol. 1
Visitors

Available from ARCHWAY Paperbacks

This one is for my mother.
—C.G.

For my sisters, Elise and Leslie Jones.
—N.H.

Acknowledgments

Christopher and Nancy would like to thank Joss Whedon, Caroline Kallas, and the cast and crew of *Buffy;* our editor, Lisa Clancy, her assistant, Elizabeth Shiflett, the Pocket team, Debbie Olshan, and each other. Christopher would also like to thank Connie and the boys; his agent, Lori Perkins; Tom Sniegoski, Jose Nieto, Stefan Nathanson, and Jeff Mariotte. Nancy would like to thank Wayne and Belle; her agent, Howard Morhaim, and his assistant, Lindsay Sagnette; the Babysitter Battalion; Stinne Lighthart, Brenda Van De Ven, Lydia Marano, Maryelizabeth Hart and Jeff Mariotte, David Hinchberger, Charlie and Kathy Grant, Yvonne Navarro, and many other dear friends who have been so good to me.

Acknowledgments

Christopher and Nancy would like to thank Joe Weldon, Caroline Kallas, and the cast and crew of Brimstone; editor Lisa Clancy; her assistant, Elizabeth Shiflett; the Pocket team; Dorrie Olson; and each other. Christopher would also like to thank Connie and the boys; his agent, Lori Perkins; Tom Sniegoski, Lee Nisco, Stefan Nathanson, and Jeff Mariotte. Nancy would like to thank Wayne and Belle; her agent, Howard Morhaim, and his assistant, Lindsay Sagnette; the Sunnydale Mansion [illegible]; Thomas [illegible]; Lydia Marano; Maryelizabeth Hart and Jeff Mariotte; David Hirschberger; Charlie and Kathy [illegible]; Yvonne Navarro; and many other dear friends who have been so good to me.

SONS *of* ENTROPY

Prologue

WILLOW SHOUTED TO THE GHOSTS SHE KNEW WERE lingering in the ether around them. "Come back! We need a little help here!"

"You guys!" Cordelia screamed, looking wildly around at the numbingly gray landscape. "You dead guys, where are you guys?"

They were alone on the ghost roads, a place filled with nothingness. Xander's still form dangled between them, and a demon raced toward them from an open breach.

So there was nothing to do but fight it.

Willow tried to lower Xander gently to the ground, but his ankles slipped through her fingers and his feet hit pretty hard. She sucked in her breath and said, "Oh, Xander, I'm sorry."

The demon lunged. "Cordelia, look out!" Willow cried.

"Oh, my God!" Cordelia shrieked. She let go of

Xander's wrists and his head whapped the ground *very* hard. Then she arced around in a circle like a shotput thrower with her hand in a fist, and smacked the end of the nearest tentacle.

To Willow's complete amazement, the piece broke off and whirled away like a Frisbee.

"Willow," Cordelia said, with a look of shock, "Willow, this thing is like, defective!"

Cordelia hit it again, and another tentacle broke off and shattered as it fell to the ground.

"Wow!" Willow said excitedly. She raised her fists and ran up to the demon. "Come on, monster thingie! We're ready for you!"

They both shouted with disappointment as it whirled around and hastily retreated.

"Willow!" Cordelia's eyes shone. "That was incredible!"

"Yeah," Willow said, shaking a little. Now that the battle was over, she couldn't believe how brave Cordelia had been. "It was."

Cordelia picked up Xander's hands. Willow looked down at him. He looked terrible. The blood on his chest from the gunshot wound had dried, but there was so much of it. They had to get him to Boston, to the Gatehouse and the Cauldron of Bran the Blessed, as soon as possible. Which was why they were on the ghost roads.

Giles had not been positive that regular humans—those not touched by the supernatural—could walk the ghost roads and live. Was simply being here killing Xander? Was that why the ghosts had already tried to lay claim to him?

Were she and Cordelia going to die here as well?

Cordy murmured, "Sorry about the bump, sweetie." To Willow, she added, "Let's get out of here. I hate this place."

Then, like the chickens they were, the phantom walkers of the ghost roads reappeared. Now that the demon was gone, their translucent faces and bodies blurred and flickered as they swarmed around the three friends.

Almost hungrily, the dead tugged at Xander's body.

"God, Willow, stop them!" Cordelia shrieked. She turned her attention to the spirits who harried her boyfriend's still form, pulling at his clothes, lifting his limp hands, and she screamed. "Leave him alone! He's not dead yet! Not yet!"

Willow felt hysteria begin to swirl up inside her, thought she might throw up, wiped away hot tears that had begun to spill down her cheeks. And then she stood her ground.

"Back off! We have safe passage! Leave us alone!"

Around them, all was gray light, as though it were permanent dusk. The featureless landscape of the ghost roads stretched out forever, and yet they could only see their immediate surroundings, as though some invisible fog blotted out all else.

But their immediate surroundings were bad enough. The faces of the traveling spirits—many of whom were lost here on the ghost roads—coalesced around them, some into full-bodied form. One, who in life had been a very old man with a bushy beard, drifted close to Willow.

"We are giving you safe passage, girl," he said, in a voice that came from everywhere and nowhere, from all the mouths of the traveling dead. *"Or shall we simply stand aside for the creatures who even now tear these walls down around us?"*

Willow swallowed. She knew what it meant. What he meant. Below her feet was solid ground, or what passed for solid ground here. She had done enough research to form a hypothesis about that, about the ghost roads existing so close to the real world, shimmering with energy an eyeblink out of reality, that oftentimes the ground beneath their feet was real. If that was so, then the farther one went into the fog on either side of the road, the farther one drifted into the limbo nothingness between the ghost roads and what waited for those traveling or lost souls at their final destination.

Deep in the fog, Willow could see ghosts battling demons. It was surreal, a mist-enshrouded ballet between the dead and the undying that made her feel like a tiny girl again, staring into the black abyss of her closet. She tried not to look.

The dead were protecting themselves, of course, but they were also giving Willow and Cordelia safe passage.

"He's one of us, now," the old man's ghost said, pointing at Xander. *"He must stay."*

"Dammit, I said he's not dead!" Cordelia shouted, before Willow could respond. "What? Are all ghosts deaf, or just you?"

Willow glanced at her. Now Cordelia was dragging Xander by his arms, as best she could. Her muscles were straining from the effort, and Willow wanted to help, but it was up to her to make sure they weren't stopped. That was more important right now.

"Move, Cordy," she said in a low voice. "Get him out of here."

"What does it look like I'm doing?" she snapped, eyes wide, on the verge of crying or laughing or screaming, but—Willow observed—on the verge of something.

"He is ours," the old man's ghost whispered.

The last thing Amy Madison wanted to be doing that night was standing in an alley across the street from the entrance to the Fish Tank, which was just about the sleaziest bar in Sunnydale. But the past couple of weeks had been ones of terrible fluctuations in magickal energy in the area, with monsters of every shape and kind flooding the town.

She'd done her part. While she didn't really hang out with the Slayer and her friends—in fact, she kept to herself mostly—and she wasn't about to start dedicating her life to protecting the innocent like Batgirl or something, well, it was her world, too.

So instead of trying to link up with Buffy and the others, all of whom had plenty on their minds, she was sure, Amy decided to just back them up. To keep her mind and her power as a witch magickally attuned to Sunnydale, and step in if it seemed the Slayer and her Watcher had overlooked anything.

With all that had been going on, how could they not?

And there had been plenty going on. In fact, Amy was certain that she didn't even know the half of it. Frankly, she didn't want to. It was enough to just do what she could, and leave saving the world to the one who actually had the job. She had a hard enough time getting her homework in on time and giving her dad the kind of quality time he liked. Well, and she liked, too.

Now it had started to drizzle a little, and the salty smell of the ocean not far away was pungent on the breeze. It helped cover the urine and garbage smell of the alley. Pretty much the old trademark alley smell, as far as she was concerned.

Her magickal searches had located something the others had not encountered, something lurking in disguise, keeping a low profile. Something inhuman. She didn't know if it was a demon or a monster, but she'd used her power to track it here, to the Fish Tank. The thing was inside.

Problem was, Amy wasn't old enough to go in, and the bouncer sure wasn't going to let her by.

She was pondering what to do about that problem when the screaming started inside the bar. A woman crashed through the blacked-out windows of the bar and landed in the street. Her face had been torn off and her abdomen ripped open through the trampy dress she wore.

The bouncer ran screaming from the bar, then turned down the street and booked it, not even looking back.

So much for not having ID, Amy thought.

Then she hesitated. This wasn't her gig. She wasn't brave. Not really. But somebody had to do something.

As Amy was sprinting across the street toward the entrance to the Fish Tank, a dead man flew through the window and landed in a broken heap. It slowed her slightly, and she thought about turning back. Then there came a long, chilling hiss, and Amy looked up to see it standing there, inside the open door, holding another corpse behind it. Its fingers were thrust into the eye sockets of the dead man, dragging the body behind it like a little red wagon. Vitreous fluid dripped from its hand.

The creature stopped when it saw Amy.

Eight feet tall, it was dark green and brown, covered with scales and gills and spikes that dripped poison. A stingerlike tail swung in the air behind it. It was like nothing Amy had ever seen before, not even in her arcane texts.

When it laughed, it sounded as though it had phlegm in its throat.

It dropped the eyeless corpse, which hit the damp pavement with a wet slap. The rain continued to fall, ran down Amy's forehead, flattened her hair. The monster flicked out a long, forked tongue like it was a New Year's Eve party horn.

Then it came for her.

"Goddess Hecate, work thy will!" she shouted, raising her hands, contorting her fingers to form the powerful spell. Magickal energy crackled between them. "Mistress of creatures great and small, confine this beast to its—"

With a savage backhand, spiny knuckles slicing into her cheek, the monster knocked Amy back against the Fish Tank. Her head struck the brick, and she collapsed to the pavement. She could feel something warm dripping down the back of her neck now, not like the cold rain. It was blood. She smelled it.

So did the monster.

Its guttural, sickening laughter increased as it strode toward her, muscles rippling, scales shining in the rain and the light of the full moon.

Blackness closed in on her vision, and she knew she was slipping into unconsciousness. She would be defenseless then, and just as dead as all of the people inside the Fish Tank.

"Confine this beast," she whispered, her lips numb, mumbling. "Confine . . . to its distant lair."

Amy fell unconscious just as the laughter stopped.

Her eyes flickered open several minutes later at the sound of approaching sirens and she realized she wasn't dead.

Where her cheek touched the pavement, it slid in something sticky. Her own pooling blood. She could taste it on her lips.

It occurred to her that she had a calculus test in the morning. Before she fell unconscious again, Amy smiled thinly, or thought she did. She couldn't be sure because she couldn't feel her face.

At least she'd have a good excuse for missing school.

Chapter 1

Buffy Summers, the Vampire Slayer, clenched her fists as she scrutinized the cars passing Oz's van left and right. Giles had brought the more spacious van instead of his own small, half-dead car to collect Buffy and the others when they'd unexpectedly burst out of the breach into Sunnydale, but, as a driver, Giles was still Giles.

As he chugged along, Buffy's heartbeat jammed into high gear. They carried precious cargo, namely, the Gatekeeper's heir, Jacques Regnier. Any of the cars whizzing past them in the night might be loaded with assassins equipped with everything from magick spells to rocket launchers.

Short and brown-haired, the boy sat beside Buffy in the first of two rows of passenger seats. That charming vampire couple, Spike and Drusilla, had held him captive for weeks. His father was on the brink of death. And a five-hundred-year-old sorcerer who hated his entire family was running him to ground like an animal. Yet he sat quietly beside her, trying to deal. Buffy figured if she was eleven and had all that weighing her down, she would have given in to the total, raw urge to go completely ballistic by now.

She had not dealt very well when she'd found out she was the Chosen One. Some weird guy comes up to you and tells you you're the only girl in all your generation who can battle the forces of evil, you figure he's read a few too many comic books. Then you find out it's true.

A couple times, you try to quit.

Once, you even die.

But in the end, you get back up, you come back home, you go back to work. At sixteen, though. At seventeen. But not at eleven.

"Damn," Giles said, stepping on the brakes as something white skittered across the road in front of the headlights.

"Keep going," Buffy said to him. "It was probably just a spirit. They're trying to escape the ghost roads. They're desperate to get out of there before Hell breaks through."

As she thought of those lost and wandering, tormented souls, Buffy shivered. She had found two Slayers among them. She prayed that trudging along the ghost roads was not her final reward, not after all this struggle.

From the seat behind Buffy, Angel said, "Oz is coming around."

Buffy sighed. "Do what you have to do."

She heard a dull smack as Angel knocked Oz out again. It was the night before the full moon, first of the three nights during which Oz was a werewolf.

Back in Florence, he had attacked Buffy and Angel. Micaela Tomasi, now sitting in strained silence beside Giles, had pretty much saved their butts.

At about the same time that, here in Sunnydale, Xander had been shot.

"When we get to the mansion, we'll call the Gatehouse," Giles said, as if he could read Buffy's mind.

"We call my mom first," Buffy objected. "Then we'll pick her up. We'll move everybody up there and—"

Giles said, "Oh, God, Buffy, you don't know."

Buffy went numb. "About a lot of things. Which one is this?" She leaned forward. "Giles? What don't I know?"

He looked into the rearview mirror and she saw the reflection of his eyes in the ghostly light of the dashboard. It was one of those moments that freeze-frame in your mind; it was a moment when everything stopped and she waited for him to tell her something unspeakable.

He didn't disappoint.

"Buffy, I'm afraid your mother has been abducted," he said. "The Sons of Entropy took her and—"

For at least five seconds, she couldn't speak, couldn't move, couldn't even think. She couldn't hear a word he said. She was a vast field of endless panic.

"Buffy?" he said gently.

She leaned forward and slammed her fist down on his backrest, very near his head.

"Where were you?" she shouted.

Micaela half turned, murmuring, "Buffy, I'm sorry."

Buffy glared at her. "Your father did this," she hissed at her. "Your *father.*"

"He isn't really my father," the woman replied weakly.

Giles looked sharply at Micaela. She dropped her gaze.

Buffy turned back to Giles. "Where is she? Where are they keeping her?"

"Xander was shot trying to save her," Giles said, and it occurred to Buffy in a vague blur of jumbled thoughts that she hadn't even asked how Xander had been hurt. Everything was so bad and they had to move so fast that all she had done was register that one of her best friends might be dying—might be dead by now for all she knew—and then she had moved on to the next bad thing on a list of very bad things.

"Where were you, Giles?" she accused him again, feeling everything slipping away from her. "Cross-indexing your stupid reference books? Making tea?"

"Hey," Angel said from the backseat. "Buffy, take it easy."

Buffy whirled on the vampire. "Don't you defend him! I risked her life by going off to Europe to find Jacques. I left her alone. I couldn't be here, but he *was* here. All he had to do was take care of her. *We* knew there were leaks in the Watchers' Council security. *We* knew there were bad guys everywhere you looked!"

She turned back to Giles. "So where were you?"

Suddenly she was aware of a small hand moving over her closed fist. She looked over at Jacques Regnier. Tears were rolling down his face. He raised his other hand and made a circle in the air with his forefinger. Buffy felt a tingle against her cheek, almost like a kiss. There was another connection between them now: they each faced the potential death of a parent. But he had been prepared for his. He had known his father would one day die.

"We all die," he said softly, as if he could read her mind. "Even Gatekeepers."

Tears welled but Buffy fought them back. Fought down her anger and the terror that threatened to completely wipe her out.

"They came to my apartment," Giles said. "They disguised themselves as floral delivery men, and she let them in."

"Mom," Buffy said, incredulous. How could she have been so careless?

She lowered her head, about to apologize to Giles, when he went on.

"They want to trade, Buffy." His voice dropped. "And you know we can't do that."

She raised her head. "I *don't* know that," she said wildly. "I don't know that at all."

Micaela turned to her again. "No, Buffy. You can't."

She shrugged. "One Slayer dies, another one is called. No big. My mom dies, that's a really big big."

Micaela shook her head. "My father needs the blood of a Slayer to satisfy his demon sponsor. If you die under my father's knife, the gates of Hell will surely open."

"They're going to open anyway." Buffy raised her chin.

"And your mother will die then, too," Micaela said mercilessly. "And she will suffer eternal torment."

Buffy took a breath and stopped the smart-ass retort that threatened to bubble over from her superheated nerves. All business, everything else inside herself tied down for the storm, she said, "When's the trade supposed to take place?"

"It already came and went." Giles signaled to the right and they began to crest the hill that led to Angel's mansion. "We tried to surprise them, get your mother back. But they were a step ahead of us. Two, actually," he added in a defeated voice. "Buffy, you know that if I could have given my own life for hers, I would have."

"No." She spoke the word as if it were a punch to her gut. "You wouldn't, Giles. Because you're my Watcher. And your first obligation is to me." And she hated that.

Giles did not respond. Buffy stared at her hands, at the smaller hand over hers.

Giles could say nothing, because there was nothing to be said.

Little Jacques said, "I have some magick, Buffy. I shall do whatever I can."

"Thanks," she said dully.

As he had helped load the unconscious werewolf into his van, Giles now helped Angel carry Oz up to the house. The vampire, though uncommonly strong, was very tired from a long night and countless battles with the Sons of Entropy, demons, and the dead who were frantic to escape their limbo dimension and reenter the world, tenuous as that harbor appeared to be.

Giles was glad of the physical exertion required, for it gave him a way to slake some of the tension coursing through his body like a live electric wire. He was acutely aware of Buffy's distress, for he shared it. Joyce Summers was not related to him; she was not his wife, nor his sister, nor his mother. Yet he cared for her deeply, and he felt entirely responsible for her kidnapping. Even though it had been she who had opened the door.

He would never tell Buffy that their enemies had signed Buffy's name to the card that had accompanied the flowers. The Slayer already blamed herself. It would serve no purpose to increase her grief.

He was also acutely aware of Micaela. Incredibly, throughout all she had been through, she still smelled of a sweet floral fragrance. Her honey-blond hair still shone as it tumbled over her shoulders.

His body still reacted to the sight of her.

So it was with distinct relief that he helped Angel carry Oz into the very place where Angel, as the evil, soulless Angelus, had once delighted in torturing him. Where he had threatened Giles with a chainsaw and worse. Angelus, the one with the angelic face, who had stalked Jenny Calendar, the woman whom Giles had loved, and twisted her head too hard to the left, and killed her with a song in his heart.

The last time Giles had come to this place, he could make himself stay only a few moments. It conjured too many painful memories. Now, if it helped in any way, he would gladly remain here for the rest of his life.

He and Angel carried Oz to a corner in the large living room. After they had secured Oz with a substantial pair of handcuffs Angel had produced from a small, ornate box, Buffy demanded that Angel drive her to her home. From there the two would fan out and begin the search for her mother. Giles thought to protest; surely the Sons of Entropy would be watching her house, lying in wait for her appearance. The

Slayer was the prize they sought; Joyce was mere bait. But Giles knew Buffy very well. She would not listen to his warnings and dire predictions. At best, they would only spur her on.

She needed to do what she needed to do. He had never been able to stay her from her chosen course of action. And often, she had been proven right in her insistence upon stepping outside the boundaries of what was reasonable and prudent. It was not his place to stop her.

Correction: it *was* his place, but there was no sense in even trying.

Next, the poor, tired child had lain down in what appeared to be Angel's bedroom, a light on, and Micaela had sung him a lullaby. Giles knew that boys of eleven generally protested against such childish things, but, peering from the doorway, he had seen the whisper of comfort that had spread over Jacques Regnier's features. Apparently his own mother had committed suicide when Jacques was a mere toddler. The prospect of life in the Gatehouse had been too much for her. Better death than madness.

Next she whispered words of magick, raising wards around the mansion. Giles stood apart, reflecting bitterly that if it were not for her father, they would need no wards.

Angel and Buffy were gone, and the boy was asleep in a room whose window was also heavily fortified with wrought iron. That left Giles alone with Micaela. As he stood by the empty, black windows, staring into the darkness and wondering if the Sons of Entropy knew they were here, she sat wearily on the couch facing the empty, black fireplace. He looked at her without turning his head. She was pale and drawn, and obviously as uncomfortable as he was. She trembled slightly, though from the chill air, fatigue, or nerves—or a combination of all three—he had no idea.

After a long, pregnant silence, he said, "I'll make some tea."

"Yes, thank you." Her shoulders were rounded. She looked as if she wanted to do nothing more than sleep.

And be forgiven.

Abruptly he left the room and went into the kitchen. Each movement seemed strange to him, as if he were inhabiting another's body, as he made the tea and got the cups. When the world was ending, the minutiae of life seemed ridiculous and self-indulgent.

The kettle screamed. No milk or sugar having been located, he set the steaming cups on a small tray and put it on Angel's coffee table.

She lifted a cup and began to sip. Suddenly she put it down and covered her face with her hands.

"I'm so sorry, Giles," she said. "Fulcanelli . . . I didn't know who or what he was. I was very little when he adopted me. He was very kind. He became my father. How could I know the things my loving father taught me were . . ."

"Evil," Giles finished for her.

Micaela only wept.

From her conversation with Buffy in the van, Giles had already deduced that the ancient nemesis of the house of Regnier, Giacomo Fulcanelli, was the creature she thought of as her father. And yet, it was a shock to hear her admit as much. To admit that she had set him up to be pushed down the stairs, or worse. And then, to have visited him in hospital in her bright red dress with flowers and a very nice volume of

Sherlock Holmes stories, acting as if she'd been attracted to him. It wounded him deeply. It angered him.

"Most demons are kind to someone, at some level," Giles said after a beat. "That's their seduction. The weakness they seek in order to recruit accomplices."

He heard her suck in her breath. Then she said, "Think about how it would be for you if you discovered now that everything you knew about Buffy was a lie. If you learned that she was more evil than the evil she was supposed to wipe out. This lovely girl you have been charged with protecting and guiding. If someone handed you a gun and told you to shoot her because she was a vile, base creature bent upon the complete destruction of mankind, could you?"

"Yes," he said firmly.

"And if someone told you to shoot me?" she whispered.

He turned to her, looked into her eyes. She had aged in the short time since he had last seen her, not very much, but more than she should have. He couldn't help the wave of sympathy that washed through him. The slight softening of his heart.

"Micaela," he said, meaning his tone to be firm and authoritative. Instead, he spoke her name like a besotted lover.

To his dismay, she began to weep again.

"Rupert, I am so sorry," she said. "I have so many regrets."

"Yes, well, now is not the time for that." He examined the interior of the mansion—anything to avoid looking directly at her. "You must explain to me exactly what's going on."

"Yes, of course." She took a deep breath. "You see,

my father . . . the man I called Father . . . is a very old and powerful sorcerer."

"Yes, I know that," Giles said, frowning. "But what does he want?"

"To do what another fallen one did." Her lovely face was very grave. "To reign in Hell."

She rose from the couch and twisted her hands together. "For years, he told me and his followers about the Otherworld, where wonderful creatures dwell. The stuff of our myths and legends. Unicorns, sprites—"

He interrupted her. "Monsters and demons. Flesh-eating ghouls, griffins and manticores."

She nodded. "From time to time, the use of great magicks in this world would weaken the walls between here and the Otherworld, many of which eventually cracked open."

"Creating a breach in that barrier," Giles said thoughtfully. "A breach the Gatekeeper would then take it upon himself to close."

"Exactly," Micaela concurred. "The Gatekeeper and his heirs kept up for a time, hunting for the breaches and binding the creatures that got through. Imprisoning them in the infinite rooms of the Gatehouse. It might have gone on like that for centuries."

She lowered her eyes. "I don't know why I didn't see it earlier, that the Watchers were vital to the world, that the Gatekeeper was a good and valiant man. I suppose I just wanted to believe that the love he had shown me was . . . real."

Micaela looked at Giles. "But when I learned the truth, which he has successfully hidden from his followers, at least so far, I grew to hate him. For he is opening up the breaches not only between the Otherworld and this world, but between these two worlds and Hell itself. Even as we speak, the ghost roads, which the Gatekeeper traveled to collect and bind the mysteries of the Otherworld, are clogged with demons from the Pit. They are swarming, massing to march on us. To obliterate us."

"And Fulcanelli is aiding and abetting this madness? In return for what?" Giles asked, though he knew the answer.

"Power," she said simply. "He alone will survive the massacre. He will rule the earth."

"And you?"

She exhaled and shook her head. "I suppose I was exempt as well. But surely now that I've betrayed him, I'm scheduled for slaughter just like anyone else."

Giles was silent as he took in all that she had told him. She extended her hand as if to touch him, then quickly withdrew it, cradling it in her lap.

She said, "When I saw you at the library party, of course I knew who you were. I had your picture in my purse. I had my orders. But you . . ."

She trailed off, then laughed shortly. "You made me feel warm, despite the cold."

"Come now," he said, a bit impatiently. There was no need for her dishonest flirtation now.

She tried to smile, and failed. "I have been alone my entire life." She looked at him very steadily, although her cheeks turned bright red. "I was to seduce you, if necessary."

"How unpleasant for you," he said unkindly. Wanting to be unkind. Wanting to make her admit that she didn't mean it.

"I wish . . ." Now she did smile, very sadly. "And

now, it will never happen. You will never let me get that close."

Giles said nothing. He put his tea cup to his lips. The first sip was very bitter.

After a time, he said, "It's bloody freezing in here. We should have a fire. Then, to sleep. We'll both need rest for what's to come tomorrow."

The strong scent of ammonia shocked Joyce Summers awake. She tried to draw a breath through her mouth, then realized with a start that it was covered with tape. Panicking, she sucked air through her nose, struggling to cough as the searing odor brought tears to her eyes, which were blindfolded.

But she knew the smells of her prison. She knew exactly where she was: back in the storage closet at the abandoned Sunnydale Twin Drive-In. An eyesore along Route 17, a good distance outside the Sunnydale town limits, it seemed as remote from help as Mars.

The rescue attempt had failed. She was sorry for that, not only for her own sake but because there was still the chance that Buffy would be tempted to trade her life for her mother's. That must not happen. Joyce understood that and accepted it. Though she was very afraid to die, it was by far the best thing that could happen if it meant that Buffy would survive.

"Mrs. Summers, hello," came the soft voice. Joyce swallowed hard against her fear. It belonged to the deceptively gentle Brother Claude, the Sons of Entropy leader who had magickally burned another man to death. That he could do this was a secret, and one with which he had threatened her. If she spoke a word of it to anyone, she would be the next charred mass of flesh on the cement floor of the drive-in.

"Do you know who I am, Mrs. Summers?" Brother Claude inquired gently. Joyce managed a nod, though her head was swimming. She wasn't even certain that she was breathing.

"That's very good," Brother Claude said pleasantly. "And now, I have a wonderful surprise for you. You are to be most honored."

No, she wanted to plead. She wanted to beg for her very life. She was grateful for the tape across her mouth, which allowed her to maintain her dignity.

Then the tape was summarily ripped away. The blindfold was roughly removed from her eyes.

At first she squinted against the nimbus of light around the figure before her. She wondered how long she had lain in darkness, how long she had been bound. For now she realized that her hands were tied behind her back. She was terribly thirsty.

"Signora," said the figure, bending toward her. "How exquisite to meet you."

She pulled back her head and stared at him. His features were sharp, and though his skin was unlined, there was an air surrounding him of incredible age. Long white hair gathered around his shoulders.

But it was his eyes that startled her. They were an incredible, deep blue. Hypnotic. She found herself unwillingly falling into those eyes, and when she blinked herself back into focus, she had the sensation that a great deal of time had passed.

That she had just lost part of her lifetime.

The man laughed deep in his throat. It was a sadistic, cruel laugh, and it chilled her to her marrow.

"A chair," the man said, snapping his fingers.

To her astonishment, one appeared beside him. No one carried it over; no one bowed and scraped in obeisance.

She and he were completely alone.

He sat on the chair. Joyce, sprawled like a broken doll on the cold cement floor, her blanket to her left, was forced to look up at him. He was wearing a black robe, like the men who had kidnapped her, but she saw a black turtleneck at the neck and black pants legs as he crossed his knees. He had on very nice loafers.

"Do you have any idea what is happening?" he asked her. His accent was European. Italian, she guessed, and wondered what it mattered. But she knew she must take note of anything and everything in case she might use it to save her own life.

"No," she rasped, then cleared her throat. "No," she said more firmly, "but it would be nice if you would fill me in."

"Ah." His face broke with pleasure. "Now I see where she gets her fire. I have often wondered at the difference in temperament of Slayers. The one I killed was almost meek. Yet the power I gathered from her dying body was tremendous."

Joyce swallowed hard and forced herself not to react. *That's what he wants,* she told herself. *He's a bully, that's all.*

Just a bully with the power to materialize furniture out of thin air.

He crossed his arms now, as well as his legs, and settled in.

"Well, let's begin at the beginning, shall we? Italy, the Middle Ages." He shrugged. "I was just a boy. But I was ambitious. I knew I was destined for great things. Just like your daughter."

"My daughter," Joyce said, "is nothing like you."

He touched her face. His fingertip burned like the tip of a cigarette, and she jerked her head. The spot throbbed with pain. She clenched her teeth to keep from making a sound.

"She cannot do that, it's true," he said, cocking his head as if to admire his handiwork. "But there are times when she would like to."

"Not Buffy."

"Yes, Buffy." He chuckled. "You haven't seen her stuff a crucifix down the throat of a writhing vampire to make her talk, have you? Or stand by and allow that strange pastiche of good and evil, that one called Angel, to torture one of my young followers to death. Have you."

It was not a question. It was a threat.

Joyce narrowed her eyes. "To save humanity," she said.

"Ah. Humanity." He clicked his tongue against the backs of his teeth and refolded his arms. "But if we go down that road—is humanity actually worth saving?—we move into the realm of philosophy. And I find the subject profoundly boring. So."

He leaned toward her again. And this time she smelled his breath. It was the same odor she had smelled a day and a night before: the odor of charred human flesh.

Joyce gagged.

"Oh, pardon, do I offend?" He blew his breath over her face, clearly enjoying the look of revulsion that crossed her features.

"Listen to me, *Signora,*" he said. "I am allied with a powerful demon, and he craves the blood of your daughter. I will give it to him. If I have to put you on the phone and make her listen to every scream I create as I slice the flesh from your bones, inch by inch, I will give it to him.

"If I have to murder every man, woman, and tiny baby in this dismal little town, I will give it to him."

Joyce couldn't bear any more. She raised her chin and spat at him. Her eyes widened in shock when she realized what she had done, but she fought hard not to let him see her surprise, and her fear.

His gaze hardened as he wiped the spittle from his cheek.

"I will give it to him," he said slowly.

"If Buffy knows this, she'll never trade herself for me," Joyce said.

He put his hand over his heart. "Your honesty is touching." Then he reached back his arm and flicked his fingers at her.

Blue tendrils of magick flickered toward her, lapping at her features with white-hot pain. She cried out and turned her head, struggling against the wall to move out of range.

"Don't trifle with me, woman. You cannot imagine the agony I can inflict on you."

Then he threw back his hand again.

This time he slapped her, hard enough to send her reeling back into unconsciousness.

The last thing she heard was his quiet, pleased laughter.

The last thought she had was, *Buffy, stay away.*

At dawn, Jacques Regnier sat up in bed and cried, "No!"

In an instant, the man and woman were at his side. The woman took his hand and felt his forehead.

Jacques said, "He's here. Il Maestro is here, and he's hurting Buffy's mother."

"Oh, dear Lord, he's here?" Micaela cried.

The boy nodded.

She covered her mouth. The man stood close behind her and looked over her head and down at Jacques.

"In Sunnydale," the man said.

Jacques nodded again.

Chapter 2

DESPITE THE SOFT GLOW OF THE MORNING LIGHT THAT shone upon her face, the lovely young girl with the golden hair was, at present, not very lovely at all. Her name was Amy Madison; she was a witch; her face was mottled with bruises and there was a cut over one eye that threatened to leave a scar.

"A pity," Ethan Rayne said sadly, and he meant it. He was a very bad person, it was true. He had attempted to sacrifice the Slayer's life to the demon Eyghon to save his own skin. He had opened a Halloween shop filled with cursed costumes that allowed demons and monsters the run of Sunnydale on All Hallows Eve.

And once upon a dark age, he had been Rupert Giles's dear friend in forbidden magicks, a lifetime ago, when the old boy had tried to dodge his miserable do-gooder destiny as a Watcher.

So yes, it was true that Ethan was not the best of

men. But these were the worst of times. Even penny-dreadful dabblers such as himself could read the signs and portents. And once you actually got to the Hellmouth, it was obvious to all but those most deeply mired in denial—that being nearly the entire general populace of the charming town of Sunnydale—that the end of the world was at hand.

"So, Rupert, I'm back in the saddle again," Ethan murmured. He had planned to come here, to do minor mischief during the confusion. Once here, however, he had realized how dire the circumstances actually were. Much as it pained him, he realized that he would need to lend a hand. For the imp of the perverse that resided within him needed a world in which to play his games.

Ethan Rayne didn't want to die any more than anybody else did. So he decided to help . . . and there was always the chance that there might be an advantage to be gained in the process.

From the doorway to Amy's hospital room, he gave the poor girl a salute. Her magickal emanations were what had drawn him to the hospital in the first place. The young witch was in bad shape, but she would recover. It was more important that he find the Chosen One.

The world had sincere need of Buffy Summers at the moment.

Ethan turned and sauntered down the hospital corridor, smiling at a fetching lass in hospital scrubs, raising a lazy brow as she smiled back. He had on a black turtleneck and charcoal gray pants; he was a looker if he did say so. As she walked on, giving him one more appreciative gaze over her shoulder, he feigned a nonchalance that deserted him with one glance at the wide panorama windows looking out onto the bright morning.

Next stop: Giles's quaint little hangout.

All roads lead to Rome, Rupert, do they not?

Through the lobby, with a brief, pensive sigh at the closed specialty coffee cart, and then Ethan swung through the large double doors and stepped into the day. The horseshoe-shaped drive in front of the hospital was packed with cars, and out of them people lumbered and limped. Bleeding foreheads, arms at odd angles, a weeping woman carrying a small boy who kept whimpering, "Monsters. Monsters."

In the distance, sirens blared. Grew closer. Ambulances were en route to the emergency room.

He walked up to a rotund, elderly woman who was being helped from a Cadillac by an equally aged but far more agile man. The woman's face was uncommonly white, and her eyes were wide with either fear or shock. There was a large bruise on her forehead.

"Excuse me, but I was wondering if you could tell me if there's been an accident or something," Ethan said, filling his voice with deep concern. "I just came from visiting my aunt on the third floor, and I see all these new arrivals, and all at once."

"Damn kids," the man said. "It was kids."

"No," the woman murmured. "Not kids."

"Sure it was." The man gave Ethan a look that said, *Don't listen to the old bat.* "One of those damn gangs on PCP." He shook his head. "You come for a visit, think what a nice little town it is, buy a house, this happens."

"I'm so very sorry," Ethan said. He clucked his

tongue in sympathy at the woman. "The staff here are very good. I'm certain they'll take excellent care of you."

"Hear that, Eugenia?" the man said, patting the woman's arm.

"It wasn't kids," she said peevishly to Ethan, ignoring him.

They shuffled past. Ethan couldn't suppress a shiver. If he ever got that old and doddering . . . well, he never would, would he? That was what magick was for.

More cars were skidding to a halt around the horseshoe. Ethan dodged around the bumper of one and gave the driver a jaunty wave. His own rental was in the parking garage. He fished in his pocket for the ticket, thinking it awfully cheeky of hospitals to charge one for visiting the injured and infirm. It should be the other way around, one imagined—such an odious duty surely ought to warrant a reward.

The ticket found, he hesitated a moment, then stepped into the gantrylike elevator complex. He stood for a few seconds, then allowed his intuitive sense of self-preservation to take over. The stairs were a better choice. In an elevator, it didn't matter if someone could hear you scream. There was nothing they could do about it.

He turned to the right and took the stairs two at a time, glancing over his shoulder as he went. Satisfied that no one was following him, he turned his attention to the top of the flight.

And, for his pains, was caught in a white-hot matrix of sizzling blue energy that flared out and down like a net. As he cried out, the energy web bent and shaped around him like a coat of armor.

The agony was intense.

His reaction, more so. It was as though every hair on his body was being burned away. Hissing through his teeth, he collected himself and murmured the syllables of an ancient Babylonian destruction spell. But even as the net began to cool and fade, an olive-skinned man with scarred cheeks and savage eyes hurtled himself down the stairs toward Ethan.

"For chaos!" his assailant shouted.

The force of his leap slammed Ethan backwards down the stairs. Ethan's head cracked against the first riser; then he slid down to the next step and managed to roll onto his stomach, holding himself in place while the other fellow skidded to the bottom.

Then the scarred man turned round and got to his feet. He balled his fists and flicked his fingers out, toward Ethan. Two bright orange balls of fire rocketed toward his face, but Ethan managed to raise his own hands and stop them with a binding spell. They hung in the air while Ethan grabbed the railing and pulled himself to a half-standing position. The world was a bit topsy-turvy; he was incredibly dizzy.

His attacker barreled up the stairs. Gripping the railing, Ethan swung both legs up to kick him in the chest, a feat which would have done the Slayer proud.

Then, as the other man fell back down the stairs, the entire structure began to shake. Violent tremors ran through it, setting off car alarms, and within the elevator complex, an emergency bell began to scream.

The hooded man stayed where he'd fallen. But the stairs rang with new footsteps from above, and as Ethan clung to the banister to keep from falling, half a dozen thugs, some of them wearing hats or hoods to hide their faces, charged at him.

Ethan slammed his fist into the face of the nearest

one, then leaped up two steps, to the roof of the parking complex, and threw himself to the right. The momentum of the next attacker sent the man shooting headlong down the steps, to join his fellow on the cement floor.

Ethan flung out his leg, tripping two more hoods. Then the entire structure shook again, harder this time. The front tires of a lovely red BMW rolled over the edge of the floor and teetered just above Ethan's head. A beat-up truck joined it. Metal slammed and ground against metal.

The sky had grown quickly dark, and now it cracked open, and cold buckets of rain sluiced down Ethan's black turtleneck as if someone had snaked a firehose into it. It was a hard rain, stinging, and it gave the battle between Ethan and his attackers a strange, strobe-like quality. Lightning flared overhead, impossibly close. A tree to the left of the structure burst into flame.

Below, someone began shrieking.

"Who are you people?" Ethan shouted as he struggled up the stairs and came upon yet more men. Some of them wore robes emblazoned with white, archaic inscriptions.

Ethan clapped his hand to his head and cried, "The Sons of Entropy! Of course! What the devil are you doing here?"

That seemed to startle the men so badly that they looked at one another, unsure what to do. Ethan pressed his advantage, saying, "Brother Claude, is he here? My gracious, it's been ages."

"What do you know of Brother Claude?" one of the men demanded. He had very red hair and a slight red mustache. As he faced Ethan, his eyes ticked slightly to the right, then downward. He was watching someone sneaking up behind Ethan on the stairs.

"Only that he can't be trusted," Ethan shot back, and whirled around, slamming his right fist into the solar plexus of the man behind him. The chap doubled over and clutched his stomach, lost his balance, and fell against the side railing. Ethan stooped down, grabbed his ankles, and flipped him over the side.

The man's screams were lost in the clatter of the downpour.

"That was Brother Marcellus!" the redheaded man shouted, quivering with fury.

"And who were you?" Ethan asked, as he grabbed the front of the man's robe and ran forward, forcing the man to stumble backward.

Ethan ran him all the way to the edge of the structure, then lifted him up and threw him over the guard wall. He wasn't used to this kind of physical conflict: it had been a while. But he felt good.

When he turned around, the others were scattering. With a grim smile, Ethan watched them melt into the torrential downpour.

"Ethan Rayne comes to town," he said, "kicking ass and taking names." He wiped his hands on his sodden trousers as if they were contaminated, which they were, with magickal residue, and balanced himself like a tightrope walker as the entire structure shook and swayed.

"Damn," he said angrily.

He had lost his parking ticket.

However, his car looked to be intact, and he still had the key. So he let himself in and sat behind the wheel, wondering what was the best way to keep from driving off at an angle as the structure whipped and canted.

He jammed the key into the ignition and started the engine. He was just about to put the rental into drive when something roared up behind him and grabbed him around the neck. It began to pull; Ethan had the image of his head as a champagne cork, and flailed his arms to grab at whatever had hold of him.

The monster was enormous, with ape-sized arms covered in purple-and-ocher leathery skin, pincers flashing at the elbows. Its head slammed repeatedly against the roof of the car, but it clearly didn't mind. In the rearview mirror, Ethan caught a flash of a face the color of a fish's underbelly, with jet-black eyes and a circular mouth ringed in deep blood-red. Perhaps a sucker. Perhaps the thing that had just attached itself squarely to the back of Ethan's head and was drawing it into its expanding mouth.

"You don't want to do that. I'm not quite ripe," Ethan managed to say, flummoxed as to how he was going to save his life.

Then his windshield shattered, and a large, very tall, very hairy creature covered with white fur reached past the wreckage to grab Ethan around the neck. He was caught between the two monsters, one tugging forward, the other suctioning him backward. He was certain they were going to break his neck.

He tried to whisper a binding spell, but the syllables were choked off along with his oxygen supply. Pinpoints of light danced before his eyes, and then everything began to go black.

It was then he remembered that the car was running.

Grunting, he released the emergency brake and pushed the gear shift into drive. Then he depressed the accelerator.

The car slammed forward and headed for the wall. Ethan couldn't figure out what was going to happen when it crashed into it, but he shut his eyes and prayed to the god Janus that there would be something left of him when it did.

With a resounding crash, the car rammed the concrete. The white-haired thing sailed over the hood, disappearing from Ethan's blurred view. The sucking thing also disappeared, no longer behind Ethan.

The engine roared and the car futilely ground against the wall. It took Ethan less than a heartbeat to realize this was the only chance he had to get out alive.

He pushed open the door and clattered to the oily pavement, then he got the hell out of there.

He half-ran, half-stumbled toward the stairwell, scanning for his Entropic friends. It appeared that the coast was clear, and that they had retreated into the driving rain.

As he began his descent, lightning crackled overhead. The structure started to buckle.

He knew Sunnydale would find a good, sensible reason for this all to have happened. It certainly wouldn't be the correct one.

But at least he would get a good laugh out of this.

He lurched out of there, tattered and torn, and no gorgeous women in scrubs, jeans, or business suits gave him so much as a glance. To make matters worse, Rupert would be at his dreary job at that monstrous school. The best he could hope for would be a spot of tea, when what he needed was nourishment—and brandy.

Those would have to wait.

Ethan Rayne was on a mission.

He stumbled along, sore and bruised, thinking to hitchhike, like they used to do in the seventies. He smiled grimly to himself, remembering when Rupert was known as "Ripper" and life was crazy and terrifying.

Those days had returned, at least to Sunnydale.

"Oh, ho," he said to himself, as he finally stood across the street from the school. Before him hung what could only be a breach, the portal to another dimension. It pulsed like a gaping wound, an ellipse of purple and black that promised entry or exit to things Ethan did not want to deal with at the moment. So he bound it and drew it closed, shaking his head that things like this were happening, most particularly on the Hellmouth. All that negative mystical energy. He made a face. Bad vibes, as they used to say.

Sunnydale was on a bad trip, man.

When he reached the high school, he crossed the street, limping slightly. He'd be all right once he could sit down for a spell. A handful of students noticed that he wasn't wearing the uniform of the day, which appeared to be enormous bell-bottoms pinned up to reveal yards of extraneous fabric. Far be it from him to criticize current fashion.

"The library?" he asked a thin wisp of a girl, and she gaped at him.

"Um," she said, and pointed vaguely, a gesture which included at least half a dozen different directions.

"Thanks so much."

Then he headed for the library by means of dead reckoning, wondering if anyone was going to say anything about the torrential rains and the truly ostentatious lightning of last night. Or if, like everything else, they would either pretend it had been a freak of nature, or that it hadn't happened at all.

At the doors to the library, he stopped and smoothed back his hair.

If Buffy was there, he wanted to look his best.

He pushed open the doors. And there they were, rather like a tableau in an old-fashioned music-hall act: Rupert with a teacup and a book; the beautiful Slayer, her hair all mussed as if she'd just pulled back from a lover's ardent embrace; the new boy, the musician, the one for whom the phrase was invented: "Still waters run deep."

They all turned to look.

And no one looked happy.

"Good Lord," Rupert blurted. "Ethan, what in God's name are you doing here?"

Ethan tried yet one more time. "Good?"

As one, everyone in the library continued to stare at him.

He stepped forward. "I mean it. I'm in. On the side of good."

"Good and greedy, good and ambitious, or good and plenty?" Buffy asked harshly.

"You malign me so," Ethan protested.

At this, the Slayer stood. "Last I saw you, you were carving tattoos in my back. Or no, wait, you were selling magick candy bars, right? So excuse me if I don't do backflips at the sight of you."

He smiled at her. "But you're such an agile creature."

"And you're not welcome here," Rupert said crisply.

"But I truly am here to help," Ethan insisted. "And please don't take offense, but it appears to me that you could use a little help."

"Batman, Riddler," Oz said warningly, as if introducing Giles to Ethan for the very first time.

"Oh, what?" Ethan demanded. "You're all so in control of the situation that you don't need any help whatsoever? While it's raining lightning—"

"—and toads," Buffy said. She looked at Giles. "Well, it did. At least, while we were looking for my moth—" She glanced uncomfortably at Ethan. "—balls."

He grinned at her. "I beg your pardon?"

There was another protracted silence. Then Buffy sighed and said, "One mistake, one little slip of the spellcasting tongue, and you're dog meat. Literally."

"Now, wait just one moment," Rupert protested. He put down his teacup and glared at Ethan. "You aren't simply going to trust him," he began.

"Fine," Buffy said, then glanced at Ethan. "Tell us why?"

"Why?" Ethan asked, raising his eyebrows.

"Echo," Buffy replied.

Ethan frowned. "Well, you may not appreciate the . . . art . . . in the things that I do, but it is what I do. Where would I be without a world left to do it in?"

Buffy gave her Watcher a look. "He doesn't want to die."

"You have me there." Rupert clapped his hands together. "Other comments?"

"She has you there," Oz said.

"All right, Ethan," Rupert said unhappily. Up went

the glasses. "But one mistake. One misstep. One typical Ethan gesture, and you are most undeniably . . ."

He trailed off.

"I believe the fashionable phrase is 'dog meat,'" Oz said helpfully.

At the east end of Sunnydale, still within the town limits but long past anything that actually passed for "town," lay the Sunnydale Twin Drive-In. Or what had once been the Twin. One after another, the nostalgic buyers had come along, dedicated to "doing it right" even if that meant making no money at all. Eventually, reality set in. There were people willing to operate the drive-in purely for pleasure, without any profit at all. But so far, nobody had been willing to run the place at a loss.

At least, not in the past eleven years, which was how long the Twin had officially been closed. The land had been sold off half a dozen times since then, to developers with an eye to vast tracts of land without a mall on them. But the property had turned out to be untenable for most developers. Too far out on the edge of town. Too far from just about everything else. Past the desolation that had once been the two-screened drive-in, there were only some thick woods, Route 17, several mom-and-pop stores, and then, when you started to get close to the next town over, an ice rink.

But by then, you were too far away for the drive-in property to be of any use. It was only a matter of time before continuing development made the Twin a piece of prime real estate. But for now, it was nothing but an enormous parking lot surrounded by a rusting chain-link fence, its pavement shattered every few feet by weeds that had forced their way up to fresh air.

Teenagers sneaked in often enough, mostly to drink or have a bonfire in the lot. One of the screens was ruined, half of it having collapsed during a nasty thunderstorm back in '95. Most of the speakers had been ripped from their stands, swung about some local kid's head by their wires, and thrown at the screens or at the little cement projection booth and concession stand that looked like nothing so much as a bomb shelter.

But there hadn't been any invading teenagers in the past few weeks. Anyone who even came close to the fence had the sudden and irresistible urge to be far, far away from the Sunnydale Twin. It wasn't any one particular thing, but just an overall feeling that drove them off.

It was black magick.

And this black magick spread over the Sunnydale Twin like a miasma, like the diseases in the mists and the steaming hot afternoons that used to make men sick; it reshaped and reformed the Sunnydale Twin until walls grew and puzzles formed and hedges sprouted and blocks carved themselves into vast warrens. Until the Sunnydale Twin was what people saw if they looked from Route 17.

But if they were inside the Sunnydale Twin, if they were a prisoner there—if they were the mother of the Slayer—then the drive-in was gone. In its place was a terrible maze.

And within it dwelled the lord of the maze, the king of the labyrinth, as it had been set down from the beginning of words and ritual executions: the Minotaur.

A man with the head of a bull. A creature without mercy, so dread that in various countries such as Spain and Portugal, they still sacrificed captive bulls in large arenas manned by symbolic heroes called *matadores*—killers—to assuage their sense of powerlessness when the minotaur had held sway over them all.

The minotaur was a thirsty creature. An abomination against heaven, it lusted for human flesh. It craved the gore of human tissue across its snout.

"Mrs. Summers?" Brother Claude called softly. "Wake up. We have a surprise for you."

Within the Cauldron of Bran the Blessed, Jean-Marc Regnier, the Gatekeeper, held the Spear of Longinus between his liver-spotted hands and wheezed to his mother, "He is winning, *Maman.* I can feel it. The Cauldron is all that sustains me now. And even that is not enough. I will not be able . . . to use it again. Fulcanelli will prevail . . . and the gates of Hell will open all over the world. The home of the Slayer . . ." He sighed. "It is the fulcrum. It is the central point. If we cannot hold Sunnydale, we are lost."

Antoinette Regnier, the ghostly mother of the Gatekeeper, who had died over a century before, stroked the lined, fevered brow of her son and closed her eyes against the tears that threatened to fall. In life, she had been bound through a ritual to this place and this house to aid her son. The sands had run out for him so completely; he was barely a shell housing a pulse and a mind. Yet he clung so hard; he waited for the return of his young son, so that the weighty legacy of the Gatekeeper might continue. Poor Jacques.

Poor Jean-Marc.

"Hush, my dear boy," she whispered. "Conserve your strength. As long as you hold the Spear, you cannot be defeated in battle."

"But I can still die. It is *ending,* Mother," he said desperately. "I'm of no use, and the world is ending."

Giles lifted his head.

After his long day at school, he had come to the mansion to check on Jacques and Micaela. The lad had placed wards around the mansion, as had Giles, in his own way; else, Giles would never have left them alone. There really had been nothing else to be done: with no one else to help them, and no one to trust—especially not Ethan, for all his protestations—the best they could hope for was to keep the boy out of sight.

As Giles had been asking Micaela about her day, he had fallen asleep on the sofa.

When he awakened, the shadows were thrown across the room, and a blanket had been gently bunched around his neck.

Across the room, Micaela sat in an overstuffed chair, her knees beneath her chin. She smiled when she saw him.

He looked at her with sudden clarity.

"I'm glad you're here," he said.

She closed her eyes.

She wept.

Giles moved to her, holding her; she cried against his chest, and then she said, "That strengthens me, Rupert, as nothing ever has."

Chapter 3

BUFFY HELD HER HEAD IN HER HANDS AS IF IT WERE going to explode. Giles could see how exhausted she was, and this brief rest during the ongoing search for her mother would do little to relieve her. But he could not allow his sympathy to blind him as to their priorities.

"We have to get Jacques back to Boston," he said tentatively.

The Slayer looked up at him as though she wanted to strike him. Giles wouldn't have blamed her. But there was nothing to be done about it. As melodramatic as it seemed to his sense of practicality, the fate of the world hung in the balance. Already, they had wasted most of a day. After school, he had gone to check on Micaela and the boy, and to get some rest. Now, not long after dusk, he'd returned with a renewed sense of purpose.

A purpose Buffy seemed to disagree with.

"Buffy, we must—" he ventured.

"Don't you think I know that?" Buffy snapped, but her anger was tempered with a tone of desperation that made Giles's heart ache.

"Buffy, you must know I understand," he said. "I fear for her as much . . ." But of course that could not be true.

"She's my mother," Buffy said sharply. "I can't leave her."

Oz sat at the library's study table several feet away. He'd been double-checking the chains he planned to use that night. Now he looked up at Giles and raised his eyebrows. "There's also that whole monster thing. Okay, the wolfman was passed out most of the time; preventing slaughter, rule number one. So I didn't actually observe the monster thing. But from what Angel and Micaela said, we probably couldn't use the ghost roads even if we wanted to."

Giles nodded, idly scratched his head. "You have a point. One we've addressed before. There is also the added problem of Fulcanelli's presence here. He wants the boy. He wants Buffy. He wants Micaela. And he was able to use sorcery to prevent you all from reaching the Gatehouse once before. If he could do it again . . ."

Buffy slipped off the library counter and grabbed the light jacket she'd been wearing off the back of a chair.

"It's settled, then," she said. "He's got us backed into a corner and there's only one way out.

"He wants me. He can have me. But I'm going to make sure it hurts."

* * *

"Leave him. He is ours," whispered the lost souls of the ghost roads.

"No he's not!" Willow yelled. "He's ours!"

Cordelia was pulling Xander by his hands, his feet and his butt dragging on the hard ground of the ghost road. Willow moved around them as though she were doing a rain dance or something, waving her hands frantically, hoping to startle the spirits who, even now, were pulling at Xander's clothes and legs.

To Cordelia's astonishment, it was working.

"You all listen to me! You're in trouble, and so are we. We're trying to find a way to put those demons and, y'know, other monster people, back where they belong. Which would be a good thing. For everyone," Cordelia said breathlessly. "Including you. So back off and leave us alone."

"He must stay. He is dead."

"No, he's not!" Willow screamed.

But despite Cordelia's raving, and her own denials, they had not been able to find a pulse on Xander. He might very well be dead. Or his pulse might be so faint, so close to stopping, that . . .

Forget it, she thought. *I don't want to think about it.*

"Listen to me," she said. "I'm no witch, but I know a few spells. You guys can cooperate, or I can bind you to the ghost roads, so you can never leave here, never find whatever, y'know, waits for you. Wherever you're going. Which would suck, right?"

To her astonishment, the old ghost's eyes went wide and he began to drift back. The others moved away from Xander. Cordelia shuddered with relief and bit her lip. The ghosts moved to join the others in fighting the demons, and Willow hurried to help Cordelia.

The girls each had an arm now, and were pulling as

fast as they could, hoping they would reach a breach that would open into the Gatehouse soon. That was the thing about the ghost roads, according to Giles. They knew where you intended to go, and would simply open whenever you passed a breach back into the real world that was near your destination. But there was no way to tell how long a walk it would be.

And they were out of time.

"We'll be all right," she told Cordelia. And then she lied again. "He'll be all right."

"This is the part where he'd make a stupid joke," Cordy replied. "I'd want to strangle him, and I'd totally give him the cold shoulder. But now . . . oh, God, Willow, this is worse than anything else Buffy's gotten us into, ever."

Willow sighed. Of course Cordelia knew that none of this was Buffy's fault, but Cordy always blamed the Slayer.

As they dragged Xander, the dead moved out of their way in a gray wave of souls, faces swirling in the mist, and screaming demons in the distance. Xander's wrist felt cold under her fingers. He was so still.

"Does he feel heavy to you?" Cordelia asked, frantically. "Aren't you supposed to be heavier when you're dead? I didn't think he was this heavy."

"He was hiding it from you, actually," Willow replied weakly. "His Twinkie addiction had flared up again. He was gonna go to the Betty Ford, but—"

"Willow!" Cordelia cried, staring at her even as they kept hauling Xander's still form along.

Willow shrugged. "Sorry," she said. "I was trying to help. Y'know, with the bad jokes. I just thought . . ."

She fell silent. Trying again not to think about Xander's condition.

Then Cordelia let out a yelp, and the two of them were falling backward, pulling Xander down after them. The drop was only about a foot and a half, but they tumbled together out of a breach and ended up in a tangle of limbs.

Willow was first to get to her feet. They stood at the foot of a double-wide staircase in the most incredible marble foyer of one of the most magnificent homes she had ever seen.

"Is this it?" she asked. She stared around in amazement.

Cordelia was tugging at Xander again. "Yes, this is it!" she snapped. "When you're through being magick-tourist girl, would you give me a hand? The Cauldron's upstairs in the Gatekeeper's room."

Willow went to help her, but both of them were stopped short by an enormous crash of splintering wood as the double doors shattered and a man tumbled through them and slid across the marble. A long stick flew in with him—no, it was a spear of some sort—and the man grabbed at it.

"The Gatekeeper?" Willow asked Cordy.

The man looked horrible, like a corpse himself. His eyes were sunken and his skin hung from his bones. But the magick that crackled up around his body as he rose to his feet . . . and then rose to hover above the ground, was not weak or sagging, not at all.

Cordelia only nodded, staring.

The Gatekeeper took the long spear and broke it over his knee. He took the pieces and broke them again. Then he flicked his hands at the fragments, and they burst into brilliant green flame. Sparks shot off them as if they were fireworks. Both girls jumped.

He moved to the shattered doors and floated

through them. Past the destruction, they could see a number of Sons of Entropy acolytes on the front lawn of the house. Then, in a sizzling matrix of magickal energy, the doors re-created themselves right before the girls' eyes. He hadn't even registered their presence.

The remains of the spear continued to spark and burn on the marble floor.

"Wow," Willow whispered.

Cordelia swallowed. "Yeah."

Willow added, "Looks like the place is under attack again."

"Oh, please," Cordelia sighed. "When isn't it? Now, come on, I didn't get his blood all over this outfit for nothing."

Willow blinked, a bit surprised to hear the usual Cordy tone in such a dire situation. But then she realized it was all a show. All a mask to cover her terror. Which made Willow wonder what kind of mask she was wearing to hide her own fear, especially from herself.

As quickly as they could, they began to drag Xander up the stairs.

When Brother Zachary first arrived on Beacon Hill, he did not see the Gatekeeper's house.

"Look harder, Brother," said the acolyte who had picked him up at the airport. "Are you so far from the source, so far from chaos magick, that you cannot see past the most enormous of glamours?"

Zack looked at him, narrowed his eyes and said, "Shut the hell up, you moron. Who taught you to speak like that?"

The man looked as though he'd been slapped. He

opened his mouth to reply, but no sound came out. Instead, they stood there together, two very different men, allied to a single cause. On the narrow street not far from the Massachusetts State House, Brother Zachary frowned and stared at the place where the house was supposed to be.

Then, suddenly, there it was.

It's an extraordinary bit of magick, he thought. It must have taken decades to perfect. But this house had stood here for centuries, so the Regnier family, the Gatekeeper Dynasty, had had plenty of time. Once it must have been one of the only buildings up here. Now it sat amid two long rows of brownstone apartment buildings that were among the priciest real estate on the East Coast.

The Gatehouse was a vast, rambling mansion that seemed to encompass nearly every architectural period that Zack was familiar with, and a number of which he wasn't. It had a large front yard—almost unheard of in a city as densely settled as Boston. And yet average people walking by would never see it. They would pass by a row of brownstones and walk right through the shadow of that house without ever knowing it was there. There might be a few extra seconds ticked off on their watch—seconds they would never get back—but for all intents and purposes, the house was invisible from the outside.

Unless one knew what one was looking for.

Even then, Brother Zachary had had trouble. Which was no surprise, considering that he hadn't had any contact at all with the Sons of Entropy for several years. Il Maestro had sent him to get his Ph.D. from Stanford, and he'd gone on with his life. Oh, Zack knew that it would come back to him later. The

Sons of Entropy had paid for his entire education. In some ways, he had suspected Il Maestro was grooming an heir. Or a husband for Micaela.

If that was the case, it would have been all right with him. She was a beautiful and perfectly kind person. But years had gone by, and Zack had sort of stopped thinking about it.

Until Il Maestro had shown up in his apartment, a glowing, ghostly avatar, to order him to get to Boston immediately. He was needed. Zachary would have liked to say no, but he just couldn't. For there was something he could do that none of Il Maestro's other acolytes could do.

It wasn't magick. At least, not as far as Brother Zachary was concerned. But it was his special talent. And now Il Maestro had need of it.

But this . . . this was a horror he had never been prepared for.

Once he was able to see into the Gatekeeper's estate, past the now ravaged wrought-iron gate that surrounded the grounds, Zack knew that the time had truly come. He knew Il Maestro would never have called for him if it were not urgent, but this . . . this was pure slaughter.

On the other side of the gate, dozens of acolytes gathered. Some of them had automatic weapons and were firing at the house. But this was no ordinary house, and it repaired itself even as Zack watched. Most of the acolytes, however, were spellcasters and magick users of some sort, and they muttered incantations and gestured oddly to build hexes and made direct, exhaustive sorcerous attacks on the house itself.

And on the aged, decrepit-looking man standing

atop the front steps of the house. Zack knew that this must be the Gatekeeper, and he could see why the man had the reputation he did. The magicks used against him were wearing him down, but not nearly fast enough. He shielded himself without any obvious concern, and struck back with deadly force.

From the way the grass was awash with blood, and the stacks of bodies some of the acolytes were using as bunkers, it was clear that this battle had been going on for quite some time.

"Chaos' name," Brother Zachary whispered, an epithet he hadn't used in many years.

"Indeed," agreed the other man, who then grew uncomfortable as he waited for Zack to tease him about his affectations once more. Zack didn't bother.

"Who's in charge over in that charnel house?" Zack asked.

The moron narrowed his eyes, then shrugged. "We're all doing the bidding of Il Maestro," he said. "But I think Brother Thaddeus is the highest ranking official here."

Zack didn't thank him. He didn't want to be here. He'd been having second thoughts about his involvement with magick and the supernatural in general for some time. But it wasn't practical to think he could just walk away. Il Maestro was a visionary—and also completely psychotic. But he might well be able to transform the world in the way that he claimed. If so, Zack wanted to be with him, rather than against him.

So he walked across the street. A black VW bug screeched to a halt and the driver leaned out the window, letting loose a stream of profanity so foul and so invective that Zack could only smile and think, *Home, sweet home.*

He was from Boston. And he'd never known this damned house was here. Which was the whole point, of course.

Now, as he moved through the shattered gate and began to pick his footing among the corpses of his fellow acolytes, Brother Zachary felt a bit sad for the old man on the steps of the house. He was backed up to the door, and a pair of minor magicians were threatening him with what seemed to be some kind of crimson serpents, created purely from sorcerous energy. The man just looked so . . . old. Weak and doddering, as if he belonged in a nursing home, having his bedpan drained and his linens washed and not much else.

"Damn," Zack whispered as he stumbled over a charred, blackened human arm, which lay on the ground several feet from its dead owner.

Then he was finally approaching the ranks of acolytes who hid behind mounds of the dead. There was shouting and chanting and bitching too, for many of these men had been here for quite some time. Empty coffee cups from Starbucks littered the ground. Which was a bit surreal. Most of the major magickal wars of the past had happened before there were such things as chain stores or shopping malls.

Zack blinked, and shuddered a moment.

Surreal was definitely the word.

On the steps, the old man screamed something in a language even Zack, who had spent his life as a scholar of the supernatural and paranormal, had never heard. Fire erupted from the ground in front of the house, but it wasn't just any fire. It was a purple-gray fire, which burbled rather than crackled, and seemed to flow rather than spark, and it blazed up high in front of the two acolytes now on the attack.

The crimson serpents were eaten by the fire.

The acolytes who had commanded them screamed in pain as the purple-gray fire peeled off their skin and then popped their eyes. The fire blazed as it was spattered with blood and vitreous fluid, as though gasoline had been thrown on it. The fire roiled around and over the dead acolytes, obscuring them from view, and when it receded, all that remained were their bones and their shoes. Whatever lived within those eldritch flames, it couldn't abide the taste of leather, apparently.

Zack wanted to throw up.

But he would not underestimate the Gatekeeper again. The man was a menace to Il Maestro's plans, and therefore, he had to be stopped. Brother Zachary crouched down behind a bunch of acolytes who were similarly positioned. They turned to glare at him almost simultaneously.

"Which one of you is Brother Thaddeus?" he asked.

A short, almost dwarfish man with a round potbelly and wire-rimmed glasses seemed to straighten up a bit.

"You're the professor?" the dwarf asked.

Zack nodded, assuming this must be Thaddeus.

The potbellied man looked around at the acolytes gathered nearby, and a broad grin crossed his face. "Well, boys," he said, "we've got ourselves a specialist, now. He's going to succeed where everything we've tried has failed."

It was easy to read into his words and his tone.

"Believe it or not," Zack said. "You think it makes any difference to me? You've got something you want me to try here, you let me know. If I wasted my time flying out, tell me we've lost and I'll go on home."

The dwarf glared at him, nostrils flaring. The other acolytes puffed themselves up, as though they might attack him. Zachary stood his ground. *To hell with all of them,* he thought.

"Look," he added, "Il Maestro asked me to come here. If that was a mistake, all you have to do is say so."

His words had the desired effect. The idea that they might be challenging Il Maestro's will by giving him a hard time seemed to terrify them all completely. Zack understood that terror. He wouldn't ever want Il Maestro angry with him.

Thaddeus sighed. "What you do, it isn't magick?" he asked.

"Not at all."

The dwarf shrugged. "Well, maybe that's what we need at this point. As a sorcerer, the Gatekeeper is too strong for anyone except Il Maestro himself. I don't understand why he hasn't come here himself . . . not that I'm questioning his wisdom," he added hurriedly.

"Of course not," Zack replied. "But I thought the old man was dying."

"Yeah, aren't we all?" Thaddeus remarked. "Regnier's been dying for ages, and he's still destroying us far too easily. Something's keeping him alive. Unless we can stop that . . . well, we need help."

Brother Zachary nodded. "I'll be more than happy to help."

* * *

Upon the steps of his home, the Gatekeeper faltered a moment. At the edges of his peripheral vision, the light began to dim. His body swayed. Sound disappeared—all of it. Not a car engine, not a voice, not the whisper of the wind remained.

Then he blinked, caught himself, and reached out for the railing to keep from falling. He was more vulnerable than ever without the Spear, but he could not let it fall into these men's hands. It was a calculated risk, destroying it before his son Jacques could take over. But it was a risk he had felt he must take. Whoever held the Spear could not be defeated in battle.

If it had fallen into Fulcanelli's hands . . .

He took a long, deep breath, and the darkness receded. But it would be back for him.

Soon.

Within her son's bedchamber, the ghost of Antoinette Regnier floated solemnly about the room, examining each of his possessions. She mourned him, though he was not dead yet. It was an odd feeling. All this time, all she had wanted was for him to be free of the responsibilities of the Gatekeeper, so that she could be with him in the world after, the world that waited for them both beyond the ghost roads.

Antoinette's ghost paused above the Cauldron of Bran the Blessed. It was still filled with the water that had saved her son only hours before. The last time, he had said. And they both knew it was true. It was as though a portion of his life was drained away by battle, only to be replenished by the power of the Cauldron. But his own life was nearly gone now, the Cauldron all that was sustaining him.

Without even a spark of his own life force, Jean-Marc could not survive. Even the Cauldron could not power a body whose energy had completely dispersed.

Yes, this last time had been the end. The cauldron could do no more.

And yet, Antoinette could not bring herself to empty it. *Not yet. If there is some small chance . . .*

"Help!"

Antoinette turned. Through the open door, she saw them in the hallway. The girl, Cordelia, and another she did not know, were dragging Xander between them. The Slayer's friends.

The boy was not moving.

Willow's eyes widened. Within the large room Cordelia had told her was the Gatekeeper's, the ghost of an old woman in old-fashioned clothing floated on air, her body from the waist down little more than mist. Willow knew who it must be: the others had told her about Antoinette Regnier, and how she had been bound to her son after her death to watch over him.

But seeing her was still startling.

"Oh" was all she managed at first.

"That's it!" Cordelia snapped. "The Cauldron!"

Willow blinked. Looked. And there it was. A large black pot, big enough to serve as a bathtub if one were so inclined. Or, in this case, if someone were dying. Legend said that the Cauldron of Bran the Blessed was capable of healing any wound, and even, perhaps, resurrecting the dead.

But Xander *wasn't* dead. She wouldn't let herself believe that.

"Antoinette, you have to help us!" Cordelia

pleaded with the ghost as she and Willow dragged Xander into the room.

"The boy is traveling," the ghost said. *"Xander has begun a journey away from this world."*

Willow was a bit freaked by hearing the ghostly woman's voice. It came from everywhere and nowhere at once. But she shook it off. Only one thing mattered right now. The words.

"He's begun a journey," she said. "Meaning he's dying, right?"

She hoped her interpretation was correct. Refused to believe there could be another interpretation. *Not dead yet.*

"We can't let that happen," she added. "We need him. The Slayer needs him."

"You love him."

Simultaneously, the two girls said, "Yes!"

"Please, Antoinette," Cordelia begged. "Please let us use the Cauldron."

The ghost seemed saddened. She hung her head as though she herself were grieving a loss. And then she nodded.

"It is no longer any use to Jean-Marc," she said. *"Please, immerse Xander in the waters. If he can be saved, perhaps you may savor your friend's presence for a few moments . . .*

"Before the end."

Willow tried to ignore those words as she and Cordelia shuffled over to the Cauldron with Xander. Together they struggled to lift him and slide him into the water. His clothes soaked up the water immediately, darkening with the weight of it. His head slid under.

"Cordy?" Willow asked.

Muttering something frantic, Cordelia pulled him up by the shoulders so that Xander's head lolled against the side of the Cauldron.

They stood and stared at him and waited.

And nothing happened.

Then Willow began to put it all together. The things Antoinette Regnier had said. The Gatekeeper couldn't be dead, or else the Sons of Entropy would be swarming the place already. But he must be close to death. *"Before the end," she'd said.*

Very close.

It was called astral projection. Brother Zachary didn't need to explain that to the others. Some of them would surely know a great deal about it. Others nothing at all. None of that was important. The only thing that was important was the plan.

The plan to murder the Gatekeeper.

Brother Thaddeus looked at him. "You realize, boy, that if you fail, we will all have died for nothing."

Zack smiled. "Yeah, but if it works, you might not all have to die. As long as one of you gets close enough to the Gatekeeper before he destroys you, I'll be able to pull it off."

Thaddeus didn't return his smile.

But the dwarfish acolyte nodded to indicate that their conversation was concluded. They would do it. It was insane, but they would do it. Il Maestro commanded, and his will would be done. Together, the two of them turned to see that the others had gathered up swords and daggers from their fallen comrades. They had enough ammunition for only one of the automatic weapons.

It didn't matter. As long as each of them had a weapon.

There were seventeen of them in all. Seventeen men, about to put their lives on the line based on Zachary's say-so.

The thought gave him a moment's pause.

Until he recalled that these seventeen men were magicians and murderers attempting to bring about the destruction of culture and society on Earth in favor of their own lust for power.

"Let's do it," he said.

Their shouts and curses rose in unison amid the carnage, and they rounded the barriers built of the dead and rushed toward the steps where the withered old man wielded magicks beyond belief. Lightning killed three men before they crossed ten yards. Then the ground erupted with enormous vines, covered with huge, gleaming thorns, which shot out and dragged several others to the ground, tearing them apart.

The screams made Zack want to vomit.

But some of them made it. Their own magickal energy lashed out in tendrils of power, stabbing toward the Gatekeeper. The old man's protective charms warded off the magick of the Sons of Entropy. But some of them got quite near him.

Brother Thaddeus dropped dead—his blood boiled in his skin—on the stairs only a foot or two away from Jean-Marc Regnier.

Zack blinked. For a moment, he was so surprised that it had worked that he forgot what he was supposed to do. There was another scream. A crackle of lightning. The surviving Sons of Entropy began to retreat, but slowly. Regnier followed them down the steps, furious, swaying, and took a few steps along the brick path that split the lawn.

"Now," Zack whispered to himself.

He closed his eyes, but his mind was open. He could see it all. His spirit rose from his body at his command, leaving it behind. His body breathed. It functioned, but it was a shell, waiting for him to return. He only hoped that he would be able to do so.

His astral form sped across the carnage-draped landscape of the Gatehouse's grounds. He passed the Gatekeeper beneath him as the sorcerer rained death down upon a pair of acolytes. Only two or three remained alive.

As though he were slipping into the swirling water of a whirlpool, Brother Zachary entered the corpse of Brother Thaddeus. Thaddeus's fingers tightened on the hilt of his sword. Thaddeus's face stretched into a grin. Thaddeus's body began to rise.

Zack felt constrained within the stumpy body of the dwarf, but it didn't matter. It would only take a moment.

With Thaddeus's eyes, he focused on the Gatekeeper's back. Slowly, quietly, he followed the old man down the few steps to the brick path. Crept up behind him.

With Thaddeus's hand, Zack drove his sword through the Gatekeeper's back.

Inside the Cauldron, Xander's hand twitched. His eyelids fluttered.

Cordelia held Willow's hands tightly and bit her lip.

"He's alive," Willow whispered.

"Of course he is," Cordelia said gruffly.

But she was filled with such relief that she nearly

fainted. And she would have, if she hadn't had to support Willow to keep *her* from passing out.

"Oh, God," Cordelia said. "He's alive."

With a roar of agony, the Gatekeeper turned on Brother Thaddeus's corpse, possessed now by Brother Zachary. He opened his mouth and blood poured out. His blood. Then his blood rose up, taking on the form of a dragon's head. It lashed out and bit the acolyte's head off.

The decapitated corpse collapsed to the brick, followed by a wet splash of blood as the dragon fell apart. At the edge of the Gatekeeper's land, Brother Zachary's body slumped to the ground, a soulless, empty husk. Breathing, a heart beating, but without a mind to guide it.

The Gatekeeper fell to his knees on the brick.

The battle was over.

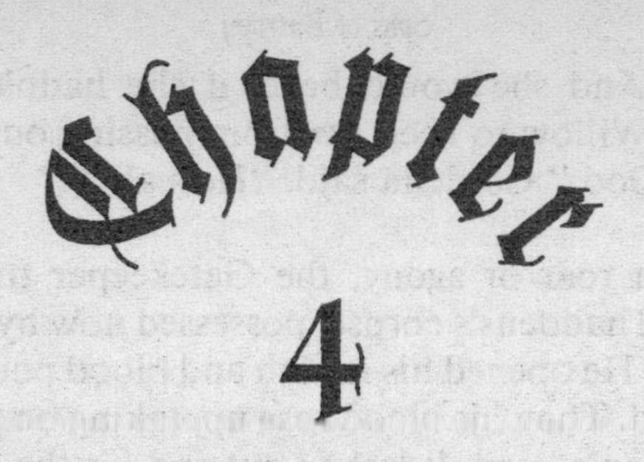

Chapter 4

AMONG THE SONS OF ENTROPY, THERE WERE MANY magicians; minor sorcerers who had trained for years to learn one bit of magick or another. Destructive energy, protective wards, healing charms, seductive glamours . . . Fulcanelli's many acolytes excelled in various ways. But he'd always been a bit disappointed that so few of them pursued the more subtle magicks.

Most merely wanted power—murderous, devastating power. He couldn't blame them, of course, but he had always believed that power was nothing without imagination. A magician who did not pursue subtlety as well as power would never be more than a novice. Some of his acolytes were quite powerful. But they were still novices compared to the man who founded the Sons of Entropy.

Which was precisely how he wanted it.

Several times in the centuries since he had set his grand plan in motion, acolytes had grown too powerful, and too curious, for their own good. Fulcanelli had been forced to take their lives before they could become a danger to him. He hated to do so, but there could be no question of who was master. No question at all.

He had spent hundreds of years adding to his arcane knowledge, studying the most unthinkable of spells. Fulcanelli, Il Maestro, had at his command a breed of sorcery very few humans in the history of that race had ever wielded. Subtle and transformational and devastating magicks, all at the whisper of a word, the flick of a wrist. And he had the black burn, *La Brûlure Noire,* which was unique among sorcerous powers because there was no known defense against it.

But for all his power, his acolytes feared him profoundly for one reason: none of them had the first inkling how he had accomplished the one thing they longed for more than anything else.

Fulcanelli was effectively immortal.

He did not age, and had not for a very, very long time. If he could manage that, his followers believed, he must be capable of anything.

It ought to have pleased him, that fear, that awe.

But it only frustrated him further.

For it was not through his own magicks that he had lived so long. Rather, his longevity was a gift, granted to him by his demon lord, to whom he had sacrificed a Slayer more than three hundred years before. He owed it all to Belphegor. No matter what he had achieved on his own, none of it would have been possible without the demon's gift.

Even then, he had begun the research that had led to this night. Over the many decades, he had punched hole after hole into the Otherworld, weakening the barrier between that place of chaos and the Earth dimension. At first, he had not even been aware that his old enemy, Regnier the magician, was still alive. Then Regnier had created the Gatehouse and founded the dynasty of the Gatekeepers. The man never realized that Fulcanelli himself was behind the breaches into the Otherworld.

Yet still the sorcerer was thwarted by his old enemy—an enemy who grew more powerful with each passing year, through his descendants. Fulcanelli's plan might have come to fruition as much as a century earlier if it had not been for the Gatekeepers.

But no matter. The time was here now.

Giacomo Fulcanelli stood, cradling his withered left hand against his body, and looked with admiration upon the enormous stone labyrinth before him. Its walls were nearly twenty feet high, and slick. It was vast, taking up nearly the entire parking lot of what had once been the Sunnydale Twin Drive-In.

It was beautiful.

"Yes, Maestro," Brother Dando said. "It is that indeed."

Fulcanelli's brow creased. He must have spoken aloud, though he was unaware of it. The thought disturbed him. *What else have I said in front of Dando?* No matter, though. He had made enough promises to the man, particularly of late, to guarantee his loyalty. For one who was hungry for power, and could not be king, what better promise than the position of magistrate.

The very idea was ridiculous, of course. Even if Fulcanelli really meant to bring chaos to Earth, rather than Hell itself, the position of magistrate would be absurd. There can be no order in chaos, nor in Hell.

"Have I spoken out of turn, Master?" Dando asked, fear making his eyes widen.

"Not to worry, Brother Dando," Fulcanelli said. "You are still my favored son."

He looked back at the labyrinth. "And we are certain the Minotaur is inside?" he asked.

"As sure as we can be," Dando replied. "This is the largest breach into the Otherworld we have been able to manage for years. I imagine that is due to the weakening of the Gatekeeper. It is logical to presume the beast is within, but to be certain, we took several people from the street and set them as deeply within as we dared to go.

"None of them have returned," Brother Dando said happily. "And we did hear screaming."

Fulcanelli nodded, pleased. "We'll have to make certain soon. But it will wait."

With that, he turned and strode away from Dando toward a concrete bunker that had once served as both concession stand and projection booth for the drive-in. When he had first arrived, the projection booth had been occupied by Brother Lupo, the man he had put in charge of the Sons of Entropy here in Sunnydale.

Lupo had given up the room without so much as a raised eyebrow. But something about him made Fulcanelli edgy. He would have to watch Lupo very closely.

As he passed through the bunker, his followers paid obeisance to him, and he waved them away as if it were not required. However, they all knew that if they failed to worship him in that way, he would take their lives as slowly and painfully as possible. When he went past the room where the Slayer's mother was held, he was tempted to stop again. Instead, he promised himself that he would return, and went up the stairs to the projection booth.

In the darkness, and assured of privacy, he called out to his lord and master.

"Belphegor most insidious, I call to your majesty. I call to your blasphemy. I bow down before your hideous beauty, worship and revile you. I beg you, appear."

The room was a bit claustrophobic to begin with, but as the air thickened and began to stink of sulfur, it only grew worse. A black, oily pool of energy began to coalesce in the middle of the room. Deep within it, something stirred. Fulcanelli didn't look too closely, partially out of deference, and partially because Belphegor was wretched to look at.

And, of course, because Fulcanelli, the founder of the Sons of Entropy, a sorcerer nearly unmatched in history, was terrified.

"You called, Giacomo?"

"Yes, Master. There are—"

"Silence. You have much to answer for, my servant. The Gatekeeper yet lives. The Slayer is also alive. You know where to find her, and yet she still draws air. You . . . disappoint me, Giacomo."

A tremor of panic ran through Fulcanelli, and he barely managed to keep it under control.

"The boy is still here in Sunnydale," he said, turning at last to look—and trying desperately not to *see*—into the abyss in which Belphegor lived. "I prevented him from going home, and even now my acolytes in Boston have the Gatehouse under siege."

"And the Slayer?"

"She has others aligned with her. Her Watcher is a much more formidable man than we were led to believe. The vampire and the wolf are with her as well."

"Your daughter has also allied herself with the Slayer, has she not?"

Fulcanelli could not bring himself to respond to that.

"She must die," Belphegor replied, his gravelly voice echoing within the projection booth. He sounded so close, and yet his voice was muffled, as though he were speaking to Fulcanelli through a wall.

Which wasn't far from the truth.

"I will take care of Micaela," the sorcerer promised.

"Yes," Belphegor agreed. *"You will.*

"You have succeeded in drawing the Minotaur and the labyrinth into your world. Use the mother as bait for the Slayer, and the boy as well. Try to get them both. Send the Slayer her mother's teeth if you must. Perhaps her eyes.

"But get her here."

Fulcanelli nodded quickly, though his mind was filled with reservations.

"Speak your mind, Giacomo," the demon commanded.

The sorcerer swallowed heavily. "The Slayer may not come. If she does not, I will send my acolytes after her. But it is possible that we will . . . that we will be unsuccessful."

There was a long silence in the swirling blackness

within that breach, the little window into Hell that Fulcanelli had opened. At length, a face seemed to surge forth from within, a face with savage-looking short horns covering it, and a long trunk like that of an elephant. Its eyes were lizardlike, a sickly green and glowing. There was a large, strange thickness in the center of its forehead. There was more to Belphegor, much more, and none of it remotely human, but this much was almost more than Fulcanelli could bear to see.

The face stretched the oily patch of darkness as though it were little more than thin plastic.

"You mean you may fail?" For the first time in the centuries Fulcanelli had served the demon, Belphegor actually chuckled. *"It would be unpleasant for you, should that happen. But fear not. Even now, the barriers have begun to fall. Hell invades the Otherworld. The Otherworld spills into the ghost roads. And there are breaches forming from the ghost roads into your world. We could use the blood of the Slayer to open the Hellmouth itself. But even without her death, the destruction of the Gatehouse will allow Hell to reign supreme eventually.*

"It isn't the most efficient way to destroy a world, but it will do if need be. Of course, if that happens, you will not be there to witness it."

Fulcanelli forced himself to breathe evenly. "Of course," he mumbled.

Belphegor was laughing as Fulcanelli stumbled from the room.

"It's all a lie," Brother Lupo said through gritted teeth.

They stood together in the parking lot of the skating rink just off Route 17, outside Sunnydale. Each had driven a separate car to this meeting, but Brother Claude suspected that Fulcanelli would be aware of their actions, wherever they went. Their cars were parked at the far end of the lot, nearest the trees, and farthest from the streetlights.

But darkness, Claude knew, could not hide them.

He stared at Lupo. The two men could not have been more different. Lupo was powerfully built, with a gleaming bald pate and a full, graying beard. A scar was slashed across the orbit of his left eye. Claude was taller, thinner, younger. He looked more like a high school teacher than a magician. Lupo was a killer, fearless in his sorcerous pursuits. Claude was vicious when need be, but in his magick he had always been a healer. It came naturally to him.

He only wished he'd had more opportunities to use that power.

Claude was stunned, not only by Lupo's words, but by the fact that the other acolyte would have come to him with something like this—something so blasphemous.

"I know what you're thinking," Lupo added.

"Oh?"

"Indeed," Lupo said. "And you're right. It was a great risk, talking to you. But I have seen the suspicion and the dissatisfaction in your eyes. I knew you would understand."

Claude considered this. Lupo was correct, about that at least.

"Still," Claude replied. "You know that I have always hated you."

"What better ally? We both know where we stand. Besides, what does personal conflict matter in light of what Il Maestro—and the very name itself makes me nauseous—has planned for our world."

"He swore we would be Kings of Chaos." Claude shook his head sadly.

"That was never his intention," Lupo said. "I have seen him, I have heard him, and I know he has deceived us. From the start. He said we could not perform the black burn, that we were too weak. But I have practiced the black burn myself—"

Claude's eyes widened. "You have achieved the black burn?"

"I have," Lupo said, with what Claude considered to be an admirable lack of pride. "But that is nothing. A minor deceit. Fulcanelli intends for Hell itself to overrun Earth, and we are not a part of his plan. How could we believe it was so, the way he throws the lives of our brothers away so casually?"

"Fools," Claude agreed, sighing heavily. "All of us."

The two men stared at each other for a very long time. Claude knew what was in his own heart, and he knew that it was in Lupo's as well. But neither man wanted to give it voice. Neither of them was willing to point out what needed to be done. But Lupo had been the one to broach the subject, and Claude supposed that it was only good faith that he be the one to make the next move.

"We'll have to kill him," Claude said.

Lupo only smiled. When, at last, he opened his mouth to speak, he was interrupted by another voice.

"Traitors!"

They turned as one. From the trees behind their

cars, Brother Dando emerged. Rage was etched on the diminutive magician's face. Eldritch flame crackled around his fingers.

"You bastards!" Dando fumed. "How dare you question Il Maestro?"

Lupo actually laughed. "Question?" he said. "You've been standing there listening to us for the past several minutes, Brother. And yet you are still so purposeful in your blindness? You are a sacrifice to him, nothing more. Fulcanelli's only plan for us, his loyal followers, is to serve us up to Hell as an appetizer when he's through with us."

"Lies!" Dando screamed.

Fire leaped from his fingers and Lupo erected a magickal shield for himself just in time. Claude was not as quick. The flames charred his face, and he screamed as he felt one of his eyes give way to the heat, bursting in his head.

He fell to the ground, shrieking, even as he brought his hands up to his face.

Magician, he thought madly, *heal thyself.*

And he did.

Shuddering with the trauma of his injuries and rapid healing, Claude rose shakily to his knees. When he looked up, his eyes widened with surprise as he saw the ebony energy boiling around Lupo's hands. He had seen it only once before, but *La Brûlure Noire* was disturbing in its perfection of darkness. Blacker than the night itself.

Brother Dando had always been arrogant, swaggering. And with good reason. Among the Sons of Entropy, he was considered quite a powerful magician.

Against Lupo, he didn't stand a chance.

He wailed in agony as his very soul was burned to cinders.

"Fool," Lupo said when the corpse hit the pavement.

"Indeed," Claude said. "And he's not the only one. I don't think we can expect any help from our brothers."

Lupo took a deep breath, then shrugged his shoulders lightly.

"We might just have to kill them all," he said.

Claude considered that a moment. Then he reached into his pocket for his keys and walked to the door of his car. Before climbing in, he looked back at Lupo.

"I don't have a problem with that."

Buffy had to meet Angel back at the library by seven, but she wanted to make a run home first to make sure her mother hadn't managed to call her somehow. In the back of her mind, she also sort of hoped the Sons of Entropy would be waiting to attack her. If she lost, they'd probably take her right to her mother. If she won . . . well, she'd make them.

But no such luck. No phone calls. No annoying zealots with daggers and spells.

Giles was still at the library, Oz was still in the cage, and Micaela and the boy were back at Angel's.

Ethan Rayne, on the other hand, was out trying to figure out where Buffy's mom was, and that was as freaky-deaky as anything else that had happened in the past few weeks. Maybe ever. But she wasn't going to look a gift magick-man in the mouth. Ethan was a dangerous man, but it wouldn't be the first time Buffy had accepted help from a dangerous man. In fact, it was getting to be sort of a habit.

I have to kick that habit. As soon as I have Mom back.

Frustrated, Buffy took one last buzz around the house, trying to see if there was anything that might indicate they'd been there. When she saw her bed, she was tempted to flop right down, curl up into a ball, and sleep for a month. It seemed like it had been that long since she'd last had even a nap. In reality, it had only been something like a day and a half.

Only.

She was running on fumes and she knew it. Even Angel had gotten a chance to sleep. If she'd been anyone but the Slayer, she would have collapsed from exhaustion by now. But she wasn't anyone else. And her mother was missing.

Buffy looked longingly at the shower, but her mother was out there somewhere, and somebody still had to get Jacques back to Boston. Giles had already called to make plane reservations for himself and the boy for first thing in the morning.

She was not convinced that Jacques would be safe aboard a plane, but the boy had assured her he would be, that he *knew,* blah-blah-magick-stuff-blah. It was on her lips to mention to him that he'd been kidnapped once already, but if she pushed too hard, she'd just feel guiltier about not escorting him herself.

Besides, morning was a long way off.

She washed her face quickly, changed into a clean shirt, and headed out to find her mother.

Joyce sat against the wall, her knees drawn up to her chest, and kept her eyes on the door to the room she had come to think of as her cell. The concrete was cold against her back, and she imagined it must be a rather chilly night outside.

She wondered where Buffy was. And how she was. And if she was even still alive. In fact, she explored those particular wonderings every fifteen to twenty minutes, always coming back to the morbid knowledge that if Buffy were dead, then she herself would have been dead long ago. As long as the Sons of Entropy kept Joyce alive, she felt it safe to assume that Buffy was in one piece somewhere.

After several days—she wasn't quite certain how many—in the hands of these madmen, these sorcerers who wanted to bring the world to an end, everything else had ceased to be important. Food. Sleep. The gallery. Her very life seemed to be the last priority. All that mattered was Buffy. Her only child.

As long as they held her prisoner—

The locks were ratcheted back, and the heavy door shoved open, scraping the floor. Joyce stared at the door as it swung wide. He stood there, silhouetted in the light from the corridor, unmistakable. Giacomo Fulcanelli. Il Maestro.

"Mrs. Summers," the sorcerer said, clutching his withered hand to his side. "Come with me."

There was something awful in his voice, something so very final. She couldn't help but think the worst. They were through with her. Buffy must be dead.

Joyce began to cry. "I'm not going anywhere with you, monster. If you want to kill me, you can do it right here!"

Fulcanelli turned slightly sideways, and the light from the hall lit up his features. He seemed to be scowling at her. But there was more to his appearance than that. He seemed greatly agitated, his features even paler than when she had first seen him, with great dark circles beneath his eyes.

"Get up, woman," he commanded.

"Go to hell," Joyce said, a quaver in her voice.

Then the sorcerer did something terrible: he smiled. "I'm not going anywhere," he told her. "After all, why go to Hell when I can bring Hell here to Sunnydale?"

Watching the gleeful expression on his face, Joyce felt sick and cold. He moved across the room toward her. Though she remembered quite well the violence he had shown her before, she prepared to spring at him, her fingers already hooked into claws. Anticipating her, Fulcanelli raised one hand, flashing red, and tendrils of energy slithered from his hand and struck like serpents at her head.

They twirled in Joyce's hair, and Fulcanelli turned and began to walk away. Joyce screamed and got to her feet, stumbling along behind the sorcerer, trying desperately to free her hair. If she refused to walk, or fell, it would be ripped out by the roots. She scrambled to keep up with him, and fresh tears began to fall.

"I'll see you dead," she whispered.

"That you might," Fulcanelli replied. "Time will tell."

After that, they walked in a silence broken only by occasional bursts of profanity from Joyce. They passed small groups of Fulcanelli's acolytes as they moved through the building, all of whom instantly stopped whatever they were doing to pay him the proper respect.

"Please!" Joyce cried out to them. "Help me. Can't

you see what he's doing? He's a madman. He wants the world to end. If he brings Hell to Earth, do you think any of you are going to escape?"

They ignored her. There were no taunts, no smiles, no questioning glances. They simply ignored her. She was there for one purpose and one purpose only, as bait for the Slayer. And at that, she was there at the instruction of Il Maestro. And Il Maestro could do with her what he wished.

Joyce screamed once. Loud and long, and more for her own benefit—for the release of it—than with any hope that she might be heard. Fulcanelli didn't seem to think anyone would hear her; he barely reacted to her screeching.

Outside, she could see one of the screens from the old Sunnydale Twin, large holes torn in it where whole sections had collapsed. Odd, because the screens looked far worse than they had only days ago. Joyce wondered idly if their deterioration had accelerated because of the proximity of the Sons of Entropy.

That was what entropy was, after all. The universal rule of corruption and erosion: things fall apart.

Fulcanelli gave her hair another yank. Her scalp tore slightly, and a small trickle of blood slipped through her hair and down her cheek. Her head was down as she followed him, but when he stopped, he relaxed the grip his magickal tendrils had on her, and she was able to look up again.

She couldn't see the other screen. In the darkness, she thought for a moment that it had been destroyed somehow.

Then, as her eyes adjusted, her brain began to take in what she was seeing. She let out a small sigh, but she wouldn't give the bastard the satisfaction of asking the question she knew he was waiting for.

"Yes, breathtaking, isn't it?" he said, watching her carefully.

She didn't respond, only stared at the enormous structure that had suddenly appeared in the parking lot.

He gave her a tug, and Joyce bit her lip.

"Yes," she said. "Yes, it is."

"This way," he said, and this time she stepped forward even before he started to move. *Well trained, just like a house pet,* she thought bitterly.

The wall was very high, at least three times Joyce's height, and they walked around its outer edges for several minutes until they finally came upon a pair of huge iron doors. The doors were barred by a long iron bar that had been slid through rings.

"Don't move," he ordered her.

Then he released his hold on her hair. The red tendrils crackled and snaked out to grab hold of the bar and slide it back, then they pulled the double doors open.

"Go," he told her.

"What?" she asked, staring at him incredulously.

Fulcanelli smiled. "There is another way out, Mrs. Summers. Joyce. If your daughter comes after you, I intend to capture her. If she does not, this is my gift to you. This door will be barred, but if you can find the other way out, I will not pursue you. By that time, your daughter's fate will have been decided one way or another."

Joyce stared at him. She did not, for a moment, think that he was telling the truth. But she could not know how much was truth and how much a lie. So she did the only thing she could do.

She walked toward the iron doors, just happy to be free of her captors' presence for the first time in days. Whatever waited inside those walls was no more life threatening than the Sons of Entropy, that much was certain. The sorcerer watched her go, the smile slipping from his face only to be replaced by a look of eager anticipation. Almost hunger.

He barred the doors behind her.

"But I'm still alive," Joyce whispered to herself. And as long as they kept her alive, that meant Buffy was still alive.

She turned to her left and began to walk along the inner wall of what she quickly realized was a huge labyrinth. She turned right. *It's a maze,* she thought with astonishment. Then she smiled wildly to herself. They just wanted to make it harder for Buffy to get to her, and to keep her busy while they tried to kill her daughter.

Left again.

But Joyce didn't mind. Joyce liked mazes. There'd been one built on the campus of a college not far from where she'd grown up. It hadn't been anywhere near as large as this, but . . . yes, she could do this. All she had to do was think, and remember the turns. To concentrate, and try to map out the maze in her mind.

Right again.

She could do this.

Then she heard the bellow of a monster, some kind of beast, not far off. Here in the maze with her.

And it all fell into place. The things Buffy and Giles and Willow had told her about the Gatehouse, and the Otherworld, and all of that. This maze. This labyrinth. And the half-man, half-bull creature who lurked inside the labyrinth, preying on those who became lost within.

The Minotaur.

She began to sweat.

And worse, she began to wonder: if they would do this to her, put her life in danger in this way, perhaps her daughter was dead after all. Joyce didn't let her mind wander too far in that direction.

But after that, she found it very difficult to concentrate.

Only a handful of his enemies remained alive outside his home, but the Gatekeeper could not raise a hand in its, or his own, defense. Even now, they were calling for reinforcements. For the moment, they were still frightened of him, still loath to come near. They had seen him on his knees before, seen him apparently beaten, apparently dying of old age or fatal wounds, only to emerge young and perfect to battle once more.

But now, as he dragged his bleeding and broken body up the stairs in front of the Gatehouse, Jean-Marc Regnier knew that it was over. He was finished. His frail form was too brittle to make the climb, but even had he been able to, the Cauldron of Bran the Blessed would have done him no good. When it had rejuvenated him, it had used part of his life force as a foundation.

He had nothing left to give. Not a drop of energy left to devote to the world.

For just a moment, as his enemies moved in behind

him, he thought of his mother, Antoinette. He was pleased that he would soon join her in the spirit world.

But then, as a young magician loosed a spell of destruction upon him, crushing the bones of his legs to powder, Jean-Marc could think only of his son, Jacques.

As he screamed in pain, he knew that his agony was more than physical. The grinning magician thought that it was he who had brought down the Gatekeeper, but it simply wasn't so.

It was just his time. No one was immortal, a lesson taught to Jean-Marc by his own father, Henri, so very long ago.

Jacques, he thought weakly. *I'm so very sorry.*

Then Jean-Marc Regnier's head slumped to his chest. The Gatekeeper was dead.

The Gatehouse, and all the strange and horrible beings inside, groaned as one, mimicking the old man's death rattle.

And the world held its breath.

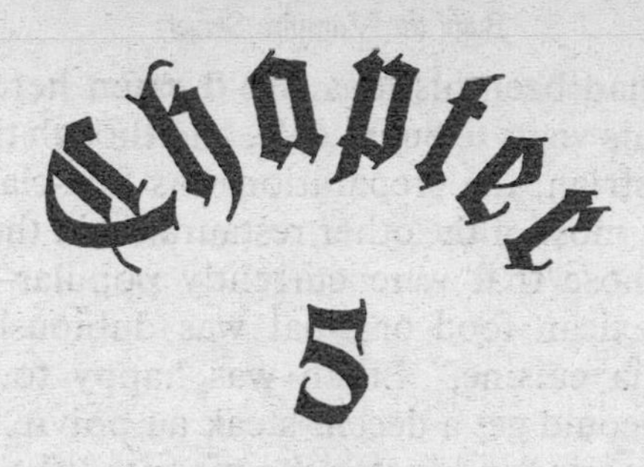

Chapter 5

IT WAS HALF PAST SIX WHEN ETHAN RAYNE STEERED HIS rental car into the parking lot of the Blue Horizon Restaurant and Lounge. Midway along the stretch of Sunnydale's coastline, and also about halfway between the beach and the docks, the Blue Horizon sat on a stony promontory overlooking the crashing surf. It was an older restaurant, built sometime in the forties, if Ethan guessed correctly, and it had long since seen its better days.

Still, with its high windows looking out on the ocean, and a fresh coat of white paint on its clapboards, it was a stately old place, frequented mainly by locals and older tourists. It wasn't hip. It wasn't happening. But the owners apparently still did enough business to keep it running. It seemed like the kind of place Americans always gravitated to when it came time to hold their wedding receptions.

Ethan smiled as he got out of the car. The Blue

Horizon had been his idea. He'd eaten here several times on his visits to Sunnydale, and though the menu was pedestrian, the preparation was first-class. And, given that most of the other restaurants in the area—at least those that were currently popular—served either Mexican food or what was dubiously called "California cuisine," Ethan was happy to go anywhere he could get a decent steak au poivre.

With a spring in his step, he mounted the stairs to the door and went in. The Blue Horizon was never really busy, and tonight was no exception. Plenty of diners, but no wait. He ignored the hostess and wandered into the lounge, eyes roving over the people at the bar. Though he hadn't seen the man in nearly fifteen years, it didn't take him long to spot Calvin Trenholm. The man's blond hair had all but disappeared, leaving a ring around Trenholm's head that was more nostalgia than actual hair. But the face was the same, without a doubt. Trenholm had wide, prominent eyes, almost fishlike, and thin lips that added to the overall bloodless, pale look about him.

The man raised his hand in a small wave, and in his smile Ethan detected both curiosity and fear. Exactly the emotions he had hoped to elicit from the man—the very same emotions he had always brought out in Calvin Trenholm, back in the old days.

Trenholm stood as Ethan approached. "Ethan Rayne, you right bastard," he said with an uneasy grin. "It's been an age."

"So it has."

"How on Earth did you find me in bloody California of all places?"

Ethan shook his head as if he, too, found this incredible. "Sheer luck, Trenholm old man. Look here, why don't we have some dinner before my stomach crawls up my gullet looking for something to feast upon, eh? We'll catch up after we've ordered, all right?"

For a moment, Trenholm looked at Ethan oddly, as though he were wondering if his comments about his stomach might hold some bizarre truth or hidden meaning. Then he seemed to exhale, and together they walked back to the hostess and let the woman find them a table.

Wanker, Ethan thought, as Trenholm ordered a drink. *Some people never change.*

Once upon a time, Ethan had been part of a small circle of young people who had wanted to tap into the power of magick. Their experiments might have been foolish games played by students in search of a thrill, or made gullible by their desire for something to make their flawed lives perfect. They might have been. But they were not.

Their magick raised a demon.

Most of the others in the group turned their backs on such dealings, recognizing the danger in them. One of those was Rupert Giles, who would later become a Watcher and combat the very things he once toyed with himself.

Ethan Rayne never turned away. The horror of that night taught him only one thing: be more careful. And he was. And so were the many other people he came into contact with over the years, in one group or another. He learned a great deal, and taught things to others in return. Sometimes, for his friends—those who had taught or given him something he wanted—he would perform certain favors.

For Calvin Trenholm, that favor was making an

extraordinary young woman named Kymberly Egler fall in love with him. Ethan had been happy to do it. He'd never liked Kymberly, and having her be trapped for life with a fool like Trenholm was quite amusing. When Trenholm left her to join the Sons of Entropy, Ethan wanted to kill him. At least, until he realized that the man's departure only made Kymberly's situation all the more ironic, and all the more agonizing.

The sadistic side of him—which was, to be honest, his only side—took great pleasure in that.

So Trenholm was still alive. For the moment.

The waiter came by to take their order. Ethan eagerly requested his steak au poivre, with the wonderful garlic mashed potatoes Blue Horizon's chef could whip up, and a side of sautéed asparagus. He asked for a scotch to be brought right away. Trenholm also ordered another glass of wine, asked for the swordfish, and then looked at Ethan nervously, waiting. Simply waiting.

Ethan let him wait. Finally, when his scotch arrived, he took a long sip, swirled the glass around to watch the ice spin, and then set it down, looking up at Trenholm and feeling the mischievous spirit that he could never quite control rising up within him.

"I saw Kymberly not long ago," he lied. "She still hates you. Because she still loves you."

Trenholm sipped his wine, trying to pretend he was not afraid of Ethan. He nearly pulled it off, too, but only because there was someone he was even more afraid of. The fact that Ethan already knew that gave him complete control over what would happen next.

"I'm sorry for that," Trenholm answered guardedly. "Sorry for . . . for her." He wiped a bit of sweat off his smooth brow.

"Yes, well, you had to do what you had to do, of course," Ethan replied. "Your friend the Maestro required that, didn't he? Complete dedication. Was going to teach you a great deal about magick, wasn't he?"

Trenholm was agitated, and nearly enough so to look it. He lifted his weak chin and clenched his teeth. "Il Maestro has taught me a great deal, Ethan. You would have done well to join him when I did. Perhaps then you would be among those who will . . ."

Ethan raised an eyebrow. "Who will what?" he asked, smirking.

The other man did not reply, but looked away instead.

"Oh, don't be daft, Trenholm," Ethan sighed. "I could lie to you about why I'm here in Sunnydale. That would be simple enough. But the truth is, I'm here because *you're* here. I know what your man Fulcanelli is up to, and I may want a piece after all."

Eyes darting like those of a frightened rabbit, Trenholm glanced about the restaurant nervously, then glared at Ethan.

"Watch your mouth, Ethan Rayne," he reprimanded. "You've always been a bit off, yourself. More than a bit. The rebel, you are. But one wrong word could have you roasted where you sit."

Ethan shook his head in amusement. "You know what's important to your boss?" he asked Trenholm. "That you believe that. He only has to make it happen once or twice, and none of you ever knows if he's breathing over your shoulder or not.

"How do you suppose he does that?"

Trenholm blinked, frowned at him. "It's magick, of course," the man replied.

With a soft chuckle, Ethan shook his head again. "So he's the great grand wizard, is he? It's amazing to me how many men, particularly those in search of power, don't even pay attention to what's going on around them.

"He's powerful, all right, but not that powerful. Not without help. Not without sponsorship. You know what I'm saying, Trenholm. You know exactly what I mean.

"He's got a plan, has he? You blokes will bring civilization down around our ears and then you'll be in charge, that it?"

Trenholm grew cold then, his nostrils flaring. He took a sip of his wine. "Something like that," he said, then sat back a bit in his chair. "You know, Ethan, you really ought to watch what you say. It could get you killed."

Ethan laughed. "I've never been very good at keeping my mouth shut," he admitted.

"That's true. Quite true."

"So you must have heard something. Whispers in the night. Seen something, even? Something that doesn't need to be there. I shouldn't have to explain this to you, Trenholm. We do magick, and we call on all sorts of ancient horrors, gods and devils and men. But for the most part, they don't attend services, eh? And when they do, there are repercussions. Always repercussions. Trust me. I know."

Ethan smiled at him. Trenholm seemed to deflate suddenly, his eyes wandering as his mind did the same. When they settled on Ethan again, he looked terrified.

"You're saying . . ."

"Quite." Ethan sipped his scotch. Made Trenholm wait. Then, at length: "Your man has a demon sponsor, old friend. And that demon is not going to help out for recreation. He's sold you out. All of you. Now I've . . . *aligned* myself with those who'd like to stop him. Hell on Earth would be a terror, wouldn't it? So much competition for attention. My little games would be mere trifles in that light.

"I need the demon's name, Trenholm. And your master's location. He's holding the Slayer's mother. I need to know where."

The man's usual deathly pallor had turned a shade of green, as though he'd died right there in his seat. After a long moment, he blinked several times as though waking from a long sleep.

"You know I can't," he whispered. "Even if what you say is true . . . he'd kill me."

Ethan leaned toward him, eminently reasonable, swirling the ice in his scotch glass. "Trenholm, dear boy," he said, "let me make this easy for you. Number one, if you don't tell me, and Hell intrudes upon Earth, you'll suffer for eternity. Which in your case would be well deserved, if only for your idiocy.

"Number two, can you feel your feet?"

Taken off guard by this seemingly inane question, Trenholm scowled, began to make some retort, and then his face froze. He glanced down. His face crumbled, and a tear appeared at the corner of his left eye and began to stream down his cheek.

The waiter brought their meals, happily asked if

there would be anything else. Ethan ordered another glass of scotch, and, out of pure kindness, asked for another wine for poor Trenholm.

When he'd left, Trenholm could only stare at his food. "What have you done to me?" he asked, without even looking up.

"Hmm?" Ethan mumbled, even as he contentedly chewed his first wonderful bite of steak. It was perfect here, every time.

"Oh, right. Well, it's just a little spell, really. Made slightly more difficult by the restrictions I placed on it. I've given you time, you see, it's going to take effect quite slowly. And, of course, I know precisely how to counter it, assuming you give me reason to."

"Ethan," Trenholm snarled through gritted teeth. "What have you done to me?"

"It's the Gorgon's Eye, I'm afraid," Ethan said, and a small thrill ran through him as he watched the tic in Trenholm's right eye begin to flutter. "It's probably moving up your legs right now, yes?

"That's right, old man. You're turning to stone."

Trenholm didn't have a response for that.

Ethan took another bite of steak, chewed several times, and then paused. "I'm going to eat my dinner now. When I'm through, I'll expect those answers. Otherwise, I'll just leave you here."

He ate very slowly. Trenholm didn't eat a single bite. He moved less and less, and by the time Ethan wiped his mouth with the heavy cloth napkin he'd had on his lap, he thought the man was likely stone from about the navel on down. When he finally met Trenholm's gaze again, there was hatred in the man's eyes such as even Ethan had never seen.

But Trenholm told him what he wanted to know.

Ethan smiled. "Thank you so much, Calvin. You may have just saved the world. And you've certainly saved your life."

"Until Il Maestro destroys me," Trenholm said.

"Well, then, if I were you I'd be off to a church as soon as I was able," Ethan advised. "I wouldn't want to die with what you've got on your soul. Not if you believe that sort of thing."

With a flick of his wrist, Ethan produced a small box of wooden matches. He reached for the white candle that burned on the table, blew it out, and then relit it with a match of his own. Black smoke burned up from the candle for a moment, and then it burned white.

"Just a whiff or two should do it," he explained.

The man complied, inhaling the smoke, and his features seemed to relax as his lower half began to return to its fleshly state. While that process was taking place, Ethan waved the waiter over and procured the check, which he then paid in cash.

"Shall we be off, then?" he asked when the waiter had gone. "You might be a bit shaky on those legs at first, but you'll adjust."

They walked outside together, and Ethan was right. Trenholm had trouble putting one foot in front of the other. But by the time they reached the parking lot, he'd fully recovered.

Trenholm rounded on Ethan, who had begun to stroll toward his rental car, whistling "Over the Rainbow."

"I should kill you, you know!" the man declared.

Ethan nodded. "I wholly agree," he said. "But you won't. If you were going to kill me, you would have done it years ago, when I first seduced Kymberly. I'm not surprised you left her, you know. Insufferable witch."

Trenholm reddened, and for a moment Ethan wondered if the man would actually attempt to attack him. It would be a change for him, at least. But then his question was interrupted, and would forever remain unanswered, as a black Jeep roared suddenly out of a space behind Trenholm and shot across the pavement at him, its lights out. The man barely had time to scream before the vehicle shattered his body, throwing him to the ground a lifeless shell.

Tires squealed as the Jeep turned, backed up, and started for Ethan. An elderly couple had come out of the restaurant in time to see Trenholm's murder, and now were screaming at him to run for his life.

Ethan rolled his eyes. He'd prepared for this. The Sons of Entropy acolytes behind the wheel knew that Trenholm was likely a traitor, but they couldn't have known who it was he'd been meeting.

Or they'd have sent sorcerers instead of assassins.

"Janus, oh golden idol," he said quickly, gesticulating with his fingers. *"Transform, begone, from human's eyes; fur and ears, now smaller size."*

The men behind the wheel turned into rabbits and the Jeep crashed into several parked cars. Ethan was glad his rental had been spared. While the people on the restaurant stairs called out to him, he climbed in, started the engine, and drove off, laughing softly to himself.

He just loved coming to Sunnydale.

Angel wasn't at the library when Buffy returned. They'd planned to meet there at seven, and from there to continue the search for her mother. But when she pushed through the swinging doors, the room appeared empty at first.

"Hello?" she called out, as she moved farther into the room.

In the cage, Oz snarled and threw himself against the metal mesh. He stalked back and forth across the small space, glaring at her, saliva sliding from his fangs.

"Down, boy," she said in a low voice. "You got up on the wrong side of the moon this morning."

The werewolf snarled.

Behind Buffy, the door opened. She turned to see Giles coming in with a cup of coffee in one hand, holding a book open in the other.

"You could get hurt doing that," she said.

Giles looked up, startled, and his coffee spilled on his hand. He hissed and held the cup away from him.

"See," Buffy said reasonably. "It's bad enough, the whole walking and reading thing. But carrying hot coffee? Major potential for household injuries."

"Yes, well, perhaps if you weren't sneaking around . . ." Giles began, even as he put the cup and book down and went in search of a paper towel.

Then he looked up, as if startled by his own words. "I'm sorry, Buffy," he said. "I've just been growing more and more frustrated, trying to figure out where your mother might be held. Sunnydale is actually a larger town than it would appear, though—unsurprisingly—not very thickly settled in most areas."

Oz growled again.

Giles looked over at him, rolled his eyes. "Oh, do shut up!" he snapped.

The werewolf paused, looked at him a moment, then went about his business of being caged up.

"Oh, great, Giles, lash out at the defenseless werewolf," Buffy said, raising her eyebrows. "Look, Angel was supposed to meet me here. Has he shown?"

"Not yet," Giles replied. "No. But there are some things we have to discuss, Buffy."

There was a tone in his voice that was all too familiar. Giles picked his coffee up again and turned to regard her. The silence inside the school was too much for her.

"What is it, Giles?" she asked weakly. "Something with my mom? Is she . . ."

The Slayer could not finish that sentence.

Giles's eyes widened. "Oh, Lord, no, Buffy. I'm sorry. I didn't mean to imply anything of the sort. But there is a connection, I'm afraid. You see, earlier today when I was at Angel's speaking with Micaela, young Jacques told us that he could sense his father, well, dying."

"That's nothing new," Buffy replied. "It seems like he's been on the verge of checking out for, okay, *ever.*"

"Indeed," Giles agreed. "But this is different. It's the first time Jacques has felt anything of the sort. It likely means that whatever has been sustaining Jean-Marc Regnier, the Cauldron, the house, what have you . . . that those things can no longer help him."

Buffy took that in, and then let its meaning sink in for several seconds. If it was true, it meant that Giles's flying to Boston with the kid, with Jacques, just wasn't going to work.

"I'm not going," she said bluntly.

Giles blinked. Ran a hand through his hair. Began to speak, then thought better of what he'd been about to say.

"You know I can't go," she said. "Angel can go. Oz

can . . ." she glanced at the werewolf in the cage. "All right, maybe Oz can't go. But Angel can. I'm not leaving this town until I find my mother, Giles. I can't just take off and leave her a prisoner of some psycho who really wants me instead."

"We'll find her," Giles insisted.

Buffy swallowed. "Sorry. You had your shot."

"This is too important, Buffy," he told her, growing angry now. "I'm sorry, but to simply pawn this off on Angel, who has several handicaps of his own, if you hadn't noticed . . . The world hangs in the balance."

"My mother's life hangs in the balance!" she snapped, and then all the energy left her, and when she spoke again, it was nearly a whisper. "Right now, she's all the world I have."

They stood together in silence. The only sound in the room was the grunting and heavy breathing of the werewolf in the cage. *Oz,* Buffy reminded herself. *It's Oz, not just some monster.* And Oz needed Willow.

Buffy needed Willow. Things just seemed to make more sense, decisions seemed to be easier to make, when Willow was around. She always seemed to know the right thing, hard as it might be to say it. *And Xander* . . . If he'd been here, he'd have volunteered to lead the charge into the ghost roads. Crazy and stupid and unbelievably brave. *But now he's* . . .

"We should have heard from them by now, Giles," she said, hanging her head in despair.

They had no idea what had happened to Willow and Cordelia, and even if they made it to the Gatehouse, Cordelia's cell phone didn't work there. There had been no answer on the regular ground line, and Buffy feared the worst.

Xander might be dead.

Her mother was a prisoner, and might as well be dead, if Buffy couldn't find her.

The world was falling apart around her, Hell trying desperately to spill into Earth. The Gatekeeper was on his deathbed. It all seemed so hopeless.

Buffy lifted her head. *No,* she told herself. *Never hopeless.*

"I'll take him," she said. "Get him here."

Giles nodded, but there was no sense of victory in his manner. He went to reach for the phone—

"And, Giles?"

"Hmm?"

"Find her."

Before he could answer, the swinging doors of the library opened again, and Angel stepped in. But he wasn't alone. Micaela and Jacques were with him. The looks on each of their faces made Buffy freeze.

"Oh, Rupert," Micaela said fretfully.

"What is it?" Giles asked. "What now?"

It was Angel who answered. "It's the Gatekeeper," he said, turning to crouch and put an arm across the shoulders of the heir to the Gatehouse.

"He's dead."

"Dear God," Giles whispered.

Buffy closed her eyes. "We're too late."

"Oh, God, Willow, what's wrong with him?" Cordelia shrieked, grabbing Willow's shoulder.

"I don't know, I don't know!"

The girls looked down at Xander, who lay in the Cauldron of Bran the Blessed. He had been there throughout most of the day. At first, they'd thought him dead. But then he'd moved, just a little. And a little more. But now . . . this.

His body was shaking violently in the Cauldron, spasming, his arms and legs pivoting, his head slamming back against the iron walls of the Cauldron. He should have shattered his entire body by now. But he hadn't.

Xander's eyes were wide open and he stared at them. Plaintively, he spoke. "Will. Cor. Help me."

Tears coursed down Willow's cheeks. Cordelia's makeup was running down her face in black streaks. Both girls tried to reach into the Cauldron, tried to hold Xander down, but it was no use.

The door to the chamber, the Gatekeeper's bedroom, slammed open and a punishing wind whipped against them, blowing them both back slightly from the Cauldron. Willow leaned forward and gripped the edge of its rim. She grabbed Cordelia, and then they were both hanging on.

"Oh God, oh God, oh God, Xander!" Willow said, terrified for him. Then she looked at Cordelia again. "We've got to get him out of there!"

"Get his arms!" Cordelia shouted over the gale-force wind.

Lamps shattered. A large bust of some Egyptian god crashed through the window and flew out into the courtyard.

"Where did Antoinette go? The ghost? We need to know what's happening!" Willow yelled.

"Just get him!" Cordy replied.

The two girls reached into the Cauldron and grasped Xander by the wrists. Both were instantly jerked upright by an electrical shock that ran through their bodies. The surge threw them back, away from the Cauldron.

With a sudden hush, the wind died.

The house began to shake.

Inside the Cauldron, Xander let out a long, chilling scream.

"Willow, look!" Cordelia cried.

The ghost of Antoinette Regnier floated through the open door and into the room. There were gossamer tears on her face, and yet, despite the tears and the rumbling of the house beneath them, the ghost seemed strangely content.

"Is this the end?" Willow asked her. "Have we . . . did we lose?"

Cordelia stared at her. "You don't think . . ."

Antoinette floated now above the Cauldron, looking down at Xander with kind eyes. Tendrils of blue light shot suddenly from every corner of the room, from the ceiling above and the floor beneath, and together they struck the Cauldron. It lit up in an aura of crackling blue light, and then, as the girls looked on, Xander floated up out of the Cauldron, jerking as the magick swirled around him.

He floated on the air.

And he smiled.

"My son Jean-Marc has joined me now," whispered the ghost. *"The Gatekeeper is dead. But when last he immersed himself in that Cauldron, he left a part of himself behind, a bit of his life force drained away. The Cauldron saved your friend, but it also washed him in my son's life force.*

"The house did it, you see. The Gatehouse thought that he was one of us, that he was a Regnier."

"What do you mean?" Cordelia demanded. "The house can't think! It isn't alive!"

"No. But the magick is alive. The spell that Richard Regnier wove so very long ago. All the power and

knowledge of the Gatekeeper will pass to the heir. Without Jacques here, the house sought out the heir."

Willow stared at Xander, blue fire crackling around him.

"Xander," she whispered. "It thought Xander was the heir."

"What?" Cordelia cried. "Willow, that's insane."

"No," Willow replied. "It's true. Otherwise, the world would have been destroyed."

"Xander?" Cordelia asked, plaintively, looking up at him where he hung above the Cauldron.

He looked down on them and smiled beatifically. Tendrils of blue magickal fire snaked out to stroke their faces, to touch their hair, but they did not burn.

The house stopped shaking when Xander spoke.

"I am the Gatekeeper."

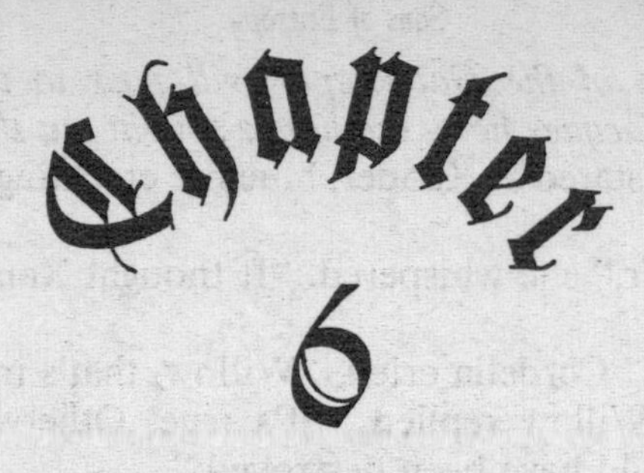

JOYCE SUMMERS'S WORLD HAD BEEN REDUCED TO THE walls of the labyrinth. There were only two things she believed in now that this was her world: that Buffy and the others would figure out a way to save her, and that there was another exit somewhere. She had to believe those things, or she would go mad.

Where the labyrinth had appeared, in what remained of the once glorious Sunnydale Twin Drive-In, there were no streetlights, nor even very much light from Route 17, not far off. In the darkness, her only savior was the glow of the full moon, which shone down on her through a clear night sky. Examining it now, Joyce thought she saw, dimly outlined, the features of a skull on the face of the moon.

There is a man in the moon after all, she thought. *A dead man.*

The walls were smooth as marble, impossible to climb. She had long since lost track of the maze itself, but had kept her wits about her enough to find a way to anchor her sense of direction. Though it wasn't heavily traveled, there was a certain amount of traffic on Route 17. The passing cars let her set in her mind where she was in relation to the highway, the projection booth, and the entrance that had been used to put her in here.

In here with the monster. The Minotaur.

She had heard it grunting not long after first entering the labyrinth, but there had been little sign of it since. Other than the smell, of course. The entire maze had a dank, musky odor, and the well-trodden earth beneath her shoes seemed to have that scent buried in every inch of dirt. Hard-packed earth. Joyce hoped that she would hear it coming. That would be her only chance of survival.

Survival. A part of her thought that she should give up on the idea. For Buffy's sake, she ought to sacrifice herself, just surrender. As long as she lived—as long as she was bait—she was a liability. But another part of her, the stronger part, wanted desperately to live, and knew that Buffy would want her to fight. The Slayer would never surrender. She wouldn't want her mother to do so either.

So Joyce went on.

Time and again she explored blind alleys in the labyrinth. Time and again she wound about, believing she had found a path through to the other side of the maze, or at least into its center. But each time she got turned around and was forced to retrace her steps, keeping the sound of the cars behind her as much as possible.

It only made sense to think there was another gate on the other side. But it was pure fantasy to think that gate might be open, or more accessible. Still, it was all she had to cling to, to keep her from drowning in hopelessness.

The musk of the Minotaur grew even more powerful, so that Joyce began to breathe through her nose. With the sound of the cars at her back, she moved closer to the center. The walls were cold and slick around her, the moonlight making them look almost alive. At each corner, Joyce would pause, heart beating rapidly, and listen for the man-beast. After several seconds, she would peek around the edge. Then she would move on.

She wanted to scream. The silence was destroying her. But she didn't dare make a sound, for fear that she might attract the Minotaur's attention.

Twist and turn. Right and left. Dead end or optical illusion. It wasn't long before she was exhausted from both terror and exertion. But she would not give up.

And then she found the bones.

"Oh, my God," Joyce whispered, before she even realized she had spoken.

Her heart trip-hammered with the fear that she might have been heard. She pressed her back against the cold wall and waited, eyes darting from side to side. After half a minute of silence, she began to breathe a bit more easily, and she allowed her gaze to return to the bones strewn along the path ahead of her. Many were half buried in the dirt, probably trampled underfoot in mud until they became a part of the structure of the labyrinth itself.

The victims of the Minotaur. *How many creatures have died within these walls?* she wondered. The question chilled her, but an even more disturbing question posed itself almost immediately. How many have ever escaped the labyrinth?

She prayed that someone had escaped. It would be easier for her to believe that. To know that it was possible.

Joyce knew she should get moving, but she could not. Her feet seemed frozen to that spot, in among the bones. There were several skulls, entire rib cages, and the various bones of the arms and legs, including a long, thick shaft of bone which she knew must be a femur. Yet she saw only one, and wondered, with a twist of nausea, where this dead man's other leg had come to rest.

That'll be you, Joyce, she thought. *If you don't get moving.*

So she moved. Slowly at first, and then with more speed. There were a great many more bones, and a pattern revealed itself. Where the bones were, that was the path to the center of the maze. To the lair of the Minotaur. It was the only thing that made sense. And if she wanted to reach the other side of the labyrinth, she would have to pass through it.

Something wasn't right, though. She hadn't heard the beast again, and it hadn't come after her. For half a second, she entertained the idea that the sound she'd previously heard hadn't been the Minotaur at all, that the thing had been dead for ages, its bones lying within these walls somewhere along with those of its victims.

But she pushed that fantasy away. It was too seductive to allow into her mind—the kind of thinking, of relaxing, that might get her killed.

A cool breeze rushed through the walls of the

labyrinth, and Joyce shivered, glanced up at the moon and the stars. Another strong wind blew her hair across her face.

Suddenly she knew. It was the wind. She hadn't been able to hear the cars from Route 17 very well for a brief time, because the wind had shifted. Her scent was being carried away from the maze, away from the beast. But the moment the wind shifted, or she succeeded, somehow, in passing by the Minotaur, well then, it would have her scent. And have her not long after.

Joyce wanted to turn, to run back the way she'd come. But there was no exit there.

Instead, she moved forward, following the trail of bones. A little more than a minute later, the labyrinth opened up in front of her. She had reached its center, a wide box made of walls broken at odd intervals by paths that led back into the maze. Bones were strewn about. Piled in certain places. An enormous chair of bones had been built at the center of the labyrinth.

Joyce threw herself back against the wall, as soundlessly as she could. Carefully, she peered around the edge.

It sat there on that throne made of its victims. Its feet were wrapped in heavy leather, tied off with thick rope. A rotting leather loincloth hung down over its upper thighs. Its legs, though hairy, were human enough. But above the waist, it was a massive, heaving bull, its face the snorting, horned head of the bull. Its arms ended in taloned hands, but huge and thick, each finger like the branch of a tree.

Its chest rose and fell.

The Minotaur was sleeping. Joyce stared at it for a long moment, the chill wind making her shiver. Or perhaps it was merely her fear. The beast shifted in its slumber. Its eyes fluttered slightly, but did not open.

The wind died. And began to shift.

Joyce fought back the tears that threatened to spill down her cheeks. She bit her lip lightly, to force herself to keep silent. Then, as quickly as she could without stumbling over the bones of those who'd come before, she began to retreat.

She'd have to find some way to get out through the front gate. It was her only hope. No hope. But her only hope. There had to be a way. The breeze shifted then, blowing into her face as she moved away. The thin sweater she wore was little protection against the cold.

On the ground, she saw the thick femur bone she had noticed earlier. Now she picked it up, hefted its weight, and began to run with it. Run as fast as she could, no longer so careful about making noise. For the wind had shifted.

The Minotaur was awake. Somewhere behind her, on its throne of bones, it bellowed with rage.

And hunger.

It had been nearly a year and a half since Ethan had vacated the costume shop he had once run in Sunnydale, and it remained empty. Considering the climate of death in the town, he wasn't at all surprised. Though it might have had something to do with the spell he had cast on the place. It was a psychic marker, almost like the scent of a skunk, but mental. Those who had come to look at the property had gone away feeling quite negative about it.

The locks had been changed, of course, but it was a simple thing to open them. When he entered, he smiled to himself. There was several months' worth of dust inside, which led him to think that, after a time, the realtors just gave up on the place. Why bother to clean it up if nobody was going to want it? If Ethan ever needed it again, why, he'd come back and set up shop under another name.

Perhaps a book shop the next time? He did so enjoy books.

Inside, he rummaged around the few racks that had not been emptied by the realtors. All the costumes were gone, of course, but there were shelves of cloth and other materials, some books and papers that he was happy to retrieve.

And the mirror.

It was prepared specifically for a night such as this; a night when he needed to call out to something very dangerous.

In the darkness of the shop, the only light coming from the streetlights outside, and from the moon, he stared into his own reflection in the mirror, and began to chant softly.

"Wanderer of the wastelands, harken now.
Lord of the Vile Flesh, hear me.
Master of the Dark Ways, show him now.
Master of the Secret Passages, let him pass.
Belphegor, Dark Wanderer, Horned Master,
Come to me now, the way is clear.
Let thy majesty be revealed."

The mirror seemed to flow, as if the reflective glass were liquid, and Ethan could no longer see his own face. The mirror was black, as though it had been burned. And then, deep in that blackness, green eyes the color of putrescent flesh stared out at him. Flashing in the dark within the mirror, the blood-red horns of Belphegor, which resembled nothing so much as huge, gnawed-upon bones, with bits of rotting meat still attached.

"You dare much, little wizard," the image rumbled.

Then it was more than an image. The horns of the demon began to poke through the shimmering silver of the mirror, into the real world.

"Not really," Ethan said. "You don't frighten me, Belphegor."

At the use of its name, the demon winced. Ethan mentally thanked the dead Trenholm—much good gratitude did anyone—and continued.

"That's right. Belphegor." Ethan grinned, though in truth he was quite afraid. He hadn't toyed with demons much, not if he could avoid it. His misadventures with Giles and the others had made him quite wary, if not exactly cautious. But he couldn't let the demon know that.

"I've called you. I know you can't make it through, not with all your power intact. That's why you're still over there, isn't it? If it was just a matter of having some weak-minded spellcaster call you up, you'd have been here centuries ago. No, you want something else. You have a plan, don't you, Belphegor?"

The demon's eyes seemed to leak something awful. Ethan could smell it, and nearly vomited. Instead, he held the mirror at arm's length and tried to breathe through his mouth.

"I'll have your heart," Belphegor promised. *"That's as much of my plan as I wish to share with you."*

"I don't particularly care what you wish."

The demon roared. The mirror shook and nearly fell from Ethan's hands. He managed to hold on until it subsided.

"What do you want, little man?" Belphegor demanded.

"For once, it isn't about me," Ethan said. Then, in retrospect. "Well, not entirely. You need to come through intact. The laws of nature won't allow such a thing, and you're trying to change those laws. That much I know. I also know that you want the Slayer. You need her power, or her blood, or both.

"I can get her for you."

Ethan saw the way the demon's eyes flared. He thought he could see its vast rows of teeth, and wondered if the thing was actually smiling. But then it drew back into the mirror, horns sinking once more. He could barely make it out, but from the darkness inside, it spoke.

"And what would you desire in return, man?"

This is it, Ethan thought. "Life," he replied. "Of the eternal variety, of course. And a small kingdom of my own, shall we say, two thousand souls of my own choosing. Not much to ask for, I believe, when you consider what you'll receive in trade."

The mirror went black. Ethan blinked, staring more deeply into it. He brought it closer to his face, and then jerked back as those hideous eyes and filthy horns shot up toward him, bloody maw of a mouth open below.

"I think I'd rather have your heart," Belphegor roared. *"I don't like you, human. You don't show the proper respect for your fear. And I certainly don't need you. If we are able to claim the Slayer, it will speed our*

invasion. It will hurry the apocalypse along, and bring my reign about all the sooner.

"But if she yet lives . . . it isn't going to stop us.

"Hell is coming, little wizard.

"I'm coming . . . for you . . ."

"Bastard!" Ethan screamed wildly. "You don't want to make an enemy of me!"

The demon's image withdrew, and one of its taloned, pustulent hands shot through the mirror and scrabbled for the front of Ethan's jacket. With a shout of fear and anger, he smashed the mirror against the wall, splintering it into dozens of tiny pieces. For a moment he saw the claw tips of several fingers poking through the larger shards of broken mirror, and then they were gone.

He'd have to prepare another mirror, when he had the time. Really the safest way to go about such things.

With a snarl, he took one last glance at the shattered mirror, and then headed out the back door once more.

Ethan might have been a useful ally to the demon, but Belphegor had spurned him. Now he would do all he could to destroy the hellspawn. The demon lord Belphegor had made a very dangerous enemy.

"This is . . . this is nuts!" Xander said, shaking his head.

He sat on the edge of the Gatekeeper's bed, holding his hands out in front of himself. His fingers were several inches away from each other, and tendrils of electric blue magick sparked back and forth between them.

With a sigh, he stood up and began to walk the

length of the room. "I can't be the Gatekeeper, you guys!" he said. "I have . . . I have school, y'know? And . . . and there's college to think of, or whatever."

His eyes wide with horror, he turned to regard Willow and Cordelia, who were both equally wide-eyed.

"And, oh my God, what about my parents? My dad is gonna kill me," he said miserably.

It was Cordelia who laughed. Of course.

"Xander, please," she scoffed. "You're, like, the Gatekeeper now. One of the most powerful sorcerers on Earth? Hello? I really don't think there's much your parents can do to you now."

"Well, they can be pissed at him," Willow offered. "And, okay, if he still hasn't graduated, they could ground him, I think. Right?"

Xander shot her a look. "Thanks, Will. Very helpful. Would you pour me a glass of hemlock while you're at it?"

Willow offered an apologetic grin and a shrug. "It's the least I can do," she said. "Xander, I don't want you to be the Gatekeeper. That would mean you, y'know, here, and everybody else three thousand miles away."

"Speak for yourself, Rosenberg," Cordelia replied, moving to link her arm with Xander's. "I think I'll stay right here with my all-powerful sorcerer boyfriend. God, wait until those stuck-up bitches at school hear about this one."

Xander spread his arms, palms up, and stared at them each in turn. A moment passed, and they only looked back at him.

"Hello?" he said at last. "Okay, saving the world. In the midst of battle? Does any of this ring a bell? Has it occurred to anyone that I'm now, like, the last line of defense for the planet Earth . . . and we're now all doomed to eternal torment of Hell on Earth."

He collapsed on the bed again and buried his face in his hands.

"Why me?" he moaned.

"Better than death, though," Willow offered helpfully. "That's something."

"Or just prolonging the inevitable," Cordelia added, her face scrunched up in that deep-in-thought look that Xander saw her get every so often. "So maybe being all-powerful isn't what it's cracked up to be. But if the kid's still alive, all we have to do is keep this place from falling apart until Buffy gets him here."

"We don't even know if they found the boy," Willow said miserably.

"Wait—" Xander interrupted. "Cordy, did you say 'if'? What happens if the kid never shows? Am I the Gatekeeper forever?"

"Well, even if he comes, I think you might have to die for him to inherit his power," Willow said.

Once again, Xander moaned.

Then, without warning, the house shuddered and the ghost of Antoinette Regnier appeared in the center of the room, above the Cauldron.

"My son's death has bought some little time," she said. *"But the Sons of Entropy are many. Those few survivors renew their assault, assuming the house undefended. And there will be more.*

"Xander, you must perform your duty."

Cordelia stared at her. "Wait just a minute, he isn't the real Gatekeeper!"

"You can't ask him to—" Willow began.

Xander cut them both off. "Guys, thanks. But she can. She has to. And I have to do it. There isn't anybody else."

He paused, lowered his head a moment, and then said softly, "Now I guess I know how Buffy feels."

None of them had anything to say to that. Until, at length, Willow slapped her hands to her thighs and stood up.

"We need Giles," she said.

"We need Giles," Cordelia agreed, and reached into her jacket pocket to pull out her thin cellular phone.

She and Willow both turned to look at Xander. He frowned and stared at them, but then he saw the phone and he understood. The Gatehouse exuded some kind of force field which didn't allow such communications to pass through, at least, not without the Gatekeeper opening a hole in that field.

Xander made an apologetic face, and shrugged. "I'm sorry, guys, I don't know . . ."

Then, suddenly, he did know. He knew exactly what to do. Cocking his head as though he were listening to something nobody else could hear, he held up one hand and twirled his fingers.

"Try it now," he said, as surprised by his behavior as the girls were.

When Cordelia dialed the number for the school library, it began to ring on the other side.

Giles placed the phone back in its cradle. He started slightly when Oz growled in his cage. Then he turned to face Micaela and Jacques again.

"Rupert, what is it?" Micaela asked. "You look so pale."

He smiled thinly. "Not to worry," he replied. "It's my natural color."

Then his smile disappeared. He'd made a joke, and Buffy was not there to remark upon the amazing infrequency of such an event. He wished desperately that she and Angel had not already gone out to search for Joyce. He needed her there, needed her to work with him to formulate a plan. As much as she sold herself short, Buffy was actually a passable strategist, and improving with time.

"What's happened?" Micaela asked.

"My father *is* dead, isn't he?" Jacques asked.

Giles went to the boy and crouched down, nodding slowly and sadly. "Yes, Jacques, I'm afraid he is," Giles told him. "But his death has, somehow, through some accident of magick, granted us a kind of reprieve."

Micaela shook her head. "But how can that be? If he's died, the Gatehouse must be in the hands of . . ."

"The new Gatekeeper," Giles replied.

Boy and woman stared at him in utter incomprehension.

"Somehow, the house itself has decided that Xander—a friend of Buffy's whom neither of you has met—is actually a Regnier. It has made him the Gatekeeper."

"With the full power of the Regnier line?" Micaela asked, astounded.

"Indeed," Giles replied.

"That's extraordinary," she said. "That means we can concentrate on the situation here. On finding Buffy's mother and dealing with my fath—with Fulcanelli."

Jacques did not seem quite convinced. "Eventually," he said, "the house will realize its error. I must return before that moment arrives."

Giles cocked his head thoughtfully. "On the contrary," he said. "I believe the house will continue to recognize Xander as the Gatekeeper—now that it has done so—until the true heir arrives. Not to worry, Jacques. We will get you home as soon as we are able."

The boy's lip quivered a moment, and then his face changed, hiding his pain. "No hurry, Mr. Giles," he said. "There isn't anyone there for me to go back to, now."

Giles thought about mentioning the boy's grandmother, the ghost of Antoinette Regnier, but refrained from doing so. He did not know if her spirit would move on now, and he didn't want to give the lad false hope.

He heard the soft shush of the library doors swinging open, and turned to see Ethan Rayne enter. Giles had hoped it would be Buffy. But Ethan was more than a disappointment. He was a constant threat, close enough to sabotage any hope for the future. Unless he was actually telling the truth, which Giles simply could not bring himself to believe.

"Hello, Ripper!" Ethan said happily.

"I've told you never to call me that," Giles replied angrily.

"Ah, of course," the other man replied, feigning regret. "But I think you'll forgive me."

Giles lifted his chin, looked at Ethan more closely. He'd known the man a long time. Too long.

"You know something, Ethan. What is it?"

Micaela and Jacques were staring at him as well,

now. Ethan winked at Micaela, and Giles felt his ire rising even more.

"Don't suppose you want to get us a cup of coffee, do you, lad?" Ethan asked young Jacques.

The heir to the Gatehouse only glared at him.

"Ah, well, I thought not." He turned back to Giles. "In any case, I've got the name of the demon behind all this, the one the old magician's been worshiping all this time. A right bastard he is, too."

How would you know? Giles thought to ask, though it was certainly possible Ethan could have just done the research.

"Well?" Micaela asked. "Fulcanelli was always very circumspect. I never heard him call his sponsor by name. Are you going to share it with us, or shall we wait for the world to end?"

Ethan looked at her wistfully. "Ah, Ripper," he said, "you always seem to gravitate towards the ones with that dry, cutting wit." His upper lip curled. "It's really not very becoming, actually."

"Ethan!" Giles snapped.

The magician rolled his eyes. "It's Lord Belphegor."

Giles's eyes widened. "The wanderer of—"

"Of the wastelands, lord of vile flesh, horned master, yes, all of that." Ethan sat down in a chair at the study desk and leaned back, his hands behind his head. "Pretty powerful, isn't he?"

"Extremely," Giles replied, already moving toward the stacks where he kept his books. After three steps, he paused and realized that his reference on Belphegor was in a box he had never unpacked, for fear some of the teachers might see it and realize how completely inappropriate it was.

The book was called *The Lords of Hell.* And it was in a box. In the library cage.

Where Oz paced back and forth in all his werewolf hunger and fury.

"Damn," Giles whispered.

"There's more," Ethan said happily. "I know where the Sons of Entropy are holding the Slayer's mother."

Giles stared at him. "Good God, man, why didn't you say so?"

"I did."

It was Jacques who spoke the words Giles was thinking. "But how will we get to Buffy now?" he asked. "If only you'd come sooner. She and Angel might still be here."

"Oh, if she's with Angel, I can find her," Ethan said. "I have a locator spell that will track him down, no problem."

Micaela shook her head. "I don't understand. After what Rupert has told me about you, I mean . . . why? Why are you doing all this? I would think you'd be trying to have as much fun as possible in the shadow of the apocalypse."

"Perhaps I do have a . . . shall we say, mischievous nature," Ethan admitted. "But it is my world, too, is it not?"

It was clear Micaela didn't believe him. Not entirely. And Giles didn't blame her. Unfortunately, they didn't have much of a choice.

"I still don't trust you," he told Ethan.

"Well, bully for you," said the magician.

"Nothing!" Buffy snapped. "This was another waste of time!"

With a shout of anger, she lashed out with a swift

kick that knocked over a large metal barrel. There was a large dent in its side when it came to rest.

Angel laid a hand on her shoulder, his gentle touch soothing her just a bit.

"Buffy, we're doing all we can," he said. "It was only logical that we look here. It was the first place you ran across members of the Sons of Entropy."

They were inside an old canning factory on the waterfront. It had stood empty for years. While they were looking into the rumors of a sea monster off the coast, Buffy, Xander, and Cordelia had unknowingly saved one of the Sons of Entropy from a savage creature called Springheel Jack.

It was the last place she could think to look.

"But it's wrong, Angel!" she said, feeling as though she was crumbling inside. "She's not here, and if I don't find her soon, I just know they're going to . . ."

"Shush," he said tenderly, and pulled her into a firm embrace. She felt the cool flesh of his hand on the back of her neck, the familiar weight of his head where he rested it on top of hers. Buffy let it all go for just a moment, let herself be comforted. In all the world, Angel was the only one who could hold her like that, who could give her a safe harbor, a world in his arms.

A world she could never have.

"Let's go," she said, pushing away from him. "This is a waste of time."

She was glad Angel didn't ask her to clarify that last statement.

As they turned to leave, a figure filled the door through which they had entered the cannery. It was tall and lithe, its arms down to its knees. Far from human.

"Well, hello, young lovers," said the thing, in a voice like silk tearing on thorns.

It stepped farther into the building, shafts of light from shattered windows all over the place making a kind of checkerboard pattern of illumination. It slipped in and out of the shadows.

"What is it?" Angel asked.

"Who knows?" Buffy sighed. "Let's just kill it and get out of here."

Suddenly it leaped from the darkness behind her—*how'd it get back there?*—and grabbed Buffy in a choke hold.

She threw her head back and felt her skull strike its face with a satisfying crack. The thing released her, and Buffy turned, spun into a high kick, and shattered one of those long arms. The thing shrieked and stumbled into a shaft of light.

It was hideous. Scales and ridges and a huge, toothless maw with tiny waving tendrils inside. It didn't seem to have eyes at all.

"Okay, I'd have to consult, oh, I don't know, the dentist! But my guess would be demon," Buffy told Angel, who came to stand next to her.

"I must have you," it said, with that voice pushed out by the little wormlike things in its gaping throat. "I subsist off the pain of love, and there is such pain here."

Buffy paused.

Angel laid a hand on her shoulder. "It's all right," he whispered. "Let's just destroy it and go. We have more important things to worry about right now."

He was right. She hated it. But he was right.

"How do you do that?" she asked the demon.

"Why, I eat the lovers, of course," it replied, and lurched at her again.

"But we're not lovers," Buffy retorted, and kicked it again. In the midsection this time. She didn't want her foot anywhere near that disgusting mouth.

"And, oh, the succulent pain of it . . ."

It rose again.

Angel came from behind Buffy, the oil drum over his head, and brought the huge metal barrel down on the thing's head. It went down under his onslaught, but he struck it again, and again. And again.

Buffy watched him, feeling each blow. Understanding. There were many things they could no longer share. What they shared now was a great deal of pain. Pain that this thing had reminded them of, at the worst possible time.

Eventually, she stopped him. "Angel. It's dead."

He glanced at her, then dropped the barrel with a massive clang. "Yeah. I wonder where it came from?"

A voice from the doorway made them both look up.

"The barriers are dropping. Slowly, but it is happening," said the voice. It belonged to Ethan Rayne.

There was someone else with him, just outside the door. Buffy saw the reflection of the moon on his glasses, and knew it was Giles.

"And it won't be the last," the Watcher said. "Not unless we put a stop to all this."

Buffy was about to speak, but paused as Giles came toward her. Something about the look on his face. There was something there . . . something . . .

There was hope.

Buffy understood, then, and her voice was a whisper.

"You've found her."

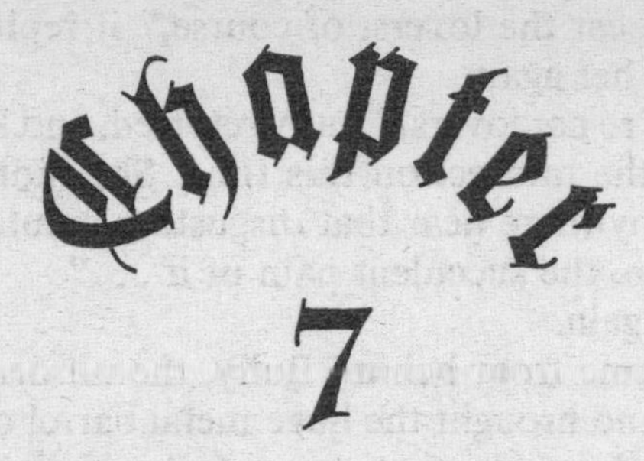

Chapter 7

SEATED IN THE DEPRESSING LITTLE STORAGE ROOM THAT had once housed the mother of the Slayer, Fulcanelli studied the sword that rotated slowly in the air. It was a very old weapon, older even than he. Hadrius had traded his soul for it, or so he claimed. Fulcanelli was inclined to believe it; Hadrius had been the cruelest and most heartless being he had ever known, himself included.

He thought back now to those days, of how his father—or rather, the man who was his father in title if not in deed—had left him bound and gagged on Hadrius' drawbridge in the dead of night. The foolish bastard crossing himself and making the ward against the evil eye.

"God keep you," the superstitious peasant had whispered, his breath like the smoke of the hellish bonfire

that still raged in the distance, "that is to say, keep you far from me and mine, you hellspawn."

Giacomo strained to spit at the man, but the tattered, filthy rag stuffed into his mouth prevented that satisfaction. He was so furious he was certain that his spittle would wither a flower, or burn a hole in stone. And as for this toothless half-wit who had actually dreamed that he was the father of such a boy as Giacomo, who had had the temerity to call him "son," while all the village chuckled at the mere thought . . .

Giacomo's spit would have sent him straight to hell.

The peasant turned and ran, his shadow trailing after like a cowardly twin beneath the smoky moon. With all his heart, Giacomo wished him ill: bad crops, a barren woman, death by hanging.

Then time passed, and while his anger smoldered, his discomfort began to rise. He shivered in the cold as the mists from the moat lapped at his body and chilled his bones to a dull, numbing ache. The tight bonds around his wrists cut off all sensation in his hands. The right one was curled around the left as if to pluck the withered fingers off his deformed hand, the miserable culmination of his useless left arm.

"Useless except in magick," his mother had whispered to him when he was very, very little, as the two stood alone before the enormous stone fireplace in the hall of a great lord. Giacomo did not know the man's name, only that he was versed in the greatest of the occult arts, and loved Giacomo's mother.

"Your hand is a sign of great favor from the king of the shadows," she continued. Whispering always. So much of their time had been spent in furtive conversation, his mother looking over her shoulder, slipping things into his hands: a poultice, a charm, a talisman.

The only person ever to smile at him, ever to embrace him. When one had a mother such as she, what else did one need?

And then one night the peasant who was her husband heard them, saw them, as they bent over the great cooking pot, conjuring.

"Hide, my darling!" his mother shouted.

Beneath the bed he had scurried, able only to see the heavily shod feet of the soldiers. His mother's bare feet.

She was screaming. She kicked and fought, and one of the soldiers laughed and said, "Struggle all you please, strega! *Not even the Devil will lie with you after we're done!"*

They carried her out the front door. In a homespun nightshirt, Giacomo ran after, sobbing, delirious with terror. He knew what all this meant. He had seen other women suffer and burn.

His feet were bruised and bleeding by the time he reached the clearing where such things were done. The enormous bonfire was already lit and blazing, a huge, infernal mountain.

His mother was wild with fear, her large, dark eyes flashing, her face bruised where they had beaten her. She knew what the fire meant. And she knew who had betrayed her.

Giacomo knew it, too: it was his supposed father, who now stood beside a pine tree and almost touched—but did not quite touch—the hand of a beautiful young woman beside him. Her chin was raised in triumph and her eyes glittered as she gazed at Giacomo's mother.

His mother reached out her hand to curse the couple and was cuffed across the back of the head by one of the soldiers. She cried out and went limp, falling to the ground in a heap of long, black hair and a flowing white nightdress far too rich and beautiful for the wife of a peasant to own. Years later, Giacomo decided that it was the nightdress that had convicted her, and had to admit that it had been foolish of her to flaunt it.

But at the time, he was only a little boy whose mother lay sprawled in the mud as one dead.

"Fool!" the local priest had shouted at the soldier. "Now she will have no chance to recant!"

"She'll not do that, not in a million years," called Giacomo's supposed father in his rugged Florentine dialect. "She's a strega puttana *and she'll burn like a piece of tallow before she'll confess. And you may as well throw that one in with her."*

He pointed at Giacomo. The boy trembled as his mother was lashed to a tall ladder. He opened and closed his fists and stared at her, willing her to turn into a raven or a bat and fly away. But she had fainted, and she could not save herself.

Some of the village women smiled as the ladder was raised over the bonfire that lit up the chilly night. Giacomo glared at them. Under cover of night, they had come to his mother, begging for love potions and philtres. "Make me beautiful. Make him love me. Kill my rival." They didn't realize that the witch's son observed all from the dark corners of the room, while the husband, drugged, snored in the loft.

"Give me children, else I die."

They raised the ladder high against the moon. The stars were the tears in the eyes of the king of the shadows, and it was to him Giacomo prayed to save her. The horned moon gleamed dully, and then clouds smothered it. The air smelled of rain, and Giacomo stared hard at the stars, willing a flood to put out the fire.

But it was not to be. It did not rain. The ladder teetered at its great height. The flames crept up the sides. Then they let go of it, and it crashed into the summit of the bonfire. His mother had awakened at the last as the ladder arced. She shrieked with terror and agony. The villagers were awed by the sight of such torment. The priest took the opportunity to warn them that similar fires awaited all unclean and unshriven souls.

As her body burned and crackled, Giacomo would have turned his head, but his "father" held it steady and forced him to watch. Then he vomited down the front of his nightshirt, and his father only laughed.

The deed completed, the villagers dispersed, though how many slept, Giacomo could not say. Such a frenzy would not yield a soft night of slumber. Passions must be spent. Guilt and horror must be purged.

Alone in the clearing with the peasant and his paramour, Giacomo had been bound and gagged. The heartless young woman smiled as Giacomo's father said, "I'll be free of you both before the cock crows."

Now Giacomo lay on the drawbridge, shaking hot, shaking cold. Hatred burned away any softness; in that moment, evil forged all that he would become.

Then the great portcullis was raised, and Hadrius, in black armor and a terrifying black helmet decorated with red devils, appeared astride an enormous black horse.

In his right hand, clad in a black leather gauntlet, he held aloft a sword of uncommon size and heft.

"Not to fear, boy," he said to Giacomo, as two

squires raised the boy across the great saddle. "This night will see you avenged."

And they rode, oh, how they rode! Cutting them all down, the smug peasantry toasting and feasting the destruction of Natalia Fulcanelli! In the tavern and in their beds, every child, every man, every woman.

The best, saved for last: the peasant and his whore, burned to death with magick.

"It is La Brûlure Noire," *Hadrius told Giacomo, "and before I die, I will make you its master."*

And he did become the master of the black burn.

Thus was he known as Il Maestro.

Now, in the rude little storage closet, Il Maestro grunted with anger. He narrowed his eyes into slits as the vicious edge flashed in a field of crackling blue energy. The blade thirsted, and he, the most skilled and feared of sorcerers on so many different planes, appeared to be incapable—for the time being—of giving it what it desired most. What it had once savored so lustfully.

The blood of a Slayer.

In 1539, Maria Regina, the Chosen One, had been easy to subdue, easier still to sacrifice to Fulcanelli's lord, Belphegor. The power of her death had coursed through Fulcanelli's veins like an incredible drug. In all his hundreds of thousands of days as a sorcerer, there had been only a handful of moments which rivaled that thrill, that ecstasy. One had been the slow death by torture of Giuliana Regnier, the wife of the first Gatekeeper. Another, when he had finally mastered *La Brûlure Noire* and burned a rival to death.

Like the blade, he thirsted for another such moment. Had believed that the glory was almost upon him. Now, however, something was going terribly wrong. He wanted the heir, Jacques, for his power and for revenge on the Regnier clan, but thus far, he had been denied the boy. It was absolutely unsupportable to Fulcanelli that that should be the case. It should have been an easy matter to pluck him away, body, soul, and small, beating heart.

Likewise, the Slayer should be dead by now, at his hand, with this very sword. And yet she still lived.

"There is no justice in the world," he groused, then smirked at his own ridiculous choice of words. He had long ago stopped believing in justice. In fact, its absence usually benefited him.

But nothing was going his way. Unbelievable as it seemed, two of his lieutenants, Claude and Lupo, had turned against him. Even more unbelievable, some of the brothers had joined the two traitors. Others were considering it, discussing it. Weakness and duplicity traveled in Fulcanelli's wake.

And while it was true that he had planned to give every single one of his followers an eternity of endless torment in return for their loyalty, and not the princely power over the earth that he had promised them, he nevertheless counted it a profound insult that he had been betrayed.

Those who insulted him once should not count upon living long enough to insult him twice.

However, Brother Claude and Brother Lupo were nowhere to be found. That concerned him further. Heretofore, none of his followers had been able to hide from him. Dare it, and they were ashes before they realized they'd been caught—

On the sword, in the field of blue, a darkness formed. Within the darkness, the familiar silhouette of horns and trunk blurred, then coalesced. Belphegor's face crystallized upon the blade, spinning slowly like a sun as Fulcanelli tried to mask his fear at the appearance of his sponsor without Fulcanelli having summoned him.

"My lord," he said, with what he hoped was humility. He inclined his head, thought better of it, and prepared to kneel.

The blade stopped moving and pointed directly at the base of his throat.

"Giacomo," Belphegor said with deceptive softness. *"I grow impatient."*

"Yes, yes," Fulcanelli said with nervous asperity, then realized what he was doing and cleared his throat. He said slowly, "Yes, great lord. I know. I'm making progress."

"Progress."

"Yes." Fulcanelli swallowed. Thus far, Belphegor had needed him as much as he needed Belphegor. But the barriers between worlds were growing weaker with each passing moment. The demon had insisted that the blood of the Slayer was necessary for his purposes, but was that true, if Micaela could serve as her replacement?

What of his, Fulcanelli's, own blood?

Fulcanelli wondered if it was time to find another sponsor. Not as a replacement—Belphegor would surely shred his flesh from his bones if he even attempted such a thing—but as protection. It would be a risky matter to approach another denizen of Hell, requiring skill and cleverness. But perhaps it would prove riskier to do nothing.

Fulcanelli glanced anxiously at the reflection of Belphegor. The demon's silence was unnerving; yet

Fulcanelli knew that the longer he himself refrained from speaking, the less worried he would appear to be. He had perfected the art of conversational brinkmanship over the centuries; yet now, faced with his failure and the dangers it posed him, he had to fight hard not to turn into a gibbering fool, intent upon making excuses he himself would never allow a subordinate to make.

He clenched his fists. He was not a subordinate of Belphegor's. He was an ally.

"You seem troubled," Belphegor said mildly.

"No, great lord," Fulcanelli assured him. "Not at all. All is going according to plan."

"Oh, really?"

"Yes."

"That the Slayer yet roams free. That your daughter helps to guard the heir. That your own confederates betray you. All this is part of your plan?"

Fulcanelli blanched, yet he retained his composure. He moved his hands and said, "It's true that there have been a number of obstacles—"

"Obstacles!"

The storage room began to quake. Rolls of paper towels cascaded to the cement floor, unfurling like party streamers. Plastic bottles thumped to the floor. A jar shattered.

The sword flew at Fulcanelli. He raised his right hand to stay it with magick, but it sailed past his thumb and sliced open his cheek.

Fulcanelli shouted in surprise. The blade clattered to the floor and he took a step back from it, touching the wound.

"Excellent," Belphegor said. *"Allow the droplets to fall on the blade. I shall taste your blood this day."*

"My lord," Fulcanelli protested. It would shame him to obey. And he didn't want the demon to know the flavor of his fear.

"Do as I say, Giacomo." The voice was deceptively gentle. *"I desire only to commune with you. You are my best beloved one in this sad little realm, you know that. I have no wish to hurt you. Only to know that you are still my friend."*

Fulcanelli had little choice. He took his hand away from the cut, his fingertips sticking to the already drying blood, pressed again, and smeared his hand over the blade.

"Ah," Belphegor sighed with contentment. *"Delicious. And filled with power."*

Fulcanelli said nothing.

But he knew his time was running out.

"Buffy, your mother is at the old drive-in," Giles said, as he and Ethan joined Angel and Buffy in the canning factory. "It's been transformed."

Buffy said, "Let's go."

Angel hesitated and looked at Giles. "Transformed into what?"

"A labyrinth," Giles said.

"Have you seen it yourself?" Angel pressed. "Or did you actually trust his word?"

"Angel," Buffy protested. "Let's just get going." She glared at Ethan. "He knows that if this is a trap, or a sick joke, I'll break his neck."

Ethan raised his brows. "For heaven's sake, you're just loaded with aggro, now aren't you? Slayer Spice. Girl power. Good Lord, why is the world still extant at all, with a hothead like you as the Chosen One?"

"Watch it," Angel said. His face morphed into full

vampire grotesquerie, which Ethan always found fascinating.

Ethan said sorrowfully, "You don't trust me. I'm crushed." He put his hand over his heart.

Angel put a hand on Ethan's shoulder and applied pressure. "Crushing can be arranged."

"That does hurt," Ethan said mildly. "All right. Listen. Not far from where we stand," he said sotto voce, "a small contingent of your dreaded Sons of Entropy recently visited the grocery store."

Buffy stared at him.

"They're fond of various forms of pasta, as one might imagine. Linguine, that sort of thing."

"Did you cast a spell to find them at this grocery store?" Buffy asked suspiciously.

Ethan shrugged. It was a poor lie, and he wasn't about to compound his trouble by elaborating. It wouldn't be wise to let them know that he'd dined with one of the Sons of Entropy earlier, then seen the man killed. It might lead to questions he'd rather not answer. He'd been trying to see what he could gain by betraying Buffy and her friends. Now his only option was to help them. Fine. But it would be best for his physical well-being if they didn't know he'd tried to sell them out to Belphegor.

"They meandered around for quite a long time, fixating on all the different kinds of coffee to be had." He shrugged. "Boring lot, those. When coffee brands consume so much of their otherwise precious time. Imagine having that much time on your hands."

The hand on his shoulder threatened to pulverize bones. "Get to the point, damn it," Angel growled.

Ethan frowned at him. "Do you mind?"

The pressure increased.

"I followed them. They went to the drive-in. And I sensed the presence of your mother with a locator spell far superior to anything Rupert's attempted."

The look Buffy gave him told him that Rupert had not recently attempted a locator spell. Then Ethan remembered they'd not gotten that far in their joint magickal studies.

"All right," he admitted. "No locator spell here, either. I heard her screaming."

The Slayer blanched and looked as if violence was not far off. She pushed past him and said, "Giles," as she raced out of the canning factory.

Angel and Giles ran to catch up with her. Ethan followed behind.

"We're in my rental," he announced.

"Where's *your* car?" Buffy asked her Watcher. Rupert obviously understood her distinct unhappiness in allowing the dread Monsieur Rayne to chauffeur her.

"His is faster."

"Bigger, too," Ethan said airily, "than that death trap Ripper pedals."

Briefly, an image flashed into Ethan's mind of Rupert on an old motorcycle, vintage World War II, with Buffy on the back and Angel in a sidecar. All of them in goggles and white scarves. It was so ridiculous he grinned from ear to ear.

Even with the world ending, it was imperative to keep one's sense of humor.

They reached his vehicle. As Rupert climbed into the front seat on the passenger side, Ethan flashed him a jaunty grin. The old boy didn't respond.

"And we're off," Ethan announced.

Angel clenched his fists. He hated Ethan Rayne. The sorcerer had put a demon into Jenny Calendar, however indirectly. Angel had been the one to save her, and ironically, it was a trauma she had only partially recovered from before he, Angel, had murdered her. Angel had often wondered if the ordeal had spurred her to find a way to restore his soul into his own demon-inhabited body. If feeling so defiled and dirty had increased her guilt over the curse she'd known her people had laid on him. Ridiculous as it was to try to pin any of the blame for her death on Ethan, Angel figured the Brit and himself both for ridiculous figures. Fatally ridiculous.

Buffy said anxiously, "Damn it, Ethan. Faster."

They hurtled through the night. Perhaps one minute dragged by. Perhaps two. When you're over two hundred forty years old, time takes on a new rhythm. As does death, and the contemplation of it.

"We need a plan," Buffy said. "We can't just pull up and ask them to give back my mother." She said to Ethan, "Did you tell them we were willing to trade?"

"We are not," Giles said, "and I will not allow you to think that way, Buffy." He cleared his throat at her steely gaze. "That is, I would request that you refrain from such notions."

"Yessir," Buffy said with mock obedience.

"They're going to know the Slayer's coming," Angel cut in. "They have locator spells. Runestones."

"I have magick, too," Ethan said reasonably. "I haven't honed my skills in the areas of violent offense, I'm afraid. My talents are for more subtle magicks. Though I've prepared certain spells, studied up a bit for the bloodshed, you might say. Also, I'm fairly certain I can mask our arrival. And our assault." He half turned from the steering wheel. "You see, dear girl, your mother's being held inside the huge maze. They've got her in there, wandering about."

Angel cast a sidelong glance at Buffy, who tensed as she listened. He understood; he, too, had the feeling that the other shoe had not yet dropped.

"That's all. Just frightening her," he said easily.

They barreled onto Route 17 and went flying out of town. Buffy's jaw was tightly clenched. A muscle jumped in the hollow of her cheek.

"I said to hurry up," she muttered, leaning forward. Angel could practically hear her grinding her teeth. He reached out a hand and touched her wrist. It didn't seem to register.

The dark shapes of trees and fences blurred across the night-blackened windows of Ethan's car. Angel couldn't shake his sense that this was bad business, a trap concocted by the British sorcerer. Who knew how many double deals he had going? How many monsters, human and otherwise, he had promised the Slayer's head on a plate?

Angel wanted to tell Buffy they should turn back. The protectiveness he felt toward her was overwhelming. But he would be wasting his time, and hers. He knew she was gearing up for the fight, and she needed his confidence in her and his own battle readiness.

Suddenly, as they flew by a large field and began to pass beneath a bridge, a fog rushed up like an ocean wave and cascaded over them. It spread out and enveloped the car, thick and oily, clinging to the windows.

"Damn," Giles muttered.

Buffy said tensely, "No, it's good."

Angel completed her thought. "It's camouflage. It means we're getting close."

Directly in front of the car, the fog thinned—the only place where it did so—and Ethan smiled proudly into the rearview mirror.

"Good work, eh? Seen from the side, they'll think their silly little trick is working. We'll pull over in a few minutes and hike the rest of the way in. Good?"

"You're a bloody genius," Giles said sarcastically. He turned to Buffy. "We still need a plan. Now, what I suggest is—"

"Okay." Buffy hunkered forward with her hands on the back of Giles's seat. "We sneak in as quietly as we can. Ethan, you make sure they can't sense our presence, especially mine. They're looking for me. You blow it, and I'll kill you."

"Not to fear, m'dear."

"Yeah, right," she snapped. "While I find Fulcanelli, Angel takes on any Sons of Entropy who notice us. With Ethan's help. They've probably got spiny-headed guards or trolls or something guarding the perimeter. Giles, you concentrate on my mom."

"That's a reasonable facsimile of what I was going to suggest myself," Giles said.

She sighed. "That's probably the best we can do. As usual, we're outgunned and outnumbered."

"Outnumbered, yeah, outgunned, never," Angel said, smiling at her.

"Oh." Ethan snapped his fingers and looked up at Buffy in the rearview mirror. "Did I mention the Minotaur?"

The three stared at him.

"In the maze. Rather keen on devouring your mother, I'd say."

There was silence in the car. Then Buffy's voice was deadly quiet. "When this is over . . ."

Ethan Rayne chuckled. "If wishes were horses, dear girl, well, let's just say my world would be a much more amusing place."

Cordelia and Willow walked closely together as they went down one of the main halls of the Gatehouse. The place was enormous, with maybe as many as a thousand rooms folding in and out of earthly space.

"It was totally freaky when we got here," Cordelia told Willow. "The house was, like, wigged. One minute we were down in the basement with this worm monster and the next, we're up in an attic with Antoinette."

She tossed her hair. "Xander almost got eaten by ghouls, Buffy had these panther people after her, and I was stuck on the roof in a fire. I would have died if the Gatekeeper hadn't saved me. Well, Buffy helped a little, too," she added.

On Willow's left, something shrieked wildly, then threw itself against the carved wooden door. She jumped.

"See, the thing is," Cordelia said, apparently unconcerned, "the Gatekeeper has to make sure all these monsters stay here. And he has to collect any new ones that come through the breaches. Oh, and pretty things like fairies and unicorns."

"Unicorns?" Willow echoed. "Cool."

Cordelia nodded at her. "Some of this stuff is neat. But some of it is, eew, possessed or something. There were these sprite things, and Giles thought they were so gorgeous, but then their stomachs started exploding and—"

There was a terrible howl, followed by a series of ferocious growls. A door down the hall burst open, and Xander appeared. He was sweaty and panting; his hair hung in his eyes, and the T-shirt he wore clung to his chest and arms.

"Xander, what are you—" Cordelia blurted, but he held up a hand.

Then he raised his arm and faced the door, saying in a booming voice, *"By the gods of old, I bind thee! I call upon Pan, my protector, to subdue thee!"*

The growls turned to yelps, then died away. Xander grabbed the side of the door and slammed it shut.

"Man," he said, wiping his forehead, "no rest for the weary."

Willow was impressed. "Wow. What was that all about?" she asked.

"Some of the rooms are losing their cohesion, the magickal bonds are loosening," Xander said casually, as if they were talking about the latest bad band to debut at the Bronze. "I'm doing the best I can, but the barriers between worlds have been battered so much, and they're still taking a beating from the inside—from things trying to get out—that I don't know if I'm up to this, Gate-boy or not." He shrugged and fell into step with the two girls as they reached the doorway.

"So," he said, "are you vixens ready for another skirmish with the losers in black? Because my spider sense is tingling, as Buffy would say. I'll bet you three chili dogs the Sons of Entropy are massing for an attack on the front lawn."

The ghost of Antoinette Regnier shimmered into form within touching distance of Willow. Willow still had not gotten used to the presence of the ghost, which was odd, considering that she—and Xander and Cordy, too—had experience with ghosts. It was hard not to move away, but she didn't want to seem impolite.

"You are correct, Gatekeeper," the ghost said. *"They are coming."*

"Oh, wonderful." Xander rolled his eyes. "When do I at least get to take a shower?"

"Oh, I like you all sweaty," Cordelia said, her eyes shining.

"I do have a sort of manly sheen, do I not?" He put his arm around her and kissed her cheek. "Kind of a B.O. *savoir faire?"*

"A what?" Cordelia asked. She wrinkled her nose at him. "Although you're right about the B.O. part. You really stink."

"There is no time to lose," said the ghost.

Without warning, the house shook and rumbled. Plaster fell from the ceiling, and the marble bust of Cupid toppled from its perch and slammed against the carpeted floor.

"You're not wrong," Xander said to the ghost. "In fact, I'd say time's up." He ran his hand through his hair. "Let's see, I'll need super heat vision and repulso rays . . . oh, and a cheese sandwich would be nice."

"I'll make it," Willow offered.

"Good." Cordelia made a face. "That kitchen creeps me out."

"Okay, Cor, you're with me, then," Xander announced. "I want you to climb out on the roof and snub the bad guys to death. Maybe wound them with little barbs about their attire."

"You're so hilarious." Cordelia made as if to punch him, then stopped and dropped her hand to her side.

"It's okay," Xander told her. "Even though I'm somewhat godlike, you can still smack me."

The house shook again. More plaster tumbled down.

Xander turned and gave Willow a wink, saying, "Sandwich." He kissed Cordelia on her lips. "Later."

Then he strode away, aware that they were watching him. He was amazed at what had happened to him. He was the Gatekeeper. He, Xander Harris, the guy voted most likely to be mediocre, to not do anything with his life except serve as Riker to Buffy's Picard.

Which actually was quite an accomplishment, when you thought about it.

But around here, he was Picard, Kirk, Sisko, and—God help him—Janeway, all rolled into one.

Okay, not Janeway. Scratch that. She talked like a Conehead and he did not get her fashion sense at all.

"So beam me up, Scotty," he muttered, as he went to battle the Sons of Entropy threatening to invade the Gatehouse.

His Gatehouse.

Raising his chin, squaring his shoulders, he marched down the curving staircase that led to the house's entryway. From there, he threw open the front door, daring the massing acolytes to attack.

One did, a scrawny man with Asian features, sending a bolt of pulsing lightning straight for him. Xander repelled it with a murmured word of magick and a flick of his wrist. Returned to sender, it exploded in the chest of the Asian man. The acolyte burst into bits.

Xander watched in satisfaction as a ripple of fear went through his enemies.

"Next," he shouted, taunting them.

"Who . . . who are you?" one of them called to him.

He grinned. "Well, I'm not the homecoming king," he replied. "But I'll do in a pinch."

Chapter 8

CLOAKED IN BLACK, BROTHER CLAUDE CROSSED HIS arms and watched as Brother Lupo directed the tying of the sacrifice to the hastily erected altar inside the service tunnel. Subterranean Sunnydale was a warren of dark and eerie passageways and sewers, and natural cave formations, perhaps speaking to a communal need, conscious or otherwise, to burrow down away from the sun and sleep in the lap of Hell.

Some of the underground places housed truly fascinating and unique demons and monsters, a smorgasbord of evil that must have kept the Slayer very busy. Claude was still mulling over the implications of a man-sized skeleton, part human, part fish, they had found while preparing the altar. Intriguing. A kelpie? He wasn't sure. Small animal skeletons and bones with a human appearance had been scattered around it—its prey, perhaps? He squinted and noted approximately a dozen or so tiny skeletons he was sure were those of Dark Faeries.

How wonderful, to revel in the beauties of the Hellmouth!

But he must pay attention to the matter at hand. As coleader of the group, he must give their ritual due reverence.

The three acolytes who bound the young girl were clumsy with nervousness. Everyone in their band—numbering almost two dozen—was anxious and uneasy. And with reason: though Claude and Lupo had managed to convince them that to remain with Il Maestro was to die, the two had not been foolish enough to guarantee their survival if they sided against their old master.

Thus, the sacrifice to chaos.

One of many sacrifices they had made in the last few hours, actually. The altar and the dirty, damp tunnel floor were awash in blood. This one, their last, was some pretty young thing they'd dragged into the car when no one was looking. Her tender beauty would greatly please the dark lords.

Claude was still sorry they hadn't taken the Slayer's mother. She would have been a very powerful sacrifice. Without the proper rituals, her death in the maze would be a ridiculous waste. And her presence had done nothing to lure the Slayer into Fulcanelli's orbit.

Proving further what an imbecile he was.

Claude sucked in his breath at this errant thought. Old habits died hard, and though he had gone against his onetime leader, he had not shed the automatic response, developed over years, of showing Il Maestro proper respect at all times, in thought, word, and deed.

The sacrifice was now fully bound, and the acolytes moved away from the altar. They still wore the hooded robes of their former order, the Sons of Entropy. Claude and Lupo had discussed it, and decided that there was no time to outfit them in something else to ritualistically set them apart from the world they sought to overrun. But now, looking upon the brethren as they moved in the dark, dank tunnel, he wondered if that had been a mistake. If they felt like traitors rather than courageous warriors.

Brother Lupo began the ritual, with Claude and the others intoning the responses. How many sacrifices had he attended, even performed? Hundreds. And yet, each one was special, if one had the discipline to make it such, and the belief that each one mattered.

On the altar, the girl moaned in terror and tried to struggle. They usually did. It was always a wasted effort. He found it in his heart to pity her, although usually he felt very little, if anything, for sacrifices. At least the end would be quick. Once Lupo stabbed her through the heart—now the bald man held a dagger aloft—she would struggle no longer.

As all held their breath, Lupo paused. Then he put down the dagger and said, "Stand back."

Claude frowned slightly and cocked his head. That was not part of the ritual.

Lupo stood apart as the others gazed at him uncertainly. His body began to glow almost imperceptibly, with an aura of oily black flame. Claude opened his mouth to speak, but he was mesmerized. The black fire crackled all over Lupo's frame, engulfing him. Even the girl on the altar was distracted from her plight as she stared, goggle-eyed.

Lupo extended his arms almost casually. Perhaps

then the sacrifice understood what was to come, for she strained against her bonds and shrieked behind her gag.

It was not pleasant. The tunnel filled with smoke and several of the acolytes had to move farther down the passage, doubled over with coughing.

But Claude could not stop watching.

Neither could any of the others, who watched in mute astonishment.

Then, as the corpse fell in upon itself into a pile of ashes, anger and excitement mingled in Claude as the acolytes began to fall on their knees in obeisance to Lupo. He must consider his next move carefully. Lupo had been grandstanding, true, but on the other hand, morale among the acolytes had sunk dangerously low. Now they were smiling. Cheers rose up. They had seen one of their leaders achieve the black burn, Il Maestro's most dangerous weapon of destruction. Their side stood a chance after all.

Lupo gazed levelly at Claude and smiled. Claude did not smile back. If they both survived their war with Fulcanelli, a confrontation between them was inevitable. And Claude could not perform the burn.

But if Lupo did not survive the war . . .

Now he did smile.

Lupo looked mildly uncomfortable.

Claude said, "It's time to go, brothers. We fight for our lives. We fight for chaos."

"For chaos," they intoned.

Lupo moved away from the altar and cracked open a wooden crate. Inside lay a cache of automatic weapons. He picked one up and said, "I want each of you fully armed. No man leaves here without one of these."

He began to toss them to the brothers, some of whom scrambled eagerly to catch them, others who shied away as if they were hand grenades. The weapons were another surprise, and again, Claude had mixed feelings. He had often argued that the Sons of Entropy should be better armed, especially the ones who were not magickally adept. But the fact remained that Lupo had not consulted with him, and again, he was establishing himself as the generous benefactor of the group.

Claude walked over and picked up one of the weapons. It was an AK-47, and he had used one before.

Many times.

"They're simple to use," Lupo said. "Watch."

While he ran through a quick demonstration, Claude flicked his fingers at the ashes of the sacrifice. They rose into a column in the air, then resettled upon the altar. He examined them for signs and portents, smiling as he found evidence of personal victory.

Lupo was temporarily distracted by Claude's actions. Claude shrugged and made his face a blank; Lupo narrowed his eyes and returned to his training session.

So. Lines were being drawn. Post-Fulcanelli plans must be made.

Claude walked the length of the tunnel and closed his eyes. He formed a mental picture of an imp sitting on his shoulder, chittering in his ear like an organ grinder's monkey. Its mottled gray face was elongated, its eyes mere slits of glowing scarlet.

He concentrated until he could feel the pressure of the imp's weight, the pinpricks of its talons as it balanced on his shoulder. The graveyard smell of it. Its grating, frenetic voice.

"Find the heir. Find Micaela," he told it.

It gabbled and gibbered, and then it unfurled its leathery wings and flew away.

Maybe this time, Claude thought. He had sent other familiars and other creatures out searching. None had been successful, and he had destroyed each one when it had failed him.

"O great dark gods," he murmured, "make me the king of this world, and I will gladly become your imp. I will be your dog. I will do your bidding with every breath I take."

Nothing happened. With this particular prayer, nothing had ever happened.

He tried again. "I will give you power. I will not rest until I have given you the Slayer."

An icy shiver passed through him and he involuntarily arched his back in surprise. Then he realized that something had passed inside him, and taken up residence.

At long last, his prayers had been answered.

He turned and impatiently clapped his hands. The sound echoed down the tunnel, eerily louder than the movements of the Sons of Chaos as they learned how to use their new toys.

All heads turned in his direction.

"I've received direct word from the ones we serve," he announced. "It's time."

"We're not finished," Lupo said haughtily.

Claude felt the presence inside him stretch against his muscles and tissues. The bony ridges of his forehead pushed forward at an oblique angle, then sank downward. The cartilage in the ridge of his nose pushed through the layers of sinew and skin and pressed its features onto his. His mouth stretched almost to the breaking point, and froze into place.

His teeth elongated, and sharpened.

He looked at Lupo, who blanched. The others drew back. Then slowly, one by one, they fell to their knees.

"We're finished *here,*" Claude retorted, but it wasn't his voice that spoke the words. Gravelly and deep, it was the voice of something ancient and very evil. One of the old gods, the Lords of Chaos.

"It is time to face Fulcanelli," the voice continued, "and it is time for him to die."

Buffy looked down from their vantage point on the hill behind the drive-in and muttered, "Well, this is just terrific. The one time I need you to be a liar, and you're telling me the truth."

Ethan shrugged apologetically. "Sorry."

Giles raised an eyebrow and glared at the magician. "Ethan, what did you hope to accomplish by keeping the Minotaur a secret until the very last?" He stared angrily at his former friend, now his very untrustworthy ally.

"Dramatic tension?" Ethan quipped. He held out his arms as if he wanted a big hug. "It's just that side of me, Ripper, the one that likes things to be a little uncertain. That's what I like about the Sons of Entropy. They're into it. Entropy, I mean. Disorder. Confusion. That's the stuff that gets an opportunist like me all hot and bothered."

He covered his mouth with his fingertips. "Oops. Begging your pardon, Miss Summers, you with your tender youth and all that."

"Stifle yourself, Ethan," Buffy sneered. She dismissed him, and returned her attention to the maze. "Can you see her?" she asked Angel, then glanced at Giles.

Giles shook his head. "I'm sorry, no."

"But I can smell something," Angel offered, sniffing the air. "Something very musky."

"It's the Minotaur." Ethan shook his head in mock sorrow. "I keep explaining to it that if it would only bathe, it could reel in the ladies."

"Oh, yeah, and *you're* such a babe magnet," Buffy said flatly.

Then she started moving carefully down the hill, murmuring, "Which way is the wind blowing?"

Giles followed after, and Angel after him. Bringing up the rear, Ethan grumbled, "But I *am* a babe magnet."

They reached the outer wall of the maze. For a moment they stood still, clearly stymied, until Buffy took a breath and slammed her foot into the wall. To Giles's utter shock, she disappeared inside the maze.

Then she popped back out and said, "Yikes."

"Whoa," Angel said, looking at Giles. "What happened?"

"Like the Flying Dutchman, and any of the other oddities we've encountered, the labyrinth is not supposed to be here. It may have been pulled through from the Otherworld by magick, or simply slipped through, now that the barriers between worlds are disintegrating," Giles explained. "But with the magickal war being waged, and all the barriers so tenuous, its presence may be only temporary."

"Meaning?" Angel prompted.

Giles frowned. "At any moment, the maze might be sucked through, and rematerialize in the Otherworld. The Gatekeeper could never return those things that slipped into our world before, but I'd bet now, with the walls so thin, it would be a simple task. In any case, that's got no bearing on the labyrinth. It was never bound into the Gatehouse, as far as I can recall."

"Wonderful. So if we go inside, we may be whisked away to another dimension, never to return?" Ethan turned to go. "I'll sit this one out, if you don't mind."

Angel grabbed his arm. "We mind. We mind very much." He looked at Giles. "The sooner we get in and find Joyce, the sooner we can get the hell out of here."

Giles closed his eyes. There was not a single part of him that wanted to say what he was going to say. It would only make Buffy angry, and she certainly wouldn't listen to him. But he had a duty, and so he went through the motion, useless as it was.

"The Slayer cannot risk this," he announced. "The world—"

"Oh, please!" Buffy cried. "It hangs in the balance, okay? How many times am I going to have to hear that!"

Giles persisted. "If we are taken to another dimension, but not killed, I'm not sure another Chosen One would be called. You would be impotent and—"

"Hey, no need to get personal," she growled. She put a leg back through the maze wall. "That's my mom in there. I'm going in. There's nothing you can do."

She lifted her chin. "Except help me."

"All right." Giles bowed his head. "I knew that would be your answer."

She flashed him her best little-girl pout. "And I knew you would tell me not to do it."

She ducked into the maze.

One by one, her team followed after.

The maze was pitch dark and smelled of rotting meat. Buffy gagged once, then resolutely hunkered into stalking position and began to move forward over the hard-packed earth.

"We need to keep track of our route," Angel said.

"There's the right-hand rule," Giles replied. "Keep your right hand on a surface at all times. If there's a break, find the adjacent wall and keep touching it with your right hand. It works on any maze. In England."

"Okay, Alice in Wonderland," Buffy muttered. "But I'm not doing that. I'm from the guess and stumble on, guess and stumble on school of mazes."

"Very well, I'll do it," Giles said, "but if we get separated, then listen for my voice."

"Hey, where's Ethan?" Angel said.

Buffy whirled around, tackled the retreating magician, and threw him to the ground.

"Oof," Ethan wheezed. "Please, this isn't a rugby match."

"Get up." Buffy was disgusted with him. She got to her feet and yanked him to a standing position.

"All right. Good Lord, who died and made you Xena?"

"Same people who made you Dr. Smith."

"Sorry, I don't follow," Ethan told her.

"Lost in Space?" Buffy prompted. "The cowardly bad guy?"

"We're from Britain, Buffy," Giles informed her. "We had *Dr. Who."*

"Whatever." Buffy flung Ethan forward. "One more time, and you won't be watching any TV ever again."

"I love it when you're angry."

Buffy gritted her teeth and walked behind him. She wished she had a flashlight.

Or not.

The clouds shifted. The mist cleared away, and the full moon shone down upon the labyrinth. The walls were lit up, the ground, littered with bones, was cast in long, jagged shadows.

Everyone froze. Directly before them stood a creature Buffy dimly recalled from her mythology class: a muscular, filthy man wrapped in a piece of cowhide, his head that of a huge bull. Massive horns glinted in the waxy light.

Something trickled down the side of its face.

"No," Buffy moaned.

With a bellow, the creature charged.

"Oh, yes," Fulcanelli rejoiced, as he heard the roar of the Minotaur. His face quivered with delight; he rose from his chair in the projection booth and flung open the door. Instantly, a small throng of hooded acolytes froze in their places, awaiting his bidding.

"The Slayer has arrived," he said, certain of it with every fiber of his being. "Go into the maze and retrieve her."

"Go—go into the maze, Maestro?" piped one of them, a very young Australian with a goatee and an earring. "With the . . . beast?"

"I'll follow in less than a minute," Fulcanelli assured him. "I have a quick spell to cast, and then we'll take her down." He rubbed his hands together. "With any luck, the heir will be with her." Too much to hope for, surely, but then, Fulcanelli was such an optimist.

The brothers looked at one another. Fulcanelli flared with anger. He threw back his arm and flung a blue net of energy over the Australian. The man screamed. Fulcanelli pulled back his hand and the man collapsed, dead.

The others trampled over his corpse in their eagerness to obey.

Suddenly, the corridor exploded with gunfire. A hail of bullets riddled the bodies of the acolytes, dismembering them and spraying the walls with blood and gore. Shrieks of pain and terror rent the air as Fulcanelli dove back into the projection room and slammed the door.

He crawled beneath a desk that had been pushed into a corner and caught his breath.

Who dares? he wondered, livid. He closed his eyes and murmured a few syllables in ancient Sumerian.

At once the faces of Lupo and Claude glowed across his eyelids. Then Claude's face dissolved and in its place, the face of the Ancient, one of the Lords of Chaos, glared at him with contempt.

"Foolish man!" it thundered. *"To align yourself with Belphegor. No matter. Now you shall die."*

Fulcanelli shook his head. "Hardly," he whispered, and, falling deep within himself, he pulled forth the strongest of his magick and mentally hurled it at the demon face. It melted in an instant, leaving the demon's image writhing in a silent scream of pain.

Alerted now, he created a field of energy around himself and rose to his feet. Dozens of bullets slammed into the energy, and were absorbed. Fulcanelli felt nothing as he crossed the room and went back into the corridor. Many of his followers lay dead in pools of blood and organs. Others cowered behind one another.

But there were those brave few who were defending their positions with magick, and one new brother who was manfully thrashing at the empty air with a chair.

At the same moment, the door at the opposite end blew off its hinges and the corridor began to fill with men dressed identically to Fulcanelli's own. They were armed with machine guns, and they began to fire upon Fulcanelli's remaining acolytes.

"Not while I live!" Fulcanelli shouted.

He began the black burn.

Recognizing it, the first rank of attackers faltered and fell back. In that moment of hesitation, Fulcanelli's men pursued them, wresting their weapons from them and shooting them point-blank. The next rank, caught between the defensive sweep and the rest of the raiding party, had no choice but to stay where they were, sitting ducks for Fulcanelli's infuriated men.

Then Fulcanelli recharged the black burn, and another man blazed like a torch, screaming as he died.

Another.

Fulcanelli was a dervish, employing every magickal weapon he had, repelling the invaders in a furious storm of energy and shock. They kept falling back, and in the confusion, Fulcanelli's troops began to give as good as they got.

Fulcanelli heard Brother Lupo shouting, "Forward, you fools!"

Il Maestro smiled grimly and kept up the attack.

* * *

"Now!" Brother Claude shouted from his vantage point on the hill. "Bring the Slayer. Wound her if you must. Hurt her by all means. But don't kill her. Not yet. Without ritual, it would be such a waste. Go."

The Sons of Chaos spilled into the maze, shooting everything they saw—bushes, an unlucky deer, the Minotaur's throne of bones. They began to race down the main arteries of the labyrinth, calling to one another, maddened by the chase like hunting dogs catching the scent of the fox.

Buffy heard the pop-pop-pop of gunfire as she ran as fast as she could from the charging Minotaur, then propelled herself off the end of the stone corridor, flipped backward and slammed into its face. It roared and tried to grab her.

"Look," she said, as she gave it a bone-cracking roundhouse for good measure, and then clipped it behind the knee, "give me my mom and we'll get you out of here."

"I doubt he speaks the Queen's English," Ethan shouted.

"That's okay. I don't either." Buffy side-kicked the thing in the groin, then lunged forward and jammed her fingertips underneath its diaphragm.

Three hooded figures leaped from the top of the maze wall, one dropping on the Minotaur and two dropping on Buffy.

"Buffy!" Angel cried, brutally punching a young acolyte in the temple and throwing off another attacker as if he were a bad fur coat. The man's AK-47 went off, spraying the sky with bullets like a water sprinkler.

By the time Angel reached Buffy, she had put some

distance between herself and the monster . . . in the form of two whimpering acolytes who had somehow dropped their weapons. The Minotaur lashed out at the first one and decapitated him.

Another hooded figure dropped down on Buffy.

"What, do you guys have one of those stealth helicopters?" Buffy demanded, pummeling the new arrival. He got off a barrage, peppering the wall with bullets. He almost got her, too, but she jumped into the air and executed a spinning kick that took him out cold.

Buffy dropped to her knees and grabbed his gun. As she rose, she saw the Minotaur looming above her. It stared down at her, and she saw that it was bleeding from several bullet wounds. She almost struck out at it, or let fly with a barrage of gunfire. Instead, she held the gun up for the Minotaur to see and looked hard at the monster.

"They have guns," she said. "It's only a matter of time. Get my mom and we'll all get out of here."

The Minotaur gazed back at her. Its eyes were enormous, and very blank. She had a sinking feeling it couldn't understand a word she said.

Then it abruptly turned its back and began to lope away.

"Chicken," she called after it.

Gunfire exploded everywhere. Buffy could barely hear herself think. Then there was a pause, and Giles was shouting, "Buffy! We have her! We have her!"

"Giles, where are you?" she cried.

"Right-hand rule," he shouted back.

"Not now," she groaned, but she plastered her hand on the right wall of the maze and began racing through it. The walls shook. Where her hand met a corner, the entire wall shimmered and disappeared, then reappeared. *The breach is weakening,* she thought. *This baby may blow any minute.*

"Ethan! Angel!" she cried.

"Buffy, I'm behind you," Angel said. She felt his hand on her shoulder.

Then the gunfire recommenced, sending both of them diving to the earth and covering their heads. Dirt spit at them as the bullets stabbed into the ground. Something grazed Buffy's back, and she gritted her teeth.

Finally, she dared to look up, and for one terrible moment, she wished she were dead.

Bathed in moonlight, her mother's body lay limp in the arms of the Minotaur.

"No," Buffy whispered. She began to get up.

"Buffy, stay down!" Angel whimpered.

The Minotaur came closer. Her mother's head was canted at an odd angle. Her eyes were closed, her mouth slack.

Buffy staggered toward the Minotaur. It looked down at her strangely, and then it yielded its precious cargo.

Buffy took her mother into her arms.

"Buffy, run!" Giles yelled, running up from behind the creature. He took the unconscious Joyce from Buffy and gestured with his head. "They're after you!"

"Run?" she said, incredulous.

Then the labyrinth flickered. There was no word for it. The Minotaur reached out a hand toward Buffy.

She said, "C'mon," but as she did so, the structure shook and flickered again.

Without another thought, she leaped over the bodies of their attackers and made a cannonball run for the end of the corridor. As she reached the wall, she closed her eyes, lowered her head, and charged.

"Buffy, no!" Angel yelled.

For an instant, she felt the impact of her skull against unyielding stone.

Oh, great, wrong guess.

Then her momentum propelled her forward, and she tumbled through the wall and onto the mist-dampened night grass.

Angel rolled out after her, followed by Giles with Joyce.

The Minotaur was halfway through when the maze vanished. It screamed, sounding utterly human, as it was cut in two. Its torso and head flopped wetly on the ground. The rest disappeared with its lair.

Buffy and the others raced for the car.

"Where's Ethan?" Angel asked.

"Who cares," Buffy snapped. "I hope he's in Hell."

"Or in the Otherworld," Giles said.

"Same diff," Buffy answered.

The stench of dying choked Fulcanelli where he crouched in the tunnel beneath the Sunnydale Drive-In. The labyrinth was gone, and those traitors who had been in it.

"And the Slayer?" Belphegor demanded.

"We'll have her," Fulcanelli said. He was wounded, shot in the leg. A rosy glow enveloped the wound, and he was whole again.

"As we have the heir?"

"He'll never leave Sunnydale alive."

"Apparently he has," Belphegor said in an even, very calm voice. Fulcanelli knew that tone: the de-

mon was gripped by an ungovernable fury, which threatened to erupt at any moment.

"What?" Fulcanelli demanded, cocking his head.

"Did you not feel it? The Gatehouse has a new keeper. The energy is far too vibrant, far too young, to be that of the old man, Jean-Marc.

"Jacques Regnier has slipped through your fingers."

"Impossible!" Fulcanelli cried. "Absolutely impossible! I have set barricades, wards—"

"He has gotten past them. And now, your life is forfeit."

"No," Fulcanelli said quickly, panicking. Then more calmly, as he hatched a plan, "No."

He nodded to himself as the pieces fell into place.

"I'll deal with this personally. I'll go to Boston."

"And?" Belphegor prodded.

"I'll kill this new Gatekeeper."

He smiled to himself.

"And when he is dead, the Slayer will have no one to turn to, and I'll kill her as well."

Chapter 9

IT WAS NEAR DAWN IN SUNNYDALE. INSIDE ANGEL'S mansion, Buffy and her mother sat in chairs pulled up before the warm fire, drinking tea. The room was chilly. Angel's place might be stylish, but it was hard to heat all the stone and cement. Buffy had managed to keep track of her backpack all this time, and her English sweater was around her mother's shoulders, where it looked at home.

Note to self: curb impulse buying, she thought, but no part of her self was listening. No part of her self cared about fashion or shopping or any of that right now.

Instead, Buffy watched her mother's hands shake as she brought her teacup to her mouth. Not for the first time, and not for the hundredth, Buffy wanted to tell Joyce how sorry she was for everything she put her through. Although Buffy had not chosen to be the Slayer, she felt guiltier about it than all the trouble she'd purposely caused as a smart-mouthed airhead back in Los Angeles. Shoplifting a lipstick now and then and sneaking out to party had strained her parents' marriage to the breaking point—she'd never get over *that* guilt—but none of that had put her mother's life in danger. Being the Slayer did.

That knowledge would never go away. And neither would that threat. If they survived all this, it could easily happen again.

"Mom," Buffy said slowly, "now that we know what's going on, maybe you should leave Sunny—"

Her mother raised her chin, smoothed Buffy's hair away from her forehead, and briefly cupped Buffy's cheek. Her eyes glittered.

"You look older," Joyce said.

Buffy tried to swallow, and couldn't. "I am older."

Joyce took Buffy's hand and gave it a little shake. Her laugh was broken and sad. "I remember when you lost your two front teeth, and you tried to stuff cotton balls in your mouth before your second-grade class picture to hide the spaces."

"Vanity, thy name is me," Buffy said, trying for a light tone, not getting anywhere near it. She set down her teacup.

"Mom, I'm serious. It would be safer . . ." She took a breath. ". . . *easier* if you weren't here. Sunnydale is on the Hellmouth, Mom. When bad stuff happens, it happens *here.* We've been putting Band-Aids on it, sure, but when everything blows—"

"Buffy, if the world ends, I want to be with you when it does," Joyce said. "You and I are a family. We need to stay together."

Buffy sighed hard. "I'm not getting through to you, Mom. I'm the Slayer."

A tear slid down Joyce's cheek. "And I'm the Slayer's mother. And I didn't choose it either, Buffy. But you know, I would rather be your mother than anyone else's."

Buffy laughed shortly. "Yeah. Except maybe Willow's."

"Oh, honey." Joyce pulled Buffy into her arms and Buffy laid her head on Joyce's shoulder. Buffy closed her eyes and listened to the strength in her mother's voice. Drew from it. "Not even Willow."

Buffy said quietly, "When Giles told me they'd kidnapped you, I refused to take Jacques to Boston. I think Jacques has been lying to me, telling me that he's safer here. Because he lost his father, and he knew how it felt. He didn't want me to lose you." Reluctantly, Buffy pulled away and sat up. "That shouldn't have happened. I should have gone."

Joyce cocked her head. "But we live in a world where you stayed. And I like that world, Buffy. Very much."

"Me, too." From somewhere deep inside herself, she dredged up a lopsided grin. "Except we could let the school blow. That'd be okay."

Joyce chuckled. "That's my girl."

"Yeah."

Shyly, Buffy pulled away and picked up her teacup. She drank, savoring the warmth. She was very, very cold.

Giles cracked open the door to the bedroom, letting in a sliver of light. It gleamed golden on Micaela's blond hair as she stood over Jacques, tenderly staring down at the boy with her arms crossed over her chest.

Giles moved to join her. She smiled gently at him,

then gazed back down at the boy. The heir's right hand lay outstretched on the pillow, as if he were reaching out for something. Someone.

Micaela sat down gently on the mattress and took his hand. He sighed and shifted slightly in his sleep.

Leaning over, she pressed her cheek against his. Then she rose.

Together they left the room, Giles first. Micaela shut the door and pressed her hand against it.

"He's so young," she said softly. "Just a little boy. He should be dreaming up pranks."

They walked down the dimly lit corridor. "I don't suppose you had much of a childhood," Giles said, "being what you were." When she flushed, he took her hand. "Sorry. I didn't mean that to sound harsh. What I meant was, having to lead a double life as you did. Your loyalties split."

In the gauzy light, she looked incredibly young. But there was a careworn maturity in her face that belied her appearance. For all her apparent softness and youth, Giles saw steely resolve in her expression. In peril of her entire existence, now and in the hereafter, Micaela had turned against one of the most powerful sorcerers ever born, an ancient creature capable of ending the world. And she had done it not to save someone she loved, nor even to save herself: she had done it because it was the right thing to do.

One had to respect a person like that.

"I want to tell you that I'm sorry for your loss, but of course that would be ridiculous," Giles said, and again, he thought he sounded cruel. Upon their return, Jacques had informed them that he could not sense Fulcanelli, and that he believed the sorcerer had been killed in the battle and disappearance of the labyrinth. It was a tremendous relief, but Jacques also stated that the work of the sorcerer appeared to have remained in motion.

The world was still in jeopardy.

"You look like you're about to cry," she said. He was floored, for until she'd said it, he had no idea he had felt so sorrowful. She added, "Or maybe you're just tired."

"Yes, perhaps." He gazed at her; she caught and held his look.

Giles stirred; she was so very beautiful, and he did not need to hide what he was from her, nothing of his double life as the Watcher, nor of the special kind of aloneness that created. He was not given to self-pity, but upon occasion, he did feel rather lonely. . . .

"Micaela," he murmured, touching her fingertips with his. "When this is over . . ."

She studied his face. "Would you be able to forget everything that's happened? Everything I helped cause to happen?"

He cocked his head. "I find it the most remarkable thing that we who are so intimately involved in the battle between good and evil are even more involved with the shades of gray between them. I've done many things in my life I'm not proud of, and I'm certain I shall do many more.

"And many of them will be in the name of good."

She looked down. "But what I did . . . you were nearly killed because of me."

"No, not because of you. Because of Il Maestro. You were trying to please your father," he said. "It seems we're all fated to some version of that. Pleasing them, inheriting their expectations. Most parents insist they only want their children to be happy." He smiled crookedly. "But you and I, and Buffy and Jacques—we have rather bittersweet legacies, and our happiness is secondary to what we must do."

"Said without resignation," she noted.

"Upon occasion." He smiled faintly at her. "When I'm trying to impress a lady."

They walked into the living room, where Buffy and her mom sat in silence, drinking tea. When Joyce looked up at Giles, he saw that her eyes were red with tears. Her face was drawn and she looked very tired.

"Hey," Buffy said to Micaela and Giles. "It's almost light. Where's Angel?"

"I'm sure he'll be along shortly," Giles told her, though he had been wondering the same thing. "I'm going to have to leave soon to retrieve Oz from the library," he added. "Then we need to start talking about Boston."

"Oh," Buffy's mom said quietly, the softest of protests, but one that tugged at Buffy.

"Yeah," Buffy murmured. "Boston-bound. We're overdue on that front, too."

"Buffy, Angel will be here," Micaela said. Maybe she didn't understand the look on Buffy's face.

Or maybe she did.

"Now, I've phoned the Gatehouse to tell them we believe Fulcanelli is dead," Giles said. "Which, of course, pleased Xander enormously. But the fact remains that he is not actually the Gatekeeper, and should not be doing what he's doing."

"My bad," Buffy murmured. Then she shifted, realizing everyone was looking at her. She picked up her teacup, which was empty.

"Do you want some more?" her mother asked,

noticing, and got up, very momlike, to get it. "Giles? Miss Tomasi?"

Giles began to shake his head, but Micaela said, very warmly, "That's so nice. Let me help you." Smart one, that Micaela.

That left Giles and Buffy alone.

Buffy said again, "The sun's almost up."

"Maybe he's resting somewhere," Giles offered. "He knew he couldn't make it in time, so he holed up."

She nodded. "Yeah." She shrugged. "Y'know, I can see why Kendra's Watcher wouldn't let her have any friends."

"She was a good Slayer," Giles said. There was a moment of silence, during which Buffy painfully recalled cradling the murdered Kendra, dead at Drusilla's hands. Her blank stare.

"But you're still the Slayer, Buffy," Giles continued. "Your specialness, your uniqueness has often been remarked upon by the Council. Which is probably why Ian Williams knew so much about you." Ian Williams had been one of Fulcanelli's followers, who had managed to infiltrate the Watchers' Council and set up Buffy, Angel, and Oz in London to be massacred. In the end, Il Maestro had killed him for failing to do so.

She chuckled slightly. "My uniqueness. You mean the fact that I don't follow the rules."

"Yes. Neither of us does. You know, back when I was a rebellious kid, they talked about kicking me out. I wanted desperately for them to do it."

"Getting kicked out would be nice," she agreed, sighing.

"But one's destiny is one's own. You can't hand it off."

"Willow's parents would definitely agree with you," Buffy said. "I'm sure when she gets back, they're going to ground her for life. Unless she gets accepted to Harvard," she added with mild sarcasm.

He raised his brows. "Oh, she applied there, did she? Good. I was after her about that. Yes, well, as for the other, your mother and I are working on that. We've been concocting a story about an art exhibition and extra credit . . ." He pushed up his glasses. "I must say, my admiration for your skills in prevarication has grown during this crisis."

Buffy worked on a translation, came up empty. "My skills?"

"You lie very well, when you have to."

She dimpled. "You're such a charmer."

"I've been told that, yes."

She grinned at him and slid her glance in the direction of the kitchen. "Lately?"

Just then, Micaela and Joyce came out of the kitchen. Giles said nothing more, but his cheeks were tinged with pink.

Slayers noticed things like that.

The ghost roads.

Clad in a flowing black robe, Fulcanelli glided over the landscape in a deep, ebony shadow of such cold and evil that even the dead stayed away. Monsters of the Otherworld, demons from Hell, they all kept their distance. Nothing could penetrate the darkness surrounding him and the Sons of Entropy who traveled with him, and only the fires of Hell could warm it.

And Hell *was* advancing onto the ghost roads. Though no one could see Fulcanelli, or his men, he alone could see everything that was happening beyond the shadow he had created. Demons and imps burst through several breaches, terrorizing the desperate dead who knew that if Hell came, they would be damned for eternity. The phantoms were running along the roads, faces elongated in terror, wild to reach their final destinations, whatever they might be. The earthbound dead, the confused dead. Some of them had been wandering for centuries. Some had even forgotten who they were, and where they were. They staggered madly along, hopelessly lost.

They would provide fine fodder for Belphegor's minions, once they crossed over from Hell into this plane of existence.

Boston, Il Maestro thought, imagining the Gatehouse. Long practiced in traveling the ghost roads, he was very good at moving himself rapidly from place to place upon them. His powers of concentration were formidable; his ability to visualize, unsurpassed, even by Jean-Marc Regnier. For centuries, the Regniers had reacted to crisis after crisis. They had never *acted.* All their magick was defensive.

Very little of his was.

Like Death himself, Fulcanelli's cloak billowed and moved as he rushed. With Belphegor's patience at an end, the hand of death was upon him. His followers sensed his urgency, and responded to it. Since their defeat at the drive-in, they had grown fearful. They, too, needed a victory.

Fulcanelli would see to it that they received one.

At the Gatehouse.

* * *

Ethan Rayne turned a page and glanced over at the cage where they kept the wolf boy. The creature was finally asleep, thanks to a combination of its own ravings and rantings, and Ethan's well-executed sleep spell. Ethan was deeply grateful for the silence. It had been difficult to concentrate with all the growling.

He was reading up on Belphegor from Giles's text *The Lords of Hell,* retrieved from the werewolf's cage. Drumming his fingers on the library study desk, he turned another page. Big stuff, this. Ethan was used to small mischiefs, pranks really, when compared to what was going on now. End of the world, rule of Hell over all creation, quite something.

But Giles's text was old and faded, and Ethan had just run into something he found a bit troubling:

> *The following pages, containing as they do vital spells and occult wisdom, must be perused only by eyes of magick. Other than those will render the material useless and none who gaze upon the words will ever make sense of them again. Therefore, a cautionary note: Go no further, Reader, unless you are to magick born, or you will doom the world to rule by the fearsome Lord Belphegor, Warmonger of Hell.*

"To magick born," Ethan repeated. "Which I don't suppose I was." He had learned all the magick he knew, beginning back when he and Ripper ran together. And he wasn't certain the werewolf qualified either, nor the mutant. Were their conditions considered magickal? He was afraid to find out. For according to what he had just read, if someone who wasn't qualified read the section in question, they would never discover how to defeat Belphegor.

Then he smiled.

For he knew where to find someone born to magick.

God, he loved being resourceful.

Slamming the book shut, he tipped an imaginary hat in Oz's direction and said, "Sweet dreams, Mr. Hyde. I'm sure Rupert will be along shortly to collect you."

He went outside. The lawns of Ripper's depressingly trendy schoolyard were wet with dew. Songbirds chirruped. Ethan was glad that dawn would come soon. The Sunnydale nights were clogged with more horrors than good old London town had seen in centuries. Ethan was surprised Giles had kept his good looks, what with all he had to do around here to maintain the balance between good and evil.

Ethan tried to feel guilty, but he just couldn't. It was such a useless emotion.

With the book under his arm, he fished in his pocket for the keys to his rental. At the same moment, a large golden retriever bounded across his path, barking lustily. It was chasing a very small troll, who looked over its shoulder and screamed at the bounding, eager dog.

Ethan frowned. A breach must have opened—they might all be opening, now that the barriers were so thin. He'd better check on the ones the little spellcaster, Willow, had closed, and see if there were any new ones, as well.

But first things first.

He got into his car, and ferried over to Sunnydale Hospital.

The parking structure was closed off, as was most of the surrounding lot. With a few well-chosen words, Ethan opened the parking barrier to the area marked "Physicians' Parking Only" and pulled into a space between a Mercedes and a Porsche. American doctors did so very well. Next life, perhaps he would be a brain surgeon.

He got out and locked the car, then strode into the main entrance. This time, the coffee cart was open, and he got himself a double espresso, which the dear clerk carefully poured into a huge paper cup. The small dollop of potent coffee splashed about inside, and Ethan thought to tease the clerk by complaining, "What? This is all I get?" but it was sure to slow things down.

Quite a lot of hospital personnel were about, and he looked for his lovely in scrubs—or one of her friends. For his trouble, he got a few perky looks, and he grinned as he wheeled down the corridors.

How fortunate that the patient he sought had been so badly hurt that she was still here.

He hung in the doorway of Amy Madison's room and smiled.

"Gatekeeper!" came the shout from the center of the weird black cloud that suddenly appeared in the middle of the Gatehouse lawn. Around it, the Sons of Entropy began cheering and whooping. Xander raised his eyes questioningly and looked at Antoinette.

"Let me guess," he said. "Publishers Clearing House."

"Oh, no," Antoinette murmured, and then she did something very wild: she turned solid. Her hands

went around Xander's biceps and she held on to him as she swayed like she was about to pass out. *"No, it can't be."*

"Um. Okay. So we're not rich. Let's try again. Siegfried and Roy?"

Antoinette let go of him and buried her face in her hands. *"Jacques,"* she whispered.

"Jacques? Which is a good thing," Cordelia ventured, looking at Xander and Willow. "Right?"

Willow shrugged.

Then Antoinette Regnier resumed her ghostly form and raised her face. Whoa. Talk about wigged. This lady's hair would turn gray if it hadn't already.

"It is our old enemy. It is Fulcanelli," she said. *"He has come at last."*

"Wait a minute," Xander cut in. "Giles said he was dead."

"So, not true. Not a good thing," Cordelia said. She moved her shoulders. "But it's okay. Xander can deal."

"Xander can?" Xander asked. He took a deep breath. "This is the main bad guy, right? Everything else has been the lackluster half-time show, during which the rest of America hit the fridge or flushed. And I'm the pinch hitter. Which is the wrong sport, sure, but I was always into figure skating, myself.

"So. This guy is like, who? Katerina Witt? Who was that really bad girl, the one who tried to take out that other skater, Tonya—"

As if on cue, the Gatehouse burst into flames. As Xander closed his eyes and concentrated, flames erupted in each one of the thousands of rooms contained within the house. And in each of those rooms, the magickal barriers that bound the creatures of the Otherworld—the stuff of myths and legends—began to fall. The Gatehouse's captives were escaping, both into the house and onto the ghost roads.

The burning house thundered with the shrieks of wild, unthinking beasts, the cheers of evil beings released from their imprisonment. Monsters rammed the walls in frenzied terror as the flames lapped at their bodies, causing huge sections of the house to crumble into mountains of rubble.

The curtains around the window where the four had stood billowed with orange flames as Willow and Cordelia glommed on to Xander and he eased them away.

"Yow." Xander looked at Antoinette. "Houston, do we ever have a problem."

"All is lost," she said.

"No way," Cordelia said, frowning. "My man is the Gatekeeper. He'll fix everything." She lifted a brow. "Right, Xander?"

"You don't get it. I may have the tools, and the knowledge, but not the skill, y'know. It's like being given the fastest race car in the world for your driver's ed test! I've gotta learn fast."

"Or we've gotta get Jacques back here, so he can take over," Willow added quickly.

"I'm not certain that is even possible at this point," Antoinette told them.

"So, wait, I may be Gatekeeper forever?" Xander asked, suddenly frantic. "Y'know, it's cool for a while, but I can't keep this up indefinitely."

"Men. Always with the excuses," Cordelia sniffed.

The glass in the window shattered.

Xander cried, "Hit the dirt!"

He threw himself onto both Willow and Cordy,

slamming them against the floor, as a barrage of blue flames and strange black objects rocketed into the room and exploded near the blazing ceiling. The floor was burning, and both girls shrieked with pain. He leaped off them and pointed at their smoldering clothes, putting out the flames.

Then he wheeled to face the window. Fire and energy poured from his hands in a torrent as he returned fire. He didn't know how he did it; he didn't even think about doing it. It just happened.

Then he attended to the house, quenching the flames and healing it all at once, strengthening the barriers around the imprisoned creatures.

Then he staggered backward, and might have fallen if Cordelia and Willow hadn't caught him.

"This is not looking so good," he said dully. His forehead was dripping with sweat and he was so tired he felt like he was floating into little pieces around the room.

"It has barely begun," Antoinette announced.

Angel's back was aflame as he crashed into the sunken garden of his mansion and doused himself in the fountain. Luckily, the last gray shadows of night sheltered him the rest of the way into the house.

"Angel!" Buffy cried, leaping to her feet. The teacup she had been holding shattered on the floor as she put her arms around him and held him briefly. Then, as if she remembered who he was and that she shouldn't do that, she pulled away. "You're hurt."

He touched his face and felt the scratches and bruises.

"I . . . needed to pick up something to . . . some sustenance. I didn't think I was going to make it back here on time," he told her, "so I decided to bunk down in the Master's lair."

"The what?" Buffy's mother, Joyce, said.

Buffy turned to her. "My first big enemy here," she informed Joyce. "Ruined church. Underground."

Joyce blinked. "I thought that was an urban legend."

"Buffy," Angel said, "I ran into a bunch of demons down there. I think they got out of Hell via the ghost roads, and I think there's going to be more of them."

Angel winced with the pain, reminding himself that soon it would be gone. As a vampire, Angel healed quickly and well.

"That would make sense," Giles noted. "Xander is doing the best he can, but the dimensional barriers are already badly damaged. As the walls get thinner and weaker, and the monsters and demons begin to mass on the other side, they would by nature squeeze through at the weakest points. The Master's old lair would be among the weakest."

Buffy sighed. "Oh, wonderful."

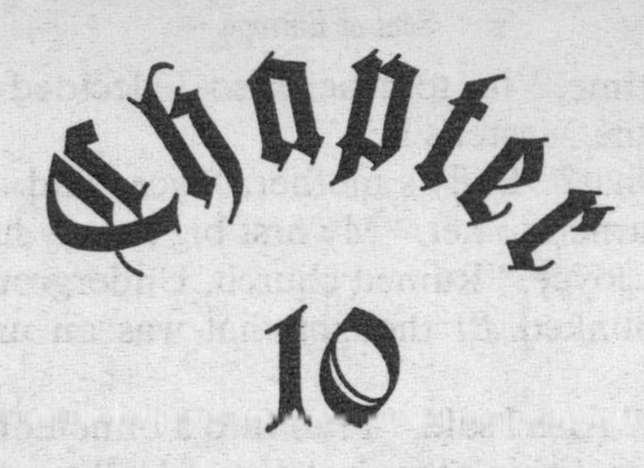

Chapter 10

THE PHONE RANG. ANGEL PICKED IT UP AND SAID, "Hello. Hello?"

He shook his head at Joyce and shrugged. "Just static." He punched *69. "Caller ID blocked. Well, their loss."

His tone was casual, but Joyce detected an edge to his voice.

She sat across from Angel in the large parlor of his extraordinary home. He sat in the shadows, and she couldn't really see him. He had offered her every comfort, shown her a room where she might sleep if she desired. Given her tea and scones and the run of the kitchen. Of course, she'd have to go out to buy anything more substantial, since the cupboard was pretty much bare. Angel didn't have to eat. When he did, it was usually to be social, or to enjoy the flavors he had once coveted.

All of that he'd explained to her in friendly conversation.

Friendly conversation during which they both pretended it wasn't awkward for them to be together. She knew everything, now, about Buffy and Angel. Or, at least, as much of everything as she could bring herself to hear. But none of that was the primary reason for the awkwardness of their situation.

No, the real reason was sleeping in a room not far away. The real reason was an eleven-year-old boy sound asleep, chest rising and falling with each breath. Joyce was exhausted, yes. And she didn't relish the idea of running off with Buffy before she'd had a chance to shower and rest and, well, recover a bit.

But she wasn't about to do any of that. Not just now. Because the real reason she was there, the reason nobody wanted to talk about, particularly not Angel, was that none of them had been comfortable with the idea of leaving that boy asleep in a bed in that mansion with only a vampire for company.

Buffy's faith in Angel notwithstanding, it was something that went unspoken. Someone else would stay with Jacques. Someone human. And since Ethan Rayne had, Joyce was told, disappeared for the moment, and was at any rate even lower on the trustworthiness scale than Angel, Micaela was much needed to help Buffy and Giles with the current crisis. That left Joyce.

"Do you need to sleep?" she asked Angel.

"I'm all right," he replied.

Which wasn't really an answer. But it would have to do. Joyce, on the other hand, needed desperately to sleep. But to sleep in the presence of a vampire, even

Angel . . . she just couldn't bring herself to entertain the thought.

She watched Angel's face. He met her gaze, smiled gently, understanding. Joyce looked away. After a moment she rose.

"I'm going to look in on the boy," she said.

"Call if you need me," Angel replied, also rising. "I have some things to attend to around the house."

He disappeared into the shadowy reaches of the unlit corridor, and Joyce shivered. Outside, the sun shone down. But here, it was black as night.

She opened the door to the room where Jacques lay sleeping soundly. The boy slumbered on, and Joyce felt a moment of envy. He had been through an ordeal not unlike her own, and now he had the chance to recover from it. To rest.

Then she shook herself. She could not envy him. First, because he was only a boy. Second, and more important, because of the responsibility that lay before him. He was to become the Gatekeeper. He was resting now, yes, but this might be the last opportunity he had to do that for several hundred years. The rest of his life.

The similarity between the boy's dark destiny and her own daughter's did not escape Joyce Summers's notice. She simply tried not to think about it. Instead, she returned to the parlor and set about the familiar tasks of worrying about her daughter and waiting for the phone to ring.

"This feels so odd," Buffy observed, as she walked through the cemetery with Giles, Micaela, and Oz. "I mean, usually the patrol thing is done after dark. Plus, y'know, it's sort of surreal to know that the rest of the world is going on without you, that everybody's at school, and the bells are ringing, and teachers are giving out homework and tests and . . . we're all completely screwed when we finally go back to school."

Oz offered a small shrug. "You get used to it after a while. The surreal part, that is. The screwed thing? When it starts to matter, that's a bummer."

Giles raised an eyebrow, and shook his head slightly at the celebrated highest-scoring-student-ever-to-fail-to-graduate.

"Forgive me," Micaela said softly, "but are we getting near? I only ask because—"

"You feel something," Oz finished for her. "Yeah. There's kind of a, I don't know, current or something. Got my hackles up, too."

"So to speak," Giles said.

Oz only nodded.

"Right over here," Buffy told her, and gestured toward a large crypt perhaps twenty yards away.

"I guess all those empty storefronts and 'For Sale' signs are just a fluke. If someone's living here, quality real estate in this town must be at a premium," Oz observed.

"Nobody lives here," Buffy countered, a dark expression crossing her face. "Not anymore."

"Maybe not the last time you were here," Micaela corrected. "But that might have changed. It seems likely this crypt has new residents. Or at least, it may be being used as a conduit of sorts for the creatures appearing underground to emerge into Sunnydale."

"That's precisely what we're here to find out," Giles noted.

He exchanged a meaningful glance with Micaela, and Buffy wondered if there was something really brewing with them. For Giles's sake, she hoped so. It would be nice to see him fall for someone. Maybe the memory of Jenny Calendar would stop haunting him so much.

"Door's open," Oz noted.

They all paused. The heavy iron door to the crypt hung open and to one side, as though it had been torn away. Buffy wasn't sure if Angel had done that getting away, or if some demon had done it chasing after him. Or later, coming out into the world.

"Y'know, I thought maybe doing this during the day would make it less creepy. But it's actually more creepy, if that's possible. Stuff like this shouldn't happen during the day."

Together, they entered the crypt. Buffy led the way, with Oz and Micaela behind her and Giles taking up the rear. The dusty gloom of the crypt was disturbed by their passing, and a pulsing purple light from Micaela's hands threw eerie shadows on the walls. There were several large, marble tombs within, their heavy lids inscribed with the names and the life dates of the deceased. Buffy noticed that one of the lids was new, to replace the one shattered the last time she faced evil within these walls.

At the far side of the crypt, the heavy iron door that led down into the tunnels also stood open. Fortunately, it was undamaged.

"A thought. Cork the bottle, withdraw to examine the big picture," Oz suggested.

"We've got to know what we're dealing with," Buffy argued. "If Fulcanelli's over, who—or what—is running the show?"

"I concur," Giles said, and glanced at Micaela.

"Perhaps you'll be able to shore up the barricades, so to speak, before it grows any worse."

Micaela didn't respond.

Together the four of them descended along a narrow stairwell. It had occurred to Buffy the first time she'd been here to wonder who had built these stairs in the first place. There were electrical tunnels, sewer tunnels, and natural cave formations beneath Sunnydale. There were also portions of the town, including an old church, that had been swallowed by an earthquake nearly a century earlier. But there were additional passages beneath the town, tunnels that someone had built, but not for any obvious reason.

One of these days, Buffy figured, she'd have to fill the entire system with concrete or something. Keep the undesirable element from setting up shop down there.

Like now, for instance.

They followed the dank underground path, eventually entering some of the town utility tunnels. Their way was lit only by the crackling purple light of Micaela's meager sorcery. For the most part, they walked in silence. From time to time, Buffy allowed herself a sarcastic comment. Oz would counter with a dry yet telling observation. Giles would raise his eyebrows, maybe clean off his glasses.

It felt like forever. In reality, it was only a few minutes.

"This is it," Buffy said as they entered a small cavern, littered with bits of existing architecture to indicate that this might have been a building once, when it stood above the ground.

"This is the Master's lair."

She felt a firm hand on her shoulder, and Buffy turned to see Giles gazing at her.

"Are you all right?" he asked.

Neither of the others would have noticed it, but there was a great deal more in his manner, in his question, than those simple words. The last time Buffy had been here, at the end of her sophomore year, she had died. Only for a few seconds, of course. But nevertheless, she had been dead. Only Xander's quick action, giving her CPR, had brought her back.

"It's empty," Micaela said.

Buffy wanted to say, "No, there are plenty of ghosts here." But she kept silent.

"Not empty," Oz observed, glancing around, his brow furrowed. "Doesn't anyone else smell that? All of that?"

But none of them did. Only Oz. And it was Oz who began to back up, glancing from side to side with a look of grave concern on his face. He held out a hand to them, beckoning.

"I think we'd all be much better off if we were elsewhere," he said.

"I'm not sure I . . ." Giles began. Then he stared hard at Oz. "You *sense* something?"

"In a wolfy, supernatural kind of way?" Buffy prodded.

"That's not usually the way it works, but . . . there's something here. Definitely," Oz replied.

Micaela turned to face the cavern. "Well, then, why don't we shed a little bit more light on the subject."

From her hands a blazing purple flare erupted, bathing the cave in violent violet hues. Picking out, in great detail, every crack and crevice. Every fang and claw. Every snarl and slither.

"Dear Lord," Giles whispered.

They were everywhere. But they were nowhere. Monsters. Nightmares. They were somehow between worlds, frozen, it seemed, just below the surface of the stone or the earth or the metal. Even the puddle of water at the center of the cavern had a face beneath it. A horrifying visage like nothing any of them had seen before, except perhaps in the sketches of the mad.

"Giles, talk to me," Buffy said.

Just as the thing beneath the water burst forth, thrashing and roaring with fury. The water held for a moment, as if the demon's head had crowned like the skull of a newborn. Then it crashed through, a savage newborn into this world.

A blood-red newborn, with scales covering its squat body, spikes on the whipping tentacles that served it as arms.

"Micaela," Buffy said.

That was all. She reached into a black bag she had slung low on one shoulder and retrieved a long machete Giles had dug out from his weapons cache. Micaela held up her hands and a bright green light danced from her fingers and seemed to trap the thing, momentarily, in a web of power. It froze. Its tentacles no longer whipped murderously from side to side.

Before Giles or Oz could speak, Buffy waded in and brought the machete whistling through the air. The blade cleaved the demon's head from its body in one furious chop. Buffy felt it catch for a fraction of a second on bone or gristle, and then she was through. For a moment, while Micaela's magick still held it, the thing's head did not fall.

When she let the net of sorcery drop, the demon's

head slid unceremoniously to plop into the pool from which it had emerged.

Buffy backed off as the tentacles twitched. They all stood together, looking around at the demons who were in the process of traveling from one world to another. Forcing their way through. The barrier to Hell had not fallen, but they were punching holes in it, finding where it was worn thin, and pushing through.

"Are you guys all pondering what I'm pondering?" Buffy asked.

"If it involves Cheez Whiz and bananas, then no," Oz replied. "But, okay, if we're talking strategic retreat, and fixing our major problem before these walls fall completely, then—"

"Let's get the hell out of here," Micaela agreed.

They all turned to go. Except for Giles. He stared at the walls, and Buffy reached out to grab his hand.

"Rupert," Micaela said.

"Giles, come on," Buffy urged.

"Angel fought several of these things," Giles noted. "It's likely they're coming through at a relatively consistent rate, and yet, we haven't seen them in Sunnydale yet. Not really."

"So what happened to the ones who have already come through?" Oz asked.

"Precisely," Giles replied.

"They may be waiting for dark," Micaela suggested.

At that, there was a loud roar from a tunnel across the cavern. In the darkness, something slithered. Something else walked with cloven hooves. Wings fluttered. From the shadows, things began to emerge.

"Y'know, Giles, the problem with questions like

yours?" Buffy said angrily. "I always hate the answers."

"Running," Oz informed them.

But by then, they all were.

"You said it was a strategic retreat," Buffy snapped at Oz.

"Which, loosely translated . . . running," he told her.

The demons were on their trail, the appalling sounds of Hell's minions echoing up the tunnels after them. Still, somehow, they made it to the stairs and up into the crypt. When Buffy turned and slammed the heavy iron door, something screamed, a talon was shorn off and dropped to the floor of the crypt, still writhing on its own. Oz stamped on it until it stopped.

Giles, Buffy, and Micaela put their shoulders to the door. There was a place for a chain and a lock. But the chain and lock were gone.

"Oz, help," Buffy said.

And Oz was there. Helping as much as he could. Which, since he was relatively small when not a werewolf, wasn't that much. He didn't have a lot of weight to throw against the door.

Which was what they needed.

"Hold it!" Buffy shouted.

She leaped away, jumped over one of the heavy marble tombs that lined the crypt. The Slayer put her back against the marble and her feet against the wall of the crypt, and she pushed with every ounce of her strength.

Nothing happened.

Buffy allowed herself two breaths.

"They're coming through!" Giles snapped. "Micaela, can you seal the door?"

"It doesn't work that way," she said. "Nothing . . . not what I've studied. And there are so many, I can't . . . I can't concentrate."

"Can you push them back, just for a second?" Buffy called.

After a second of silence, she heard a huge, cacophonous roar. Then Micaela shouted, "Yes!" and Buffy knew she'd done it. It would buy them only a few breaths of peace.

"Help me!" she shouted.

And they were there. Giles and Oz were by her side, their backs set against the marble. With all their might, they pushed. And the tomb moved. It slid toward the door. Oz stayed low, and Giles and Buffy stood and bent to the job, moving the huge marble sarcophagus.

"This is too easy," Oz said.

"Speak for yourself," Micaela replied.

Buffy looked up and saw her face, red with effort, sweat dripping down her forehead. She was standing in the middle of the crypt, doing nothing. But apparently doing something after all.

"Micaela?" Giles asked.

"This, I think I can do," she said.

The first tomb slammed against the iron door just as the demons began to pound on the other side. Then Giles was up, not helping anymore.

"We're not done here, Giles," Buffy said.

He turned to look at them, flustered. "I'm sorry, all of you. But we've got to look at the big picture. If memory serves, there may be an enchantment—a very powerful enchantment but of limited range, you understand—that could buy us the time we need to attend to the 'big picture' the way it ought to be handled.

"The way we ought to have handled it already."

Buffy flinched. He was talking about her reluctance to deal with the crisis at hand before rescuing her mother. She knew he meant nothing by it, but it still hurt. Buffy knew that she had been selfish, that putting her mother's safety ahead of the fate of the world was nothing short of abhorrent. But she would do it again if it came to that.

"Go," Micaela said.

"We'll handle it here, Giles," Buffy said. "You go do your thing, and we'll muzzle the Hellmouth."

For a moment Giles looked at her oddly, processing the humor. Then he smiled wanly and was gone, heading off toward school at a trot. Buffy, Micaela, and Oz continued the process of blocking the iron door as best they could.

But in her mind, Buffy saw an image of that cavern below, where demons were slowly emerging from their own dimension into this one. And she knew that no matter what they blocked the way with, it wouldn't be enough. Nowhere near enough.

And, of course, there were plenty of other ways out of that underground warren.

"Faster," Buffy said, shivering a little, though the sun shone through into the dusty crypt.

It was barely noon.

Ethan Rayne sat at the desk in Giles's small office, sipping whiskey from one of the cups from the antique tea service that had sat on top of a squat bookcase. There were books strewn all around the room. Books stacked on top of the desk. Several of them were open on the desk, and he'd had the temerity to tear pages out of another. He knew old Ripper would have his knickers in a twist over that one, but he hadn't time to seek out the copy machine.

He'd managed to shake the beautiful young witch, Amy Madison, out of a deep sleep, in order for her to read the selection about Belphegor in *The Lords of Hell*. Only one born to magick could read the pages, but Ethan copied down every word as she read it aloud to him. Only then did he let the injured girl go back to healing sleep.

The nurses never saw Ethan. He didn't let them. And when he'd returned to the library, it had been a relatively simple matter to cast a glamour over the glass of the door to Rupert's office, so that anyone looking inside would see the office as it had been before Ethan entered. Empty. Neat. A bit stuffy.

He'd even taped a small note to the counter out in the library proper. "Back in 5 minutes," it read. The weasel of a principal had come in at one point. Ethan had watched him stomping angrily about the place through the window in Giles's office door. The man had even come to peer into the office, but he'd seemed to be looking right through Ethan.

The glamour was working just fine.

Now, as Ethan took another shot of whiskey—horrid stuff he'd acquired at a liquor store near the hospital—he frowned. He'd read Amy's translation dozens of times. Most of it, he understood. But there were several things that still puzzled him.

When he'd called up Belphegor for their little chat—and even now, Ethan was still a bit irked with the demon for being so dismissive of him—he'd called the Hell lord by many of his names: Lord of the

Vile Flesh, Wanderer of the Wastelands, Master of the Secret Passages, and so on. But there were others here. Dozens of others, in fact. A boring grocery list of references to the same blasted demon. Most of them were gibberish, or hinted at some of the abilities Belphegor could brag about.

But there were passages Ethan just didn't understand.

Born from the bowels of the Old Ones;
The Lord of the Vile Flesh;
His heart a whisper of shadow;
He watches the world of man with human eye;
The eyes of man, the darkest passage;
The path he must follow, the world which he covets;
Belphegor, scion of worlds old and new;
Wanderer in Darkness, shying from infernal flame;
Yet the dawn of man shall not burn his eyes;
Yet the sword of man shall not cut him down;
For man's only weapon must be himself.

Yeah. That was pretty damned confusing. *"Man's only weapon must be himself,"* Ethan thought. *What the bloody hell is that supposed to mean? And the old man certainly doesn't have human eyes.*

From outside in the library he heard the sound of the double doors swinging closed. With a quick glance over his shoulder, Ethan folded up the pages of young Amy's recitation and slipped them inside one of Rupert's books.

He looked up just as the Watcher opened the office door.

The look on Rupert's face was priceless.

"Hello, Ripper," Ethan said, and grinned.

The Watcher's eyes narrowed. His nostrils flared. His eyes roved across the books strewn around the office, moved to the volumes open on his desk, then settled back on Ethan.

"These are my things," he said coldly.

Ethan shrugged. "Sure, but, y'know, one for the team and all, eh, old man? A spot of research is all."

Rupert moved farther into the room. There was an edge to everything about him now, a change in the very air of the office. Ethan tensed. There had always been a dark side to Rupert Giles, no matter what face he put on it later. He was the Watcher, now, all right and proper. But he was capable of anger and violence of great magnitude. Had been, even before his lady love had her neck snapped by the Slayer's dead boyfriend. Even before said boyfriend had tortured poor Ripper until he was half a moment shy of mad.

Or was he?

"Where the hell have you been, Ethan?" Rupert demanded, removing his glasses and setting them on top of a bookcase. "You disappeared in the labyrinth. Now you're here. What are you up to?"

"Doing my best to help, Rupert."

Ethan didn't even see it coming. Giles's right hand whipped out with ferocious speed and strength that belied the mild-mannered librarian exterior. Knuckles cracked across Ethan's nose and mouth, splitting his lip, and the magician tumbled out of the chair to the floor, where his head cracked the glass front of a bookcase. The antique tea set slid off the top and crashed to the ground, shattering.

But Ripper wasn't through.

With his lips curled back in fury and his eyes narrowed dangerously, he hauled back his right leg and kicked Ethan hard in the ribs. Ethan grunted, but he didn't fight back. He was frightened, but there were several valuable pieces of knowledge that came from having been in the same position with Ripper Giles in the past.

The first was that he had no chance in a one-on-one against Giles, and no time to concentrate enough to defend himself magickally, not without Ripper noticing his attempt to use magick and caving his skull in or something.

The second was that Giles wasn't going to kill him. Not this time.

Ripper grabbed Ethan by the hair, hauled him up and screamed into his face.

"Liar!"

Ethan didn't even reply. He knew what that would do, and he was right. Giles seemed to deflate suddenly, the rage going out of him. He let go of Ethan's hair. But he didn't withdraw. Instead, he loomed over Ethan and scowled down at him.

"You've got something going on the side, Ethan. You wouldn't be here if there wasn't a percentage in it for you. I want to know what you're up to, and I want to know now. You lie to me, and I'll know it. Or don't you remember, Ethan? I know *you,* you cowardly bastard."

Ethan didn't move. But finally, he did respond.

"I've said all I can, Rupert," he replied calmly, nursing his bleeding lip and mashed nose, feeling to see if anything was broken in his face. "You don't believe me, and of course, I'm not at all surprised. But there isn't a bloody thing I can do about it, old man.

There's certainly no percentage in the world ending, is there?

"I don't think there's a way I can convince you to believe me. If there is, I wish you'd tell me what it is."

Giles only stared at him, still fuming. Then, suddenly, he spun on his heel and walked out of the office. Ethan rose and went to the door to watch him. Ripper went into the library cage and fished through several boxes there until he pulled out a dusty leather volume, apparently just what he'd been looking for.

Then he strode purposefully across the library and pushed past Ethan into his office. The Watcher carefully closed and moved the various volumes on his desk, but he ignored those stacked on the floor. He slapped the dusty book on the wooden desk and glared at Ethan.

"There's a certain wonderful irony, even a perversion, in this," Giles said, a mad smile playing at the corners of his mouth. "You recognize that volume?"

Ethan nodded. "*Slaves of Order*. It's the opposite of everything I love about this world. Order is sterility, Rupert. It's gray death and the boredom of perfection. Inaction and impotence. It has its own horrors, as you well know."

"Indeed," Giles agreed. "But today, it is the only hope we've got."

They both looked at the book. Ethan sighed. His entire life was dedicated to the perverse exploitation of magick for his own amusement. Chaos was a joy. That was the whole point of it for him, really. Or, at least, one of them. Which was how he had become aware of the Sons of Entropy to begin with. But they were just a bit too psychotic for him. He enjoyed chaos for its own sake. But in a world of chaos, with chaos become the norm, he knew he would grow bored very quickly. Even if Fulcanelli hadn't sold out to Hell, he might have helped Giles and the Slayer.

But this . . . this was an insult to everything he lived for. Everything he believed in. If chaos was everything, then order was nothing. And this book was a compendium of magick and arcane power rituals performed for and drawing upon the power of the Lords of Order.

"What are my options, hmm?" Ethan asked aloud.

Ripper began to reply, but Ethan cut him off with a wave of his hand.

"A rhetorical question, I assure you. Now, what do you want me to do?"

A short time later, Giles arrived back at the cemetery. Buffy, Oz, and Micaela were piling large stones pried away from the cemetery wall on top of a manhole cover in the middle of the graveyard. Giles knew immediately what they were doing. There were other exits from that underground.

There was no way they would be able to get to them all. And even if they did, the demons would still escape eventually. Which was why he was now counting on Ethan.

And several others, for that matter.

"Giles, are you all right?" Buffy asked when she saw him.

He ran his hands through his hair, pushed up his glasses, and smoothed his jacket as best he could.

"A bit tense, of course," he told her, avoiding the subject of Ethan, and his behavior at the library. He had that violence within him, but he wasn't proud of it.

"Can I ask a question?" Oz ventured.

All three of them looked at him.

"Where are all the creatures from the Otherworld? I mean, I think I saw a troll down there, and something else that looked vaguely like a hairy dragon, but it's mostly demons now, right? Why?"

Giles grew contemplative a moment. It was a good question.

"Perhaps," he said thoughtfully, "perhaps it is simply that the creatures of the Otherworld fear the demons. They were attempting to enter our world before, but now, many of them may be withdrawing, letting the demons hold sway. Most of the creatures of the Otherworld are not truly evil, but rather savage, killing by instinct. Some are malicious, but many simply primitive. Either way, they would fear the denizens of Hell."

Oz nodded. "See, now that's what I thought."

"Great," Buffy said, clapping her hands together. "Now that that's settled, what's the plan?"

Giles glanced away a moment. When he looked up again, he was sorely troubled. "Micaela," he said, "you and Oz must come with me to Angel's home. Jacques must be returned to the Gatehouse immediately, and I'll need you both, as well as Angel."

"But Angel can't go anywhere while the sun is up," Buffy said.

"And, I hate to bring it up, but this is the third night of the full moon. I'll get all wolfy by sundown," Oz noted.

"Yes, yes," Giles replied, even as he turned to walk back toward his car. "I've taken all of that into consideration."

He started for the car, and Micaela and Oz followed after.

"Hello?" Buffy called.

Giles turned to face her.

"Have we forgotten about the Slayer here? Trying to keep the forces of Hell from breaking out of the underground and swarming over the sleepy town of Sunnydale?" she demanded.

"Ah, yes," Giles said. "Keep at it. If all goes as planned, Ethan should have that all taken care of shortly."

He turned toward the car again.

Behind him, Buffy called out, "Ethan. *You're* trusting Ethan?

"We're all gonna die."

Chapter 11

TIRED AND WORRIED ABOUT BUFFY, OZ SAT BEHIND Micaela and Giles in the Gilesmobile on the ride back to the mansion. In addition to processing everything that had just happened, he was wondering exactly how Giles was taking his third night as a werewolf into consideration. No dignity there, no matter how you looked at it. Not a lot of help to the others, either. The world was in danger of ending, and he might just go out looking like the lead in a frame-by-frame color remake of *I Was a Teenage Werewolf* instead of kissing his Willow good-bye.

Speaking of kissing, the two big people were not talking; now that they were coming down from the battle, there was lots of unspoken intensity between those two. Oz thought they'd be a lot better off if they really hashed it out about her father and got through it. Maybe did some, ah, grappling. However, no one was asking his opinion. No one was even speaking to him.

But that was cool.

He sat back and watched Sunnydale go by. It was almost two P.M. By five-thirty or so, he would be transformed. Three hours to go.

When they arrived at the mansion, he climbed out and stood by the car while Micaela unbound her wards and spells of protection over the house. She remarked casually that Jacques's spells were still in good shape, and she wished she were as good at magick as he was.

Oz figured she was lucky. Next thing you knew they'd be forcing *her* to be the Gatekeeper. Which maybe could not happen, because, hey, chick and all. On the other hand, one of the rules was also that your last name had to be Regnier, and last time he'd seen Xander's ID, it had said Harris. So maybe the only rule was that rules were made to be broken.

"Right, then," Giles said, and the three walked through the garden and into the house.

Despite the hour, it was very still, very quiet, a marked contrast to the situation at the cemetery. Oz wondered again how Buffy was doing back there.

"Everyone must be sleeping," Micaela remarked. "Jacques has been out for a long time."

"Grief can have that effect on a person," Giles replied.

"This must be an unbelievably hard time for him." Her face was very gentle, very sad. "He has no one in the world. He'll have to go live in that house all alone for hundreds of years, except when he leaves to bind some monster or other. I don't think I could stand it."

"It's all right, Miss Micaela," the boy said from the

entrance to the hallway, where he stood with Buffy's mom. "I'm ready to take up my duties."

He looked different, somehow. Older than eleven, but still not exactly grown up. Maybe the way Oz and the rest of the Scooby Gang looked these days.

Buffy's mother had one hand on the boy's shoulder, comforting him.

"I'm sorry you heard that," Micaela told Jacques.

"Don't be." He smiled thinly. "It's not a surprise."

"But perhaps it is a shock," she persisted.

He inclined his head. "Perhaps." He regarded the three of them. "But you know it's time for me to go to the Gatehouse. Past time, actually."

Joyce cleared her throat. "It's time I went home as well," she said. "Nowhere's safe now, and I want to be there until Buffy comes back or the world ends, whichever comes first."

She looked at Giles as though he might protest. Instead, he nodded slowly.

"Be well, Joyce," he said.

The mother of the Slayer looked at the Watcher a moment longer, and then she departed.

"Okay," Oz said, "about Boston."

Jacques spoke up. "We'll stand a better chance if I travel only with those touched by the supernatural," he said.

"My thinking also," Giles replied. "However, as it seems likely the demons will soon break through in force, and Sunnydale has proven to be ground zero, Buffy must remain here. Which leaves only Angel and Oz."

Oz frowned slightly and raised his hand. "Um, question here. It's light out, so Angel can't leave the mansion to get to the breach that leads into the ghos roads. Unless we hide him in the back of the van, I guess. And if we wait until dark, I'll be a werewolf."

"Right." Giles cleared his throat and pushed up his glasses. "Here's my thinking on that. Micaela has the ability to open the ghost roads where she wishes." He bobbed his head in Jacques's direction. "And one might assume that when you inherit your powers, you may do so as well."

"True," Jacques answered, "but I haven't inherited them yet."

"Quite so," Giles said. "So, we open a breach right here. Jacques, Oz, and Angel leave immediately, which is a little after five Boston time."

"But—" Oz began, but Giles held up his hand.

"One must assume you'll arrive there after dark. At which point you will, indeed, transform into a werewolf. My suggestion for that is that Micaela work a spell to render Angel and Jacques invisible to you."

"I can do that," she said.

"So we won't see each other on the ghost road?" Oz asked. "What if somebody attacks us?" He looked at Micaela. "Can you time it to happen at a certain point, like right before we arrive in Boston?"

"I also thought of that," Giles cut in, "but the problem is, we really don't know how long it will take you. It's rather certain you'll be attacked, plus there's still the relative newness of the experience. In the sense of controlling it, I mean. Think of it this way: we assume it will take a certain amount of time for me to drive from the cemetery to this house—approximately ten to fifteen minutes—but if there were a traffic jam, it would take considerably longer."

Especially if you're the one who's driving, Oz thought, but kept that to himself. Instead, he nodded.

Micaela warmed to her subject. As she talked, she moved her hands expressively. "You can each carry something, maybe wear an armband or a vest. Once they realize you've changed, Angel and Jacques take theirs off, and stay invisible until Xander deals with you."

Oz raised a brow. "Deals with me?"

"I would assume he'd bind you into the Gatehouse," Giles said. "I've tried phoning them to tell them about all this, but the line is out again, which would seem to indicate that the conflict in Boston has heated up once more. Xander may be Gatekeeper now, but it was clearly presumptuous to take comfort in that. He is not a Regnier. It's possible that fact has handicapped his ability to access the power he has received. Still, we have little choice as to our course of action."

"That's not new," Oz said unhappily. Getting bound into the Gatehouse did not particularly sound like his idea of personal bliss.

"I won't give up trying to reach them." Giles scratched the back of his neck and moved his head slowly, as if he had a kink. "I think you'll be in good hands, Oz. Whether Xander is the Gatekeeper or the mantle passes to Jacques."

Oz was a bit embarrassed that he was putting up such a fuss. He didn't mean to. He was cool with the program, and he didn't want to be any extra trouble.

"I'm in, totally," he said.

"Which leaves only one, final problem," Jacques said. "Angel's asleep."

"No, I'm not," Angel murmured groggily from the pitch-dark hallway. "I can deal. I've had enough rest."

Micaela nodded to herself. "I can open the ghost roads in the hall as well as anywhere."

Angel replied, "That would be best."

"All right." Giles looked very serious, very concerned. Oz felt a chill down his spine. He hadn't died yet, he reminded himself, and he'd been on a lot of thrill rides with Slayer and Company. Problem was, for most people, the first time one died was also the last time. Except for bad guys. They usually got extra innings. What was up with that?

"I guess we may as well proceed." Giles gestured for Oz and Micaela to join him as he walked into the hall.

Angel was there, hair tousled. He was buttoning his shirt and tucking it into his black pants. He looked up and nodded at Oz. Oz nodded back.

Jacques moved to join them. They stood shoulder to shoulder, and Oz took a deep breath.

"I think I saw this on *Sliders,*" he said.

Angel actually chuckled.

Somehow that made it all a little better.

"Wait. Armbands," Oz said.

Angel went into his room and returned with a white T-shirt and a pair of scissors. While the others waited, he cut three strips and handed one to Oz and one to Jacques. They tied them around their upper arms.

"Make sure it's easy to take off quickly," Angel said to Jacques.

Jacques practiced tearing it off a couple of times, as did Angel. They nodded at Micaela.

"All right. I'll begin," she said.

She extended her arms and closed her eyes. Her voice was breathy as it dropped to a whisper. Oz could make out only a few syllables, and he was pretty sure they weren't in English. He licked his lips and braced himself, not sure what to expect. The last time Micaela had intervened on the breach thing, he had been unconscious.

Suddenly the hall filled with a bright white light. Micaela said, "Move toward it."

Oz was a tad not okay with that; how many books and movies had he read or seen where moving toward the light entailed dying? Okay, Micaela wasn't a squeaky-voiced dwarf woman, and Angel was no Carol Ann, but still, creepy.

"You're certain," Giles said, adding to Oz's concern.

"Yes. Move toward it, all three of you."

Oz took the first step.

In an instant, he was surrounded by nothingness. Around him, everything was the color of the pewter chess set in Aunt Maureen's TV room. Twilight time in the twilight zone.

So they were on the road again.

Beside him, a piece of white T-shirt floated in the air, and Angel said, "Can you see us?"

Another piece of white T-shirt floated on the other side of Oz.

"No. Can you see me?"

"Yes."

Oz took that in. "Freaky."

There was a brilliant flash, and then the landscape shadows around them snapped into focus: a throng of dead swarmed around them, terrified and screaming, as four or five slathering demons raged after them. Hulking and bent over, they were the color of rotten flesh, and smelled just as bad. Their faces looked like wet, loose clay, with black teeth and milky eyeballs pressed into it. They'd expected something like this, given how overrun the ghost roads had been the last couple of times. But still. So not what Oz wanted to see.

Just ahead of the pack, a pale, slack-jawed wraith slammed into Oz and clung to him, screaming, "Stop them! Stop them!"

"Hey," Oz protested, "let go. I can't help you if—"

The demons were on them in an instant. Oz crashed to the ground, landing on the ghost, whose fragile skull shattered in an instant. As Oz caught his breath, he got to his knees, then ducked back down as another demon sailed into the air, wings flashing open. One of the white armbands went into combat mode, slashing and swinging, while the shorter of the two—Jacques, obviously—did something magickal, creating some kind of barrier that held for a few seconds as the demons slammed into it. Then it broke down, and the demons tumbled into themselves and rammed forward, borne by sheer momentum.

Again Oz was thrown to the ground.

Immediately he was surrounded by shrieking spirits, so panic-stricken that they flitted back and forth wildly, passing through him, trying to grab hold of anything, screaming in his face. It was like a bunch of drowning people attacking a lifeguard.

"Hey!" he shouted as he struggled to his hands and knees, but they were beyond listening to him. One actually tried to crawl underneath him, like that would help anybody.

With supreme effort, he staggered to his feet and extended his fist, connecting at last with the slimy, bulgy side of the tallest demon as it waded into the pool of terrified dead and began crushing their heads with what might be its mouth. Hard to say. Whatever it was, it did the job. The ghosts exploded.

Oz had hit the demon. He'd felt his blow land. But the thing didn't even register Oz's punch, which made Oz angry. He was used to holding his own. Okay, he wasn't Buffy, but he was a fairly strong guy, for a musician, and Willow liked to feel his arm muscles, so at least he had some, or she was just being nice. But it wasn't like her to lie, really.

So he tried again, really going for the gusto, and knocked the living hell—so to speak—out of the demon, who stopped, blinked a whole lot of eyes, and took a step backward.

It roared so hard Oz's teeth rattled.

Then something stepped between Oz and his opponent—Oz felt the pressure—and the demon was hurtled up and into two of his closest personal friends. The three fell over, and while they were down, Oz and—it had to be Angel—advanced on them and punched and kicked for all they were worth.

"You know, we should have told her to make all three of us invisible to everyone else," Angel's voice sounded in Oz's ear. One of the demons was screeching as several of its eyes deflated and black liquid streamed down its front.

"Yeah. Oversight," Oz agreed, wrinkling his nose in disgust as he kicked at the demon directly in front of him. It didn't look as damaged as the one Angel had taken on.

"You look terrible," Angel went on. "You okay?"

"Yeah. Great."

Then suddenly, a howl erupted from Oz's throat

He looked down to see the hairs on the backs of his hand sprout and begin to grow. His fingernails became vicious claws.

"Sorry," he growled.

"We'll take care of you," Jacques called to him.

But Oz could no longer understand the words.

"Now, boy, concentrate," Hadrius said to Giacomo, as they stood before the pulsing wound in the world. "This is called a lacuna. A breach."

Giacomo wanted to draw back from the pulsing circle of purple. He was afraid, as he often was during his training sessions. But to admit fear was to invite a beating, and he had not recovered from the most recent one.

He had been with Hadrius a full lunar year—thirteen months—and still he dreamed of his mother and her smiles and her elixirs. He woke in the night with tears on his cheeks and remembered her shrieks of terror and pain, and vowed that such would never happen to anyone he loved, ever again.

What Giacomo Fulcanelli did not realize, as he moved toward the breach with his breath held and his back stiff within the cassock he wore, for his back was crisscrossed with whip marks, was that the price Hadrius paid for power was the ability to love. And that if he stayed in the terrible lord's service, he would all but lose that ability as well.

Power would become what he worshiped.

And he would admire Hadrius' hard-heartedness, striving to emulate it. He would be known as a cruel and exacting taskmaster, and his followers would do almost anything to avoid his wrath.

But for now, he was still a boy who had lost his witch-

mother to the flames and whose survival depended upon pleasing his master, whom, he suspected, was his true father. In the beginning he had assumed that such a bond might afford him a gentler life within the walls of the brooding fortress that was nightly surrounded by mist and raven's wing. But he grew to realize that Hadrius must *be proud of his own; he* must *have a son who was the coldest and cruelest. And so, whatever affection he might have felt for Giacomo, he would never reveal it to the lonely, terrified boy.*

Giacomo was fresh steel, and Hadrius was the hammer.

Together they would forge an ungodly weapon the likes of which the world had never seen.

Ethan wiped the sweat off his forehead and hoped sincerely that Ripper appreciated the amount of trouble he was enduring in order to stave off the invasion of various and sundry demonic entities into the pastel backdrop of dear old Sunnydale and other points earthbound. The old boy didn't seem to recall that the casting of spells required an awful lot of energy, and, well, one had to face facts: though he might appear to be a mere lad of, say, thirty-one or -two, Ethan had accumulated a lot of mileage over the years. Whatever proved best for your complexion, darling: some people went to spas; Ethan regularly performed sacrifices to the dark gods. Goats, mostly. Goats were always popular. He supposed he owed the lack of crow's feet to reeking, bleating goats.

"To order I bow," he muttered, bending from the waist and facing north.

"To divine harmony I subjugate myself." He shifted west.

"To balance I kneel." Kneeling now, eastward.

"To symmetry I abase myself." And for the final idiocy, south.

Funny thing about magick: sometimes one had to believe, and sometimes all that was necessary was the correct words and the proper rituals. Luckily, this was one instance where belief was not required. Else, the good guys would have been dead ducks by now. Order, harmony, balance, and symmetry: *Look them up in your thesaurus under boredom.* Ethan actually felt guilty invoking their qualities into the world. There was a reason your heart sped up upon occasion; why, in your sleep, you might startle. It was to remind your body that it was alive. Keep up that wretched thumping and pulsing for too long, and it would forget what it was doing. The same was true of the psyche. Things had to be stirred up now and then; all kinds of things hatched in a brook. Distilled water bred nothing at all.

The only way he got around his uneasiness was to promise himself that once this crisis was averted, he would wreak mischief over Sunnydale such as never had been seen before.

Slightly cheered, he continued.

"I call upon the gods of order, upon the guardians of the north, and of the south, selah! And of the west and the east, blessed be! Bring forth a sphere of order, a formation of calming influence, and let it grow and flourish in this place. Let it spread its power to all places of chaos. Let the chaos weaken, and the sphere become nourished thereon.

"I chant three, three, three.

"I chant seven, seven, seven, seven, seven, seven, seven!

"And of the perfection of the prime, I call, one!
"As it is, so shall it be."

As required by the text, Ethan closed his eyes and cleared himself of all inharmonious thoughts. He imagined his mind as a clean, clear crystal, forbidding himself to scoff at the very notion, and then took a deep, cleansing breath. Which was tainted with whiskey, and soon, he prayed, would be tainted with a little more of it.

However, all these damn guardians didn't have to know about that.

"As it is, so shall it be," he repeated.

He took another breath, exhaled, and cleared his throat. Thank God that was over with.

He opened his eyes, started, and chuckled.

It had worked.

The mess he'd made of Giles's precious books had been rectified: the learned tomes, which had once been ranged all over the floor, were now stacked on the study table in the center of the library. Not only that, but as he crossed over to them, he saw that they were arranged in alphabetical order. The chairs were each pushed in, just so.

The pencils beside the checkout counter were lined up like little dead animals, longest to shortest.

Everything was unbelievably, unrelievedly tidy. He was certain that if he checked the library bookshelves, they, too, would be carefully organized and dust-free to boot.

Over the library, a sense of calm and tranquility glowed like a Christmas carol.

"All is calm, all is bright," Ethan sang in a whisper. He wasn't at all surprised that the spell had worked.

Otherwise, what was the point of devoting one's life to the occult arts?

"All right, Rupert," he said, nodding with satisfaction. "Let's see if this did the trick where it really matters."

He picked up the phone and rang Giles up.

"Giles here," he said, in a very tense voice. The old boy also sounded a little tired. Maybe he'd finally bedded that beautiful woman. Micaela. Or was he still ever the gallant?

Foolish Rupert. Never knew how to make the most of an opportunity.

"Yes, Ripper, it's Ethan," Ethan announced. "Any sign of order up by you?"

"You performed the ritual?" Giles asked.

"Indeed I did. And?"

"Nothing as yet. That is, I see nothing unusual."

Ethan was miffed. "Then tell me, please, dear boy, that it's because you're standing in the abode of a neat freak."

"Hardly," Rupert replied.

"Humph. Well, I'll take a look round, see what I see. I can report that the library is awash in order. It's positively stultifying. Order, order, everywhere, and I think I'll drink some more whiskey."

He reached over to the checkout desk and poured himself a bit of a cuppa. Drank it down.

Waited for the delicious little burn and felt nothing.

"Bloody hell," he said. He inspected his glass. Empty. Poured another two fingers' worth and swallowed it in one gulp.

Absolutely nothing.

Drunkenness was off the menu, it seemed. Not orderly.

He smiled slowly. When you thought about it, neither was aging. Or dying.

This spell just might be the fountain of youth. And the key to eternal life.

If you could stand the aftereffects of monotony it brought with it. Perhaps later, a little tinkering with the recipe would be in order. *In order.* Ethan smiled to himself at the play on words.

"Are you still there?" Rupert queried. "We're going back to the cemetery."

"Oh, yes, I'm here. But I'll ring off for now. I'll go a-hunting to see what I've wrought."

"Very good. Ethan?"

"Yes, darling?"

"Behave yourself."

Ethan closed his eyes and pressed his hand over his heart. "Of course I will."

He picked up the whiskey bottle and raised it high. "Here's to glorious, tedious order," he proclaimed, spreading wide his hands.

"As it is, so shall it be."

That afternoon, during the last school period of the day, every student taking a test received a perfect score. Perhaps at another school, this would be a cause for alarm, but at Sunnydale, it was initially explained away by the administration, and then test papers were altered to allow for discrepancies and F's. The students, who at first had thought the entire affair was some kind of joke, accepted the paper-thin explanation that a number of answer keys had been mixed up, and those who received failing grades meekly accepted them.

Which was the sort of thing that made them failures in the first place.

Ethan sat in the teachers' lounge and listened to the stories, though: no one sent to the principal's office. No drug deals in the basement. Perfect attendance throughout the entire school. Not one single person in the nurse's office.

"It's scary," a buxom instructor of physical education said to Ethan.

"Indeed." He shivered theatrically.

She raised an eyebrow and smiled at him. "What class are you subbing for again?" she asked.

"Mr. Giles is out sick," he replied.

"Oh." She looked mildly confused. "I didn't realize there was such a thing as substitute librarians."

He leaned forward and said conspiratorially. "Oh, no one could fill Rupert's galoshes, do you know what I mean?"

She dimpled. "He is kind of cute." And sighed. "You know about Miss Calendar, don't you? They used to date. She was *murdered.*"

"No." He covered his mouth.

It was remarkable how fast the perfection of the day was lost to small-minded gossip, but there it was.

Ethan marveled.

The hits just kept on coming:

At the hospital, every single terminal medical case of any sort went into spontaneous remission.

There were no car accidents.

There were no accidents of any kind. The ER was devoid of customers.

So it said on the telly in the teachers' lounge, where he pretended to be reading some nonsense handbook about cross-referencing while he gave the sphere of order time to work.

Ethan was dying—*ha ha*—to go to Restfield Cemetery to see if the buried corpses ceased to rot.

But it was his job to ensure that the spell was working on the little problem in the Master's former lair, and so at the end of the day he hied himself up off the couch, politely declined the physical education instructor's invitation to join her for coffee, and meandered in a straight line (order working its wonders upon him, as well) over to the cemetery.

There he ran into none other than the exquisite Miss Summers, who was seated on the floor of the crypt checking her blond tresses for split ends.

"Hello, Buffy," he said, standing in the doorway of the crypt with his hands raised, rather as if she were a sheriff who had ordered him to reach for the sky. His experience with this young lady was that she thrashed first and asked questions later, and he didn't want to investigate the possibility that punches delivered by the Slayer might actually still hurt.

"Where's Giles?" he added.

"Ethan." The venom with which she spoke his name was awe-inspiring. "What are you doing here?"

"Had any action lately?" he queried. When she blinked at him, he hastily added, "Of a demonic sort? I mean, has anyone tried to get out?"

She narrowed her eyes at him. "You want to know why?"

He decided it would be more efficient to tell her the truth. Or perhaps the guardians of order had decided that.

"Your Watcher bade me do a spell," he said. "I have established a sphere of influence. It's spreading outward. It's like carbon monoxide—odorless and colorless but it packs quite a wallop."

"Influence," she repeated.

"Exactly so. Of order. The opposite of chaos. Or entropy." He looked at her. "Are you following me?"

"Oh, whatever." She stood and opened and closed her hands, which Ethan found somewhat discomfiting.

And he was right to feel that way.

The punch came out of nowhere.

But it didn't hurt. He didn't fall over.

The Slayer was clearly shocked.

"What the hell?" she blurted.

He grinned at her. "Were you about to take me to task for abandoning you at the labyrinth?"

She shook her head. "No. I was about to take you apart."

"Ah, well. That doesn't appear possible for the moment." He gestured to the door. "I think they've probably all gone to sleep. Or something."

At that very moment, something rammed against the heavy metal door, almost dislodging the sarcophagus wedged against it.

Buffy looked questioningly at him as she slammed her body against the sarcophagus. To Ethan's astonishment, it moved under her weight.

"Oh?" she asked. "Asleep, you say?"

"Or not." He moved quickly away. "I'll just, um, check outside for strays."

"Ethan, you're such a coward," she yelled at him.

The crypt resounded with pounding as something tried to get out. Ethan judged it best not to bother with a clever riposte, and left the crypt.

The most extraordinary thing happened in that

moment. A Wendigo capered across the cemetery, its huge, hairy white body a blur of movement as it darted from headstone to headstone. Then, as if it were a vampire exposed to sunlight, it burst into a flash of light. But instead of burning to cinders, the flash subsided, leaving the Wendigo's image on the eye like the remnants of a camera's flash. For a moment its transparent image hovered in the air, and then it disappeared.

Ethan stood stock-still. Then he clucked his tongue and said, "Very good, Ethan," and continued on.

All the while, the pounding in the crypt continued, a sort of counterpoint to his footsteps as he took himself off. He wondered about that; he sincerely did.

Across town, Giles's car sat in Angel's driveway and would not start.

Neither would Oz's van.

Giles got out and walked around to the front of his car, explaining that he knew it better and was thus more likely to repair it quickly.

Micaela sighed deeply. She didn't like this.

Not at all.

Deep within the buried church that had once housed the vampire called the Master, Belphegor pressed against the breach and felt the thinnest of membranes between it and freedom. Someone had cast a spell that was holding back its minions down here in the fragrant, rotting earth. Above, those who had already managed to go aboveground were being destroyed.

A pity, since the invaders of this realm numbered ten to one in favor of Hell-spawned demons. The

Otherworld was yielding up her population at a much less prodigious rate.

Hell was coming to this little town of Sunnydale, and to the world.

For some, the spell would stop them.

But not for Belphegor.

It pushed against the membrane. It required just a little more strength, a small amount of power more than it currently possessed. For want of just a little energy, it was still imprisoned in Hell.

If it had the blood of a powerful being, it would be out: the blood of the Slayer would have been necessary before, when the barriers were still fully formed. But now they were so thin that another might be made to take the Slayer's place. The blood of a master sorcerer might do. Or, if necessary, even that of one with the potential to master the black arts.

Fulcanelli's daughter was such a one.

Still, the best would be a Slayer.

Ah, yes, a Slayer.

It couldn't help but laugh.

For a Slayer stood on guard less than a quarter of a kilometer away.

"My dear," he whispered, *"can you hear me?"*

In the crypt, Buffy froze. Her blood turned to ice in her veins.

Belphegor was in Sunnydale.

The banging on the door stopped. Panting, she took a step away.

"My dear?"

She breathed in, out, didn't know what to say. A hundred smart-ass remarks died on her lips. From the part in her hair to her toenails, she was terrified.

"All will soon be lost, Slayer, and you will die," it said. *"But if you come to me willingly, I will be merciful."*

"That's what they always say, and then they pull the trapdoor lever," she said, fighting to stay calm.

"It is not a joking matter," Lord Belphegor insisted. *"There is no smile on the face of one who dies in agony."*

"Yeah, well, I'm not planning on dying any time soon."

"Mark it well, my dear," Belphegor told her. *"This day is your last."*

There was a terrible ripping noise far beyond the door. Maybe that was the sound of the demon lord ripping free of the breach, and maybe some demon babe had caught her Morticia Addams dress on a nail.

And maybe it was the sound that the fissure made as it separated the floor beneath her feet, each half of the dirty concrete splitting apart to reveal sulfurous flames that shot up like party noisemakers and singed Buffy's thighs.

"Hell is opening," Belphegor thundered. *"Welcome us."*

Chapter 12

As his followers were picked off by the false Gatekeeper, Giacomo Fulcanelli smiled grimly and waited for just the right moment to end things. For all the power in that house, it would fall to him this very evening. Its exterior shifted even as he looked at it; a Victorian-style turret on the upper left face of the house simply disappeared, subsumed into the massive structure.

On the lawn, several of his acolytes screamed. Fulcanelli raised his eyebrows.

Rank amateurs, he thought.

Their enemy was not the Gatekeeper. That much he had ascertained only moments after his arrival. He'd traveled the ghost roads, and made his trip even shorter by crossing over, just for a moment, into the Otherworld. He had never done that before, and there had been a chance that he might be trapped, but with the barriers so thin, it was a chance he'd been forced to take.

After all, if he did not resolve this situation quickly, Lord Belphegor might not have any need of him.

He couldn't allow that.

Not when the battle was so nearly won. Fulcanelli was displeased with the way things had gone thus far. At every step, it seemed he had been betrayed. By the vampires, Spike and Drusilla, by his acolyte Albert, by Claude and Lupo and so many others, and worst of all, by the girl he had raised as his own daughter. The defeats had been far too frequent.

He had failed to offer up the Slayer's life to Lord Belphegor. Thus, the barriers between Earth and dimensions that bordered it, specifically Hell and the Otherworld, in this case, remained intact. Belphegor would have eaten his heart already, if not for the fact that Fulcanelli's constant efforts had thinned the barriers significantly.

The walls between Hell and the Otherworld and the ghost roads had, for all intents and purposes, fallen. Thus, the demons and monsters of those realms were using the ghost roads to try to gain access to Earth just as their brothers were battering at the walls between worlds.

It was chaos.

It was beautiful.

Belphegor would be pleased. Still, Fulcanelli had not kept up his end of the bargain. Without the Slayer's blood, his own life was forfeit if Belphegor should breach the veil between Hell and Earth. If the sorcerer didn't do something about it first. He had to find a way to make it up to his demonic master. Some way to prove his power, and his value.

Sunnydale had proven a more difficult battlefront than he'd expected. With the treason of some of his most trusted acolytes, the escape of the Slayer's mother, and the death of the Minotaur, Fulcanelli had sought desperately for a way to please Belphegor.

And now he'd found it.

Jean-Marc Regnier, the Gatekeeper, was dead. But somehow this boy Xander, a friend of the Slayer's, had been invested with the power of the Gatekeeper. The war in Sunnydale was under way, and would be won or lost based upon factors that had nothing to do with whether or not Fulcanelli was present.

The war in Boston, however, raged on. Somehow, this boy who had become the Gatekeeper had managed, thus far, to hold together the house and to help hold back the creatures of the Otherworld trying to break free. It was extraordinary, certainly.

Fulcanelli smiled.

It was dark now, and a fire burned on the front lawn that moments earlier had been one of his acolytes.

It didn't matter.

A black panther bounded out the front door and down the steps, past the burning man, and fled out into the Boston night to prey on some unsuspecting civilian.

Fulcanelli chuckled.

The Harris boy was doing well. He had managed to fulfill the job of the Gatekeeper. But barely. And thus far, aside from a handful of moderately adept acolytes, some of the last, really, he had been presented with no opposition.

That was about to change.

It was all about to change.

With a whispered prayer to all the demons in Hell,

Giacomo Fulcanelli walked toward the entrance of the Gatehouse, intent upon winning the favor of Lord Belphegor once more.

Before it was too late.

"Why doesn't he do something?" Cordelia shouted across the huge marble foyer of the Gatehouse. The white-haired old man with the withered left hand just stood there with some kind of force field around him.

"Oh, thanks for giving him the idea, Cordy," Xander muttered, as the man started walking quite calmly toward the front of the house.

"Try Giles again," Xander added anxiously.

Willow ran to grab the phone, but even as she dialed, she figured it was useless. All their calls had been blocked. There was no way to tell the home team what was going on here. They probably thought this wizard guy was still back *there*.

Cordelia said to her hero, "Xander, just let him have it."

Xander faltered. He'd seemed more at ease, more confident, since he was infused with the power and knowledge of the Gatekeeper. Now he seemed like the old Xander again.

"Let him have what?" he cried.

"It!" Cordelia shouted at him, barely under control herself.

They were all terrified of this man. Willow could see that. Even the ghost woman who hovered only a few feet away. And she was already dead. When people who were already dead were afraid, okay, maybe it was time for that golden parachute.

Problem was, Xander couldn't retire. Not and have any world left to retire to. Not unless Buffy and Giles had something up their sleeves back in Sunnydale that they hadn't told anyone about. Which would be nice, especially since they didn't know the sitch. So that was more like wishful thinking as far as Willow was concerned.

Nope. Until they knew different, they had to assume that it all rested on Xander's shoulders.

And Willow had always thought he had kind of skinny shoulders.

Fulcanelli could see the panic on the boy's face as he walked steadily toward the steps. Rather than smiling, however, his face contorted with sudden disgust. Pleasing as victory was, this way of getting it was wrong. It was not supposed to happen this way. He had spent centuries battling the Regnier family, long before there was even a Gatekeeper. First Richard, and later Henri, and Jean-Marc. He had destroyed each of them, in a way, and scarred them as often and as deeply as possible.

They were the greatest of his enemies, and as such, their destruction had afforded him the utmost pleasure. Now he was poised to take away the greatest accomplishment the Regnier family had ever achieved, and not a single Regnier was present to appreciate the indignity of it.

It was wrong.

But Fulcanelli didn't have the luxury of worrying overmuch about such things. The end of the world would soon be at hand. If he wanted to be saved from the agonies of Hell, he would need to prove himself once more.

At the front steps of the Gatehouse, three more acolytes made a final, fatal attempt to gain entrance.

The ground erupted around them, swallowing two of them whole. The third was electrified by a bolt of blue light that streaked from the Harris boy's hands and jolted him where he stood. He sizzled, and then seemed to wink out of existence like the image on a television as it is turned off.

The teenage boy playing Gatekeeper looked as though he might be physically ill.

There were nine acolytes left alive here in Boston. As one, they swept toward the front of the house. A suicidal assault, and one they would not even have dared attempt if their master hadn't been present.

"Stop!" Fulcanelli shouted.

The nine men froze. They turned to regard him, fear on some of their faces, and hope on others. These few were so far down the chain of command that he recognized only a handful of faces, and those he could not put names to.

"Go," he said, waving his hands.

"Maestro?" one of them asked, a Russian man who stepped forward from the group.

"Leave!" Fulcanelli boomed. "You're doing nothing here but embarrassing me. Stay another second and I'll kill you myself!"

He thought they might argue, or at least ask what would happen if they left. They had been made promises after all. They were to be the kings of chaos, or at least, that's what he had told them. But faced with the horror of what had happened to the others they had arrived with, and given a few seconds to consider it, they did what he'd expected of them.

They fled.

Fulcanelli watched them go, considered destroying them as they ran from the premises, and then thought better of it. They were resources, and until the day was done, until the world had ended or his life had, he wanted to conserve what little he had left by way of resources.

Instead, he turned to look up at the dark-haired young man who stood in the open door of the Gatehouse.

"I know who you are!" cried the boy, this new, faux Gatekeeper.

Fulcanelli laughed. "Yes, young fool. And I know who you are not! You could save yourself a great deal of suffering, you realize, if you were to simply walk away. Leave the house and everything in it to me. I give you your life. Your friends as well. You can all go."

Xander's eyes went wide. He glanced around at Willow and Cordelia. Cordy looked at him hopefully, but Willow only frowned, chewing her lower lip.

"I'll do what I can to help," she said.

That was all the answer Xander needed, and really, he hadn't even needed that. He knew what hung in the balance here.

Xander looked at the old man. Deceptively old. He felt the house around him, felt it breathing, felt the power of the Gatehouse and the magick and knowledge of the Gatekeepers within him. Sorcerous energy crackled around his fingers and thrummed in his every muscle. His face felt flushed and his skin itched as though he had a sunburn.

It was power. Power like he'd never even dreamed about.

But he wasn't the Gatekeeper, and he never would be. He was Xander Harris, from Sunnydale, California. And he was here with his girlfriend and his best friend, both of whom now looked to him for heroics and strength in a way that they never had before.

He was just Xander.

But that would have to be enough.

"Xander!" Willow screamed, her hands contorting even as she started to babble, trying to weave some kind of protection spell, he figured.

Willow was valiant, but she would be too late. She was only a minor spellcaster, and Xander had barely a moment to react. Fulcanelli must have sensed his resolve, he reasoned, for the sorcerer was on the attack. Tendrils of a sickly orange magickal light sparked out at him, at the house itself. The stairs crumbled beneath his feet and Xander hopped backward across the threshold.

A tendril of magick touched his face, and Xander shouted.

Then the pain was gone. Almost by instinct, he had erected a circle of protection around himself, buzzing with a purple light that reminded him of the bug zapper in his parents' backyard. Blinking, stunned that he wasn't dead, Xander rose quickly and glanced around. He stretched out his arms and spread the protective field to include Willow and Cordelia, even as Willow herself continued to chant spells, doing all she could to back him up.

He didn't bother with Antoinette Regnier. As a ghost, she was already dead.

Then he sneered angrily and stepped up to the open door again.

He saw Fulcanelli's white eyebrows rise at the sight of him, and Xander smiled. *Tougher than I look, old man,* he thought. He raised both hands, palm up, as though he had been born to perform magick. In his left hand, a sphere of white energy began to form. A kind of mist leaked off it, filling the room like steam in a shower. In his right hand, magick swirled, and then solidified. It looked almost real there, in his hand, but it was pure sorcery.

A sword.

Fulcanelli took three steps toward the house.

"Come, then, boy," Il Maestro said darkly. "Come and die, and then all of Hell will be my reward."

Cordelia and Willow, safe behind the protective shield he'd given them, moved farther back toward the massive, double-wide stairs. Willow looked frustrated, and Xander knew why. She wanted so badly to help, and there was nothing she could do. The ghost of Antoinette Regnier hung in the air by Xander, silently lending him her strength and belief, just as Cordy and Willow did.

Xander was completely still. "You want Hell? You can have it, you evil son of a . . ."

He hurled the sphere of white, steaming light with his right hand. It struck Fulcanelli full in the face, and the sorcerer made no attempt at all to stop it. When it struck his flesh, it burst and spread white fire across his features. Fulcanelli screamed. His face seemed to melt and his features to run in gobs of blazing fat down onto his chest.

For a moment, Xander froze. He'd done it. And it had been easy. Fulcanelli was one of the most powerful sorcerers in the history of the world, and just like that, he'd . . .

"Xander, my God!" Cordelia cried.

"What is it?" Willow asked, horrified.

Well, Xander thought, *maybe not just like that.*

Fulcanelli had stopped screaming. He reached up with his good right hand and peeled away the ravaged flesh that had once been his face. Beneath it, his face was inhuman, yellow as parchment and hard as bone, pitted and run through with stiff, leathery folds.

"Fool," Fulcanelli said, and his voice sounded different now, strange, because he spoke through something that barely resembled lips. "Did you think I had spent all of these centuries prostituting my soul to the darkness without any repercussion at all? Oh, I am still alive. Still living, breathing. Human, even, by some definition.

"But I'm much more than human."

Around both of his hands, and in his eyes, an oily black aura had begun to form. The withered hand twitched at Fulcanelli's side, and talons ripped through the flesh of his fingers. Still, though, the arm was crippled. The blackness crackled and burned, so dark that it swallowed the night around it.

Xander swallowed. Raised his sword.

"Come on, then, you ugly bastard," he said. "There isn't anything good on TV tonight anyway."

With a roar of courage and fear rolled into one, Xander leaped from the threshold of the Gatehouse, magickal sword raised high, and brought it down toward the twisted creature that Fulcanelli had become.

From the sorcerer's hands and eyes, the black burn lanced out.

Willow and Cordelia screamed a warning and ran forward, trying to get him out of the way of Fulcanelli's attack. But they were too late.

Xander was blasted backward into the house. He flew across the foyer and crashed into the marble stairs. Pain shot through his entire body, and the magickal weapon he'd created dissipated. He was barely able to keep up the protective field around Willow and Cordelia. The girls ran to him, shooting terrified glances over their shoulders toward the open door.

"God, Xander, are you all right?" Cordelia asked.

"Do I look all right?" he grunted, sitting up painfully. "What was that?"

The ghost of Antoinette Regnier hovered near. *"That was what is called the black burn, young man. One of the most powerful forms of magickal energy on this plane of existence."*

"Great," Xander said.

"It could be worse," Willow said quickly. When they glared at her, she shrugged. "Not, y'know, *much* worse. But—"

"Willow," Cordelia interrupted.

She was staring past Willow, and now Xander saw what she was staring at. Fulcanelli. He had levitated himself up with the power of the black burn, that ebony oil swirling in the air around him, and now stood at the very threshold of the Gatehouse.

The entire structure convulsed.

A horrible, fetid wind blew through the house, and Willow and Cordelia had trouble standing in the gale. The house was trying to keep him out. But the wind didn't seem to affect Fulcanelli at all.

The leathery yellow features of the sorcerer's face stretched into what might have been a grin.

"An extraordinary house," he said with that slithering voice. "And an amazing feat of magickal fortitude."

"No!" Willow shouted. "Xander, what do we do?"

Xander stood up, green light flashing from his hands, reinforcing their protection and pulsing with power.

"Get out!" Xander snarled.

"You can't come in here," Cordelia insisted. "You weren't invited."

Il Maestro laughed at that. "I'm not a vampire, girl," he said, the black oil pouring from his mouth now as well.

"I'm something much, much worse."

Angel's mind was racing. This entire plan of Giles's had been hatched in an instant. The Watcher was one of the brightest men Angel had ever met. It wasn't that he merely knew how to acquire knowledge, but that he knew how to apply it, which was far more important. But there were times when he lacked in the strategy department.

Like now.

"Take off your armband!" Angel snapped to Jacques.

But the heir to the Gatehouse was already doing just that. He untied the white strip of cloth around his arm and tossed it away, off into the gray ether that swirled around him. The ghost roads had suddenly grown rather quiet, and it bothered Angel. He wondered if the barriers had fallen, if the final battle was over before he and Oz and Jacques had even had a chance to do their part.

"How are we going to get him to follow us without getting slashed?" Angel asked angrily, glancing around at the nothingness that was this limbo world.

Beneath the soles of his boots, he felt the solid ground of the road, and dared not look down. The ghost roads still had never made sense to him. They were the roads that the spirits of human beings followed after death. Somehow they existed in all worlds simultaneously, and supposedly had no reality of their own. But if not, then what was Angel standing on? He wasn't sure how deeply he wanted to examine the idea.

And he certainly didn't want to think about the things he'd seen here before. Even if he had the time. Which he didn't.

"I have an idea," Jacques said.

Even as Angel felt a bit of relief wash through him, he shook his head at the absurdity of it. He was more than twenty times the boy's age, and yet he was looking to the child for assistance. And yet . . .

Suddenly a red, raw light blossomed like a wound from the palms of Jacques outstretched hands. Angel stared at him, blinked several times, and then noticed that Oz had turned his snout toward Jacques and was sniffing the nothing in the air.

He couldn't see them. But whatever Jacques was doing, Oz could see or smell or taste it. Something. And he liked it.

"I thought you didn't have access to your inherited abilities," Angel said, frowning.

"I don't," Jacques agreed. "But I know a bit of magick my father taught me over the years, and I've practiced quite a bit in Europe. I will have all of my father's power and magickal knowledge once we reach the house. Now that he has . . ."

The boy didn't want to say the word. Angel let it go. His father was dead, and he was only eleven years old. Eleven, and he had to take up the responsibilities his father had left him, responsibilities that the world would never know enough about to appreciate. Angel was amazed at the boy's strength of character. Personally, he'd never been much more than a drunken, ungrateful layabout when he was alive. Only in death, and under his curse, had he found a purpose to his existence.

A child like Jacques, a person like Buffy, even her other friends, amazed Angel. They saw something that was required of them, and they did it, simple as that. It reminded him of something he'd heard said a very long time ago, something at which he'd scoffed at the time.

"A hero is someone who does what must be done, and needs no other reason." How true that was. He wished he hadn't killed the man who'd said it. But, after all, the guy had been trying to kill him. Heroes were like that.

Angel stared at Jacques a moment longer. It was amazing how much he reminded Angel of Buffy. Both of them were trapped in a life they never asked for, with the world depending on them. And both took up the gauntlet the world had thrown down with their chins held high.

"Now that he's died," Jacques finished. "But for now, this is enough."

And it was enough. Oz followed the magickal fire, sniffing the air of the ghost roads, and they walked far enough ahead that the occasional swipe of a claw did no damage.

Time slipped by. They saw several demons, but they were far off, and looked to be on their way to somewhere else. The wandering souls of the dead appeared from time to time, en masse, and then slipped away again. They were terrified. Hiding. Angel didn't blame them. Most of them—the ones who had given up traveling and been lost—had long since lost any hope of finding their way to their ultimate rest. And now, it appeared as though that rest would instead be eternal damnation in the flames of Hell.

Which, he knew from experience, was less than pleasant.

"Look," Jacques said suddenly. "I think we're nearly there."

Angel turned. In the distance, he could see a shimmering hole in the ghost roads.

Perfect order was perfectly boring. Ethan wandered the roads of Sunnydale with a roiling feeling of revulsion in his gut. The trash in the alleys was stacked like reams of computer paper. The graffiti on the walls and fences wasn't gone, but he did notice that it was all spelled correctly.

He sighed heavily.

While he was unable to seal off the ghost roads, or to reinforce the places where the barriers between worlds had grown thin, he had been perfectly capable of creating this foolish bubble of perfect order. It made him question everything in his life. Chaos magick was exceedingly difficult. It had taken him many years to rise to the modicum of proficiency he could now claim pertaining to chaos magick.

Why was it, then, that the magick of order was so damned easy?

It had to be, of course. Each spell was perfect. Orderly. And it was attractive to think of the power he might obtain through worshiping the Masters of Order.

But, God, the world would be a stultifyingly tedious place.

So the Hell with that.

Still, Ethan did allow himself a tiny bit of pleasure at seeing the rather silly results of his work. The cars in the parking lots were each parked precisely the same distance from the curb, and from one another. On the street, passing vehicles were moving at the speed limit. Exactly.

As he wandered, he saw more and more examples of the touch of order. Each lawn was cut to the same height. Passing youths spoke flawless English to one another. Which was, of course, patently impossible in America.

The sphere was spreading. Strengthening.

So, although one might claim he'd abandoned Buffy, it was fairly clear to him that the sphere needed more time to spread its influence. It was a good guess that the sphere was strong enough now that it would keep the demons back, and the monsters of the Otherworld, if any of them were brave enough to face the demons, for quite some time.

The sphere wouldn't last forever. And it wouldn't stretch out indefinitely. But as a stopgap measure, until Giles could figure something else out, or Fulcanelli could be done away with, it was damn fine work, if he did say so himself.

And he did.

Grinning, Ethan decided it was time to go back to his hotel and have a bit of room service. He was tired and hungry, and besides, there was a good movie on the hotel pay-per-view in about twenty minutes.

He'd done his bit. Let the others make a contribution.

Then an evil wind rose from the west and whistled down the street, blowing him to the ground and stealing the breath from his lungs. For a moment he couldn't breathe at all. Then, finally, his lungs sucked in fetid air, like a farmer had dumped twenty tons of manure a block away. The stench made his eyes water.

"Bloody hell," he snapped. "What the devil could—"

Then it hit him.

Nothing could. Not in this sphere of order's influence. Not unless the sphere had already been ruptured.

Ethan jumped in his car and raced down Route 17.

In the cemetery, Buffy scrambled backward out of the crypt.

"Oh, God, oh God, oh God," she muttered as she fell on her butt, then jumped up and started to run.

Just to put some space between her and . . . it.

Behind her, the crypt exploded in a shower of granite and marble. The ground split open, but it wasn't any earthquake. Six huge tentacles shot out of that hole in the ground, each of them covered with row upon row of razor-sharp spikes that moved with one mind.

It dragged itself up out of the ground.

"Slayer!" it roared.

Buffy turned to face Lord Belphegor, without so much as a weapon in her hands.

Face flushed with fury, she screamed, "Ethan!"

Chapter 13

A NUMBER OF THE SONS OF ENTROPY WERE STILL camped at the remains of their sanctuary at the Sunnydale Twin. They were holed up in the ruins of the main building, surrounded by the bodies of their fallen comrades. The place was a shambles, and, as was usual for Sunnydale, no police or other authorities were to be seen.

From his vantage point at the end of a corridor, peering from behind a reasonably intact door, Ethan softly clapped his hands and gave himself one of those natty black robes all the really fashion-forward chappies were wearing. Not that he had any notion of revealing himself. Still, one had to take precautions.

"Well, what I want to know is where Il Maestro has gone," one of the acolytes was grumbling. "Has he deserted us?"

"My runestone indicates that he's no longer in

Sunnydale," another added. This man was rather old, and his voice sounded high and whiny.

No news here, Ethan thought, and figured himself for a fool. It had occurred to him that perhaps young Jacques had been mistaken. Everyone had leaped on the notion that simply because he could not sense Fulcanelli anymore, the sorcerer was dead.

"Identify yourself," a harsh voice said behind him. A hand came down hard on the same shoulder Angel had threatened to pulverize.

Oh, dear.

Ethan thought fast. "I'm Brother Ermino," Ethan told the hand. "I've been sent by Il Maestro himself to tell you to clear out. Go back to, ah, London."

"Really?"

"Oh, yes," Ethan said brightly.

"Liar!"

Ethan was whirled around so hard his head spun, and then someone was smashing that same head in. Not using magick, just good, hard elbow grease.

"Liar! He took some of us to Boston!" the man shouted. He was amazingly ugly, with a brutish cauliflower nose, pug eyes, and jowls.

"But . . ." Ethan spit out a tooth. *Damn.* "I hate to seem confrontational, but that wasn't my understanding."

"Do you think all are privy to the plans of our dread lord?" The man's jowls bobbled with indignation. He hit Ethan again. "Now, tell me why you're here, spy."

Ethan blurted out, "His demon sponsor, Lord Belphegor, is in the cemetery." And realized that, by George, that just might be true. That might be why the sphere was crashing.

By all the gods, he thought in alarm, *it's begun.* Then he cleared his throat and continued. "He's there."

"Why don't I believe you?" the man screamed, and again started pounding Ethan's face.

"Stop!" cried another voice.

Ethan looked up at the smooth-faced lad who pointed a finger at the ugly man. Nice chap, or looked to be. He was smiling at Ethan.

Then the lad whirled and pointed the finger at Ethan. A blue net of energy dropped over him like a hood.

Not again, Ethan thought, before he started screaming.

At the apex of the breach into Boston, Jacques stopped suddenly and looked hard at Angel. Oz, who had trailed behind, started to gain on them.

"Fulcanelli is at the Gatehouse," Jacques announced. "He's not dead."

Angel closed his eyes. Not good news.

"Angel, I need to get to him *now.*"

Angel nodded, all business, and anxious to keep moving so that Oz wouldn't get too close. "Will he sense that you've arrived as soon as we enter the breach?"

"Yes, no doubt," Jacques said. He looked hard at Angel. "Angel, I cannot die."

Angel was distracted by Oz's fast approach. He could smell the musky scent of Oz's hide. There were certain legends about werewolf blood and vampires but he had no idea if they were true.

He realized Jacques was still staring at him, and tried to give the boy his full attention. "You can't die You mean, you do have some of your powers now?"

Jacques cleared his throat. "What I'm trying to say to you is, I must not die."

They regarded each other very seriously. Angel got it. He was expendable. Jacques was not.

"You want me to distract him. Act as decoy. Me and Oz."

Jacques inclined his head. "Please understand, I don't ask this for myself. If giving my own life would solve anything, I would do it without hesitation."

Angel put a hand on the boy's thin shoulder. "You've already given your life. You're the Gatekeeper."

"I should be," he said firmly. Then he looked very young, a little afraid, and confessed, "The notion of leaving Xander to it crossed my mind, I must confess. But not for long." He lowered his head. "I'm very ashamed of my weakness."

"You wouldn't be human if it hadn't occurred to you," Angel said, with a sad smile. "There've been a lot of times where I chose the easy path."

"But you were not born to fight evil," Jacques persisted.

"Sometimes I'm not so sure of that," Angel replied, and the boy looked startled.

"I'll go first," Angel went on, "and I'll lure Oz out with me. Then I'll distract him as best I can. But he won't be that interested in us. I mean, what real threat do one vampire and one werewolf pose?"

As if in answer, Oz roared and charged. Angel sighed, turned, and punched him across the snout. The bewildered werewolf jumped back and pawed at the air, seeing nothing, but sensing tantalizing prey nevertheless.

They moved away from Oz, who stood stock-still for a moment, growling and sniffing.

"I must prepare," Jacques said, as he closed his eyes. His face went as blank as a dead man's, and Angel stood respectfully by. In another situation, Oz's whining and confusion would have been comical as he wandered to their left in a zigzag pattern, searching for him and Jacques. For now, it was a welcome break, as Angel watched Jacques breathe deeply and rhythmically. The boy's chin rested on his chest.

Then he raised his face and his eyes opened slowly.

"Do you see? Do you hear? Do you understand?" he said in a slurred voice. His head swiveled as if it were on a strange pivot. He looked straight at Angel.

Then he smiled and said, in Xander's voice, "Hiya, dead boy."

"Xander?" Angel asked, impressed.

"Only part of us is known to you as Spock," Xander replied. "Listen, Jacques filled me in, I'm going to help on my end. But hey, um, hurry, okay? I mean, being the Gatekeeper is making me a real chick magnet and all, but I'm not sure how much longer I'm good for. I got somebody on my door stoop and it's for sure not the pizza delivery guy."

"I'm going to be a decoy. Oz, too. He's in beast mode," Angel said.

"Okay, here's my plan," Xander replied, sounding very out of breath. "First, you come out and—"

Jacques's entire body went rigid. His eyes narrowed and his mouth snarled into an ugly, cruel smile.

"Why do you tarry, boy?" he thundered. *"Your end has come. Accept it with dignity, and I will be kind."*

Angel took a step back.

Just then, Oz charged Jacques; his huge front paws

raised, his mouth slathering, he threw himself at the boy, and would have landed on top of him if Angel hadn't grabbed the heir, held him tight, and barreled through the breach.

Howling in frustration, Oz followed after.

Angel rolled, keeping Jacques as far away from Oz as possible. Then he leaped to his feet and prepared to take Oz on, at the same time taking in his surroundings, trying to locate Fulcanelli.

They were inside the Gatehouse, in some kind of anteroom, with statues and greenery all around.

At the sound of his name being called, Angel glanced up and saw Willow and Cordelia running toward them.

But Oz saw them too. He sniffed the air, and turned toward the girls. He was hungry. The werewolf launched himself in their direction now, his wolf brain unable to understand that Willow was his girlfriend and killing her would be, at the very least, slightly damaging to the relationship.

Willow and Cordelia stopped short, then cursed as Oz rushed at them.

Angel tackled the huge werewolf, managing only to make him stumble. Cordelia cried, "It's okay, I'm armed!" and swung at the beast with a cast-iron frying pan.

"Cordy! No!" Willow yelled, at the same time that Cordelia shouted, "Xander! We need help!"

"Don't distract him," Willow countered, grabbing the frying pan as Oz came for her. She swiped the air with it. "I mean, yes, distract Oz, but not Xander."

Oz raged at her and she smacked him across the face. "Oh, sorry." He backed off a few inches. "Okay, the hitting's a good thing."

She smacked him again. "Oooh, sorry." Then she said to Angel, "Xander sent us to get you as soon as you got here. He needs hel—"

Oz grabbed her arm and bared his fangs. She let out a bone-rattling scream.

Angel dove toward them both.

Suddenly the house began to shake violently, throwing Angel and Oz off balance. Oz released Willow, then was suddenly thrown across the room, slamming into the wall. Jacques, who had gotten to his feet, also began to shake, spasming, his back rigid, his head thrown back.

Assuring himself that Willow was, for the most part, safe, Angel tried to contain Jacques's seizure by grabbing him, yelling, "Someone get something to keep him from swallowing his tongue."

"No!" Willow cried, as the ceiling rained plaster down on them. "The same thing happened to Xander when he became the Gatekeeper."

His fall cushioned by Angel, Jacques was spread-eagled on the floor. His legs kicked and his arms flailed wildly.

Oz got back up and charged at Cordelia, who went crazy, grabbed the frying pan from Willow and really pounded on him. "Why don't they make these things out of silver?" she cried.

"Hey!" Willow shouted. "Don't forget who you're whaling on!"

An ear-splitting whistle like a teakettle added its counterpoint to the cacophony. Oz threw his head back and clutched his ears, and Cordelia shouted and accidentally dropped the frying pan.

The door to the room slammed open and a high, wild wind blasted in, blowing everyone, including Oz, to the floor. Willow grabbed Cordelia's hand, and Cordelia hung on to Angel's boot. Angel felt for purchase, and wrapped his hands around a marble column, holding on for all he was worth.

It was like being in a hurricane. The walls of the room buckled and cracked. Statuary crashed to the floor, and the floor split open in a series of fissures.

"Oh, my God!" Cordelia cried shrilly. "It's got to be Il Maestro!"

"Hold on," Angel bellowed. "Nobody let go."

"Oz, where's Oz?" Willow asked, terrified. "What's going on?"

Then Jacques let out a long, shuddering moan.

"Look," Willow said, staring at a point beyond Angel's shoulder.

Angel fought the fierce wind as he turned his head, but the column he was holding on to blocked his view, and he could see nothing.

Then two figures glided through a nearby red-velvet couch and stood beside Angel. One was the ghost of Antoinette Regnier. The other was a young, handsome man as transparent as she. He had jet-black hair and dark eyes, and he was crying. Angel stared, amazed. It had to be Jean-Marc Regnier, more youthful than they had ever seen him in life.

Tendrils of blue light undulated like electric currents all over the room, from the corners to the ceiling to the floor, and bathed the inert boy in an aura of magickal energy. Jacques was raised up, floating at the waist level of the two ghosts, and the man touched the boy's cheek lovingly.

"My son," whispered the male ghost. *"Thank you, vampire, for bringing him to me."*

The wind stopped at once. Jean-Marc stretched out

his hands and placed them on his son's forehead. He closed his eyes and murmured something in a slow, even tone. He was chanting.

Jacques opened his eyes. He saw Jean-Marc and cried out, "Father!" But in that moment, both Jean-Marc and Antoinette disappeared.

"No," Jacques whispered, lowering his head. For a few seconds, there was no sound in the room. The proverbial pin could have dropped.

Then he raised his head. He regarded them all with the face of a child and the eyes of a very old soul.

"Your friend is released," he said, "and I must hurry to take his place. Fulcanelli will know his power is gone, and kill him with the black burn."

Without another word, he strode out of the room.

"Oh, um, Mr. Gatekeeper," Cordelia called.

"Don't bother him, Cordelia," Willow said. "He's got important business to conduct."

Beneath a pile of rubble, Oz growled muzzily.

Cordelia let go of Angel's boot and shook Willow's hand away. "Okay," she said sourly, getting to her feet "I'm looking for silver."

"Hey," Willow said sharply. "Oz doesn't mean to be, um, lethal."

"Yeah, well, nobody ever cuts *me* any slack for being honest," Cordelia went on, then turned on her heel and started out of the room.

She collided with Xander, who was on his way in.

"Xander!" she shrieked, throwing her arms around him. "Thank God!"

"To coin a phrase, 'Yeah, well.'" He sat down on the couch and dangled his arms between his legs.

"What's going on?" Angel demanded. "What's Jacques doing?"

"He sent me in here. He told me we'd be in the way." Xander looked at Angel. "But I think we should figure out a way to be useful." He groaned. "I'm one tired ex-superhero."

Cordelia curled around him and gave him a big kiss on the cheek. He smiled at her and kissed her back.

She said, "We've got to get out of here anyway. Oz is in wolf mode and he's hungry or pissed off or something."

Xander nodded and got to his feet, holding hands with Cordelia.

Angel bent over Willow and helped her to her feet. She was limping slightly. When he gave her a questioning look, she said, "Someone has to sprain an ankle when the group's running away from danger. It always happens."

Oz growled again and began to move.

"Uh-oh," Willow murmured.

Before she could react to what was happening, Angel swept her up into his arms. He grinned at her and said, "You're blushing."

She got even redder. "I'm not surprised."

Angel carried her out of the room and shut the door.

Not that that would keep Oz at bay for very long.

"No!" Fulcanelli shrieked, as the Gatekeeper rushed him.

Jacques glared hard at the evil being who had tortured and harassed his family for centuries, at the monster who had threatened the entire world's existence, and attacked him with every bit of magick at his disposal.

Multicolored fields of energy erupted around and

through him. He reveled in his power. He was guardian and protector.

He was the Gatekeeper.

"What?" Fulcanelli cried, returning blow for blow of lightning and fire. Around Jacques, pieces of the house exploded like mines. "How did you—"

"You didn't realize I came through a breach inside the house, did you?" Jacques bellowed. "You thought the gale inside my house was *your* doing."

The look of wild frustration on Fulcanelli's face as Jacques made him retreat through the foyer, staggering backward under the assault, made up for a lot. It made up for the death of Jacques's normal life, if not the death of his father.

"This night will end with your death," Fulcanelli flung at him as he teetered on the threshold.

Jacques answered with another barrage, then blasted Il Maestro out the front door. As the sorcerer tumbled end over end, Jacques manifested a pair of heavy oaken doors where the former ones had once stood, and slammed them shut just as Fulcanelli got to his feet.

"And stay out," Jacques said grimly.

Crouching low, her hands flexed, Buffy forced herself to stand her ground as Belphegor emerged from the pit. Its tentacles slithered and snapped with whiplike cracks as it toyed with her, remaining just out of reach. It was covered with sharp-tipped horns and a long, weird trunk. As it raised the trunk, she counted seven mouths, starting with two or three beneath the trunk and slashing down its neck and across its chest. From inside each mouth, a set of jaws extended about three feet beyond its lips, dripping with green slime and what had to be blood.

It had two pulsing red eyes, and there was a thick mound in the middle of its forehead. Buffy figured it for some kind of scar.

"Eew," Buffy said. "Somehow I pictured you, y'know, all muscley and kind of, like, having good bones, a nose, that kind of thing. Maybe some nifty body armor. But you must have a terrible time getting dates. No wonder you're cranky."

"Still the same fire," it said, chuckling low. *"I have many forms. This is the one I choose to show you. Yet you barely respond. You are a most unusual being, Slayer."*

"Yeah, well, I'll bet you say that to all the beings."

"Only the ones I kill."

While Buffy worked on her comeback for that zinger, about half a dozen of the guys in hooded robes streamed into the crypt and herded around Buffy like stampeding buffalo. Most of them fell to their knees and held out their hands. One lay on the floor with his face in the concrete dust.

Another one got the hell back out of there, fleeing the crypt and running shrieking for cover.

The only smart one in the bunch, Buffy figured.

"Oh, Lord of Darkness!" one of the acolytes cried. "We have come to worship you. Il Maestro told us of your coming and—"

"That is a lie. He would never have told you such a thing."

The man looked very confused. "But . . . but Brother Ermino heard of it from him. He sent us here . . ."

"Your enemies have sent you to die," Belphegor

replied. *"Perhaps it was your Brother Claude. Or Brother Lupo. So that I would dispatch you for them."*

"Oh," the acolyte said uncertainly. "But we have come to worship you. I swear on my black heart, lord. To aid you."

Buffy backed slowly away. She watched the demon carefully. It was disgusting; it gave off a rank odor worse than the grave and it was leaking some kind of chunky fluid. As it loomed over the acolytes, it quivered and shifted, and Buffy thought she saw a shadow inside of a creature shaped more like a man than this thing. That creeped her out even worse.

"I don't need any help," the demon responded. *"Not anymore."*

Then it rushed the five men, encircling them with its tentacles and gathering them up like bowling pins. The jaws catapulted forward, all seven at once, and began ripping the flesh from the panicked men as they screamed and scrambled to get away. One lost half his face to one bite; the arm and chest of the next were gone, and his remains tumbled to the floor in a disgusting heap. From beneath the strange mound, talons emerged, dissecting what was left until there were only tiny bits of flesh and viscera.

Another was decapitated in the first attack, and his body swallowed whole in the next. Blood spurted everywhere, spraying the walls, the sarcophagus, Buffy.

Buffy was almost at the open door of the crypt when the tentacles looped over and behind her like a lasso. She was only barely able to leap out of range, but as a result, she was closer to the demon's clacking, blood-drenched jaws.

Just then, someone grabbed her arm and yanked

her to the left. For no good reason, Buffy glanced at her attacker before she took him out.

It was Micaela. And Giles was right behind her.

"Hello, cavalry," Buffy said, as Giles threw a punch at the demon.

"We need to get out of here. Immediately. Someone tried to prevent us from coming here."

Belphegor hissed, *"Guilty as charged."*

"I can't let this thing get free," Buffy protested.

"By the power of the old gods, I bind thee," Micaela intoned, raising her arms toward the demon as Buffy stood guard and Giles assumed a good fighting stance—give it a ten on the Watcher bell curve. *"I call upon Pan to guard me and mine."*

"A binding spell?" Belphegor hissed. *"That paltry little charm is laughable."*

But Buffy realized that the spell had worked. The tentacles still traveled along the floor, but an invisible barrier barred their progress as they tried to reach for her and Micaela.

"It won't hold," Micaela murmured in Buffy's ear. "It will only buy us time. Seconds. We must—"

The tentacles broke through. The nearest one curled around Buffy's calf. Teeth and pincers dug into her flesh and she cried out, more in shock than pain. Her Slayer's reflexes went into high gear as she curled both hands into fists and slammed down on the tentacle, stomping as hard as she could with her free foot.

Giles shouted, "Buffy!" and stomped as well, kicking the tar out of it, or maybe those were pieces of acolyte.

Micaela raised her arms and repeated the binding spell.

Belphegor laughed. *"Victory!"* it shouted as it began to yank Buffy toward the snapping jaws of its seven mouths. Giles grabbed her around the waist, but he was pulled along as well. *"Finally, I'll taste the power of the Slayer."*

She braced herself. She had always figured she'd die in battle. Somehow she'd always thought she would graduate first. Okay, maybe not graduate. But there was the prom—

Micaela raised her arms and shouted, *"I call upon Pan to protect me and mine!"*

For one, maybe two seconds, Belphegor slackened its grip. Buffy bolted free, made sure Giles was still with her, grabbed Micaela's hand, and headed for the door.

Buffy jumped as wide as she could, feinting to the right. The tentacles whipped in her direction. Like Robin to her Batman, Giles was with the program as they both made an end run around the tentacles, Buffy dragging Micaela along.

They burst out of the crypt. Micaela stumbled behind and Giles took over the dragging duties. They ran as fast as they could, Buffy not even daring to look behind them.

She bellowed, "Okay, now what?"

"My vehicle," Giles shouted, pointing to his car, haphazardly parked on the other side of the cemetery gates. "The influence finally reached it, and it started."

"We need to get to the center of the sphere of order your friend created," Micaela added.

Buffy glared at her. "Ethan Rayne is not my friend," she and Giles said simultaneously.

Behind them, something roared. The ground shook.

The sky darkened.

"Where did he cast the spell?" Micaela asked.

Buffy said, "I don't have a clue."

As the Slayer and her companions burst through, the sidewalk ruptured. One half of it jutted upward while the other half canted into the earth. A water main buried beneath it burst, geysering water fifty feet straight up into the air. Buffy kept her footing and managed to keep Micaela from falling as well.

"He mentioned Rupert's books," the blond woman said, looking at Giles.

Buffy nodded. "Okay. Library."

Giles fished out his keys and ran around to the driver's side.

"We'll have a chance there, if we can reach it in time," Micaela continued, gasping for breath as they ran toward the car. As Buffy looked at her questioningly, she grimaced and pressed her hand into her side. "Not much of a chance, it's true."

Buffy shook her head and jumped into the front seat on the passenger's side. "Why, on the last day of the world, do I have to go to school?"

Fulcanelli felt the night air on his true face as he sent tremors through the earth and rocked the very foundation of the Gatehouse. He watched with glee as the beveled windows in one of the turrets glowed white-hot. Then the turret disappeared completely.

He did not want to destroy the Gatehouse. Once he dispatched the brat, he would claim the incredible structure. Now that Belphegor had spurned him, Fulcanelli would need as much power as he could find. And he could find it here. If Belphegor continued to be a problem, he would release all the creatures of

Otherworld—the thousands of them, bound so long that most of them were now quite crazed, if they hadn't been at the time of capture—and herd them in a wild mob across the ghost roads and into Sunnydale.

Even the Warmonger of Hell would have its hands full.

From the balcony of the house, the new Gatekeeper stared down at him. Fulcanelli conjured up a spear of black burn and sent it his way, not expecting to harm Jacques Regnier, but one could always hope, could one not?

The child deflected the attack with apparent ease. But he had not had time to adjust to his new role, simply stepped immediately into it. Now Il Maestro was sorry he had sent the nine remaining acolytes scurrying away like the vermin they were. If all they had managed was to harass the little Regnier for a few seconds before the lad destroyed them, their lives would have had meaning in the grand scheme of things.

The ancient sorcerer glanced left, right, did not see them. He chose to think of them with rancor for deserting him. Loyal followers would have insisted upon remaining with their leader, no matter that he had dismissed them as useless.

There! He spied one of the Sons of Entropy hiding in a lush stand of rosebushes. His dark hooded robe was like a black shadow on the dark red blossoms, so unusual for this time of year. The Regniers always did love roses. Giuliana Regnier had died in delirious pain, muttering nonsense about them.

With a careless wave of Fulcanelli's hand, the bush burst into flame. The crouching man shouted with surprise and threw his arms over his head. The fragrance of the burning flowers was overpowered by the more delectable odor of charring flesh as the man went up, a pillar of flame.

In this very way had Richard Regnier thought he had killed Fulcanelli, during the Great Fire of London in 1666. What incredible hubris, what monumental pride, to assume one had rid himself of Giacomo Fulcanelli in that ineffectual manner.

As you thought you had rid yourself of Hadrius, came the unbidden thought. He tamped down his anger and focused on the boy, who watched impassively as Il Maestro's acolyte burned to death.

Boy no longer, Fulcanelli reminded himself. *Give him no quarter. Show him no mercy. He is the Regnier. The Gatekeeper.*

Nevertheless, he could not help himself as he called out, "Child, give me the house and you may return to your school days. I'll allow you to live." He smiled, relishing the freedom of movement of his mouth, now that his false face was gone.

"Of course, you will become my devoted servant," he added.

The Gatekeeper said nothing, only stared at him.

Beneath Fulcanelli's feet, the earth shook, and he was slightly taken aback. Only slightly, however.

For the shaking was not of his doing, but what did it signify? He was Il Maestro, and the victory would ultimately be his.

He bent low, sending something of himself into the dark places where the blackest magick was born. Shuddering, his projected persona gathered fresh hatreds and more weapons from the cache where Il Maestro kept them.

Alerted to its presence, a swarm of red demons

rushed it, talons flashing in the black light. The presence departed, and returned to its master.

Fulcanelli opened his eyes and flexed his hands meaningfully. The pitifully small figure observing him never changed his expression.

Fulcanelli made two fists, pressed them together, and whispered an incantation in a language that was already dead in another realm before this realm bore thinking creatures.

The night went completely and utterly black as, one by one, the stars winked out and the moon was choked beneath a blanket of living, breathing evil.

Inside the Gatehouse, Willow said to Angel, "Um, I can run now."

It was a very weird experience being carried around by Angel, who was in full vamp face, as he kept her safe from her boyfriend. Angel was quite muscular and his chest was very broad. It was neat, in a girl-responding-to-boy way. And that was very weird, all around, and she felt vaguely guilty, like she shouldn't tell Buffy about it. Oz either. On the other hand, she was not so good in the secret-keeping department.

So, after graduation, no X-Files for me, she thought giddily.

"Um, Angel?"

"Hey," said a voice, and it was Oz's voice.

She and Angel both turned their heads at the same time. There was Oz, her guy, Oz, only sometimes when he de-wolfed, he didn't have on a lot of clothes. Luckily, he was standing behind a chair draped with a white sheet. As Oz took in his appearance, he began to pull the sheet off the chair.

Willow practically leaped from Angel's arms

nearly falling as she landed on her swollen and rapidly numbing ankle.

"What gives?" Cordelia said, glancing at Xander.

Xander shrugged. They had been running through a small, hexagonal room, which Xander and Cordelia got all excited about, and Angel had said to Willow, "It's a twin of the room we did the Ritual of Endowment in." That was the ritual they had performed to make Buffy stronger, Willow doing her own part by remote control in Sunnydale.

"Did someone put out the moon?" Oz asked.

Then, just as abruptly as he had become Oz, he threw back his head and howled. Coarse black hair spurted over his face and body, and his face began to elongate.

"I'm thinking yes, and now it's *not* out," Xander announced. "As the former Gatekeeper, may I suggest that we all run away!"

Cursing, Willow followed Xander and Cordy out of the room, Angel bringing up the rear. Oz was slashing the air just behind Angel's head by the time they reached the corridor and flew down it.

At the end of it, there was an enormous curved stairway Willow could not remember seeing before. It wasn't the one at the front of the house.

The Gatehouse is beginning to lose its mind again, she thought anxiously. *Jacques must be overloaded fighting Il Maestro. He can't keep the Gatehouse together.*

One look at Xander's and Cordelia's faces confirmed her thought. It didn't make her happy.

Nor did the fact that everyone barreled down the stairway without considering that it might disappear at any moment.

Or maybe that did. Maybe falling twenty feet or getting whisked into another dimension was preferable to being dismembered by her one true love.

Who was gaining on them.

At the foot of the stairway was a large wooden door. Xander, in the lead, pushed it open. Willow blinked.

It was the way out, literally. Outside. Out of the Gatehouse.

"Is this good?" Xander asked. Then his eyes widened and he yanked on Cordelia's hand, shouting, "Jam it, Cor!"

They ran out of the Gatehouse. Angel followed after, stopping long enough to slam the door in Oz's face.

They stood on an expanse of lawn surrounded by trees and a small fountain. Xander and Cordelia were wheezing, staring uncertainly at the door as Oz slammed against it and started pummeling it.

"I'm thinking we need more distance," Angel said. "He may get out."

"Isn't the door magic or something?"

"I can try to bind him," Willow suggested, but she wasn't very happy about that notion. After all, this was Oz, not some Otherworld escapee. She wasn't sure what would happen to him in the unstable Gatehouse.

"We'll save that as a last resort," Angel said.

Willow relaxed, just a little.

Then the door disappeared.

"Oz!" Willow cried. "Oz!"

Just as suddenly, the lawn beneath them disappeared. Willow plunged into the murky depths of frigid, dark water, and lost sight of the others.

She broke to the surface, gasping for breath, counting heads in the weak moonlight. Xander, Cordy . . . Angel.

"Whoa," Xander said. "What the heck is Jacques doing? Hey, kid!" he shouted. "We could use some help."

Treading water beside him, Cordelia shook her head. Her hair was slicked back from her face and her makeup was gone. She looked very cold and very scared.

"He's not going to help us, Xander. We mean nothing to him. He's got to concentrate on Il Maestro."

Xander looked perplexed and angry. "No way. I subbed for him while those guys took him to Disneyland or whatever. Besides, he's the goodest of the good guys. So he can just part this sea!"

"He's not gonna help us," Cordelia snapped. She looked at the others.

"We're on our own."

"Okay, so swimming," Willow said, only she was so cold she was having trouble making her arms and legs move. In the icy water, her sprained ankle really hurt.

"Swimming to where?" Cordelia shot back.

Willow looked around. All she saw was water and moonlight.

And then, about twenty feet away, the water began o churn.

"Oh, God," Cordelia screamed. "What is it?"

"The Kraken," Angel suggested. "The Gatekeeper ound it back into the house."

"Willow," Xander urged, treading water. "Do your hing. Now."

"She can't bind it by herself," Cordelia said, splashing wildly as she tried to swim away. "Jean-Marc had to help her, remember?" She grabbed at Xander. "I can't swim! My clothes are too heavy. I'm going to drown."

"Here," Xander said, putting his arm around her. "Willow, you have to try."

She cleared her throat. She was so frightened she couldn't think of the exact words of the incantation. *"To the old gods I give all reverence and honor,"* she began.

"Pan, protect me. I call upon thee to bind—"

The water roiled and bubbled. A huge wave rushed over the four, crashing down on Willow as she sputtered and fought to complete the spell.

"Pan, be my guardian!" she tried.

"Those aren't the right words," Cordelia shouted at her. "Say the right words."

The water rushed and another wave smacked them. Then the sea seemed to dome upward.

"It's coming! It's going to eat us up!" Cordelia shouted.

Very softly, Angel said, "Buffy," and Willow spared her no-doubt last thoughts for Oz. And her parents. And the fact that it didn't matter anymore if she lost her conditional status at Bryn Mawr.

Then the Kraken rose from the depths and hovered over them. Willow realized her eyes were closed; she opened them and took a deep breath. The big, ugly lady was going to win after all.

Only it wasn't the big, ugly lady. It was some kind of dinosaur, with a long neck and a little head, and it stared down at them almost as if it were as frightened of them as they were of it.

"Oh, my God," Xander said, "it's . . ." he looked at Angel. "You're like, what, Scottish? Is it what I think it is?"

Angel nodded. "I'm Irish, and it's the Loch Ness monster."

"Oh." Cordelia brightened. "That's okay. That thing is friendly, isn't it? It's Nessie." She looked very proud of herself.

"Oh, oh, right." Xander's tone was sarcastic and a little harsh. "The Cartoon Network says so, right?"

Cordelia scowled at him. "Hey, Xander, who died and made you—"

"Gatekeeper?" he zinged back.

The creature threw back its head and trumpeted loudly. Then its head plummeted toward Xander, but Cordelia yanked him out of the way.

"Maybe it wants to play," Xander snapped, then managed to add, "Thanks," to Cordelia as the monster reared back its head and tried again.

"By Pan, I bind thee," Willow said lamely. She was drawing a blank.

Then Angel took her hand and murmured, "Think it through, Willow. You've done this a hundred times. You can do it."

She was still blank, but suddenly, she began to speak. It was as if someone else were in her head, like the time she had spoken Rumanian to restore Angel's soul.

"To the Old Gods I give all supplication, and deference, and honor."

"Now you're cookin'!" Xander cheered.

He was right. She was in the zone.

"I call upon thee to protect all within these waters," she intoned.

The Loch Ness monster trumpeted again. Then it blinked at them as if in surprise.

In the flash of an instant, it disappeared, as did all the water.

"Cool," Willow said brightly as they lay soaking wet on the lawn. "I did it!"

"Or not," Cordelia muttered, pointing.

On the roof of the Gatehouse, Jacques was silhouetted against the full moon. Bolts of lightning shot into the area surrounding him. So far he was untouched, but from where she lay, Willow could feel the force of the energy. If one of those hit him . . .

He gave them a wave. Willow waved urgently back and said, "We're fine! Go battle!"

She looked anxiously at Angel. "He shouldn't be bothering with us."

"I'm glad he did," Xander said. He got to his feet and helped Cordy up.

Angel did the same. Willow rose easily.

"Hey," she announced, "he fixed my ankle." She gave Jacques another wave.

"Your full-service Gatekeeper," Xander said. "Now, if he can also save the world, I'm for buying him a present." He moved his shoulders. "What the heck. Let's go crazy. We'll get a cake, too."

Willow flinched as a bolt landed perilously close to Jacques. He leaped to the left and fell to his knees.

"I'm not liking this," Willow murmured.

"Me neither," Angel said.

Then, as Jacques knelt and worked a ball of energy between his hands, a bolt arced directly for him, honing in like a cruise missile.

"No! Look out!" Willow shouted.

They all shouted.

And then Cordelia's shriek of terror was consumed by the huge flash of light as the lightning struck home. A direct hit, right in the center of Jacques's chest.

One minute he was there, the next . . .

"Oh, my God, Angel," Willow said. "He's been vaporized."

As if in response, the Gatehouse shifted and flickered. As they watched helplessly, it began to crumble in upon itself.

14

FOR A HEARTBEAT, WILLOW COULD ONLY STARE AS ONE entire wing of the Gatehouse began to collapse in on itself.

Then she screamed.

"Oz!"

She started to run toward the house, her mind awhirl with fear for her boyfriend, who was kind and gentle and clever—when he wasn't a werewolf. Willow had been standing in the courtyard of the Gatehouse with Xander and Cordelia and Angel. They had been watching young Jacques Regnier, the new Gatekeeper, in sorcerous combat with the ancient Fulcanelli.

And then Jacques had lost. Suddenly, and unexpectedly, it was over. The Gatehouse was collapsing, the Gatekeeper destroyed. Fulcanelli had triumphed. Now the barriers between dimensions, the walls that separated their human world from Hell, and from the

Otherworld—where so many monsters of myth and legend still lived—were falling.

"Oh my God," she whimpered to herself, legs pumping, heart pounding. "This can't be happening."

But it was happening.

The shriek of timber was punctuated by small explosions inside the house. Fulcanelli was outside, on the other side of the front segment of the Gatehouse. They had a handful of moments, perhaps several minutes, to figure out what to do, how to survive.

But first she had to save Oz.

Heedless of the danger, Willow ran toward the house as one entire wall began to crumble, pouring down into the courtyard. Strong hands grabbed her, dragged her down to the soft earth, and she lay there, panting, as dust rose from the rubble.

"Oz," she whispered.

Then she bucked, shouting, "Get off me!"

"Whoa, just saving your life. No applause required, but, y'know . . ."

It was Xander. She stared at him a moment—she'd thought it had been Angel, scooping her out of harm's way once again—but no. Xander. Her oldest friend.

Heavy-hearted, consumed entirely by the question of Oz's fate, Willow barely noticed Cordelia's screaming. Xander, though, responded immediately.

"Cordy, relax," he snapped, looking at Willow with concern. "I'm sure it's not the end of the world."

But then Willow could see past Xander. She could see what Cordelia was screaming about, what Angel was staring at in silence, and what Xander now turned to look at.

"Okay, I take it back," Xander mumbled.

But none of them found it even remotely funny. For the world *was* ending. That was the undeniable truth of it. All around them, save for the wing that was nothing but debris, the Gatehouse had begun to shimmer, as though it were a reflection in a pond rather than something real and tangible.

Out of that shimmering reflection, monsters were being born. Monsters, and a great deal more. Trolls and ghouls and horrid flying things and a woman with snakes for hair . . . all manner of creatures tore their way through that portal. All the things that the house had held captive for so long, denizens of the Otherworld who could never return to their own world, each was out now. Free.

Most of them were pretty pissed.

Willow shouted in pain and covered her ears as a sudden skyquake split the night, and the thunderous crack boomed loudly around them. Toads began to fall from the sky. Several spheres of burning ball lightning hovered about, and then moved to alight in the still tangible wooden rubble of the crumbled wing of the Gatehouse.

There was a loud clanging, as of a distant buoy, and suddenly the sky was blocked from their view by the ghostly form of the *Flying Dutchman,* hovering above the courtyard. Several of her corpselike pirates threw ropes overboard and were, even now, descending to the earth.

"We are so dead," Cordelia said, with more anger than terror in her now.

Angel appeared beside Willow. He looked at her intently. "Willow," he said. "Can you—"

Then his words were cut off as a serpent-man seven feet tall rose up on his tail and prepared to strike at him. Angel leaped first, moving in the blink of an eye, grabbing the open jaws of the snake-man and pulling them open. Willow heard the crack of its jaw from a dozen feet away, and it sickened her.

"Heh, heh, little girls. I like 'em fresh," said a revolting voice.

Willow spun to see a hunched, green-fleshed man eyeing her with a vulgar expression. *A ghoul,* she thought.

Her hands gesticulating wildly, she whispered a spell and tried to bind the thing back into the house. Nothing happened. And it should have, that was the kicker. The house was falling apart, like an intricately woven pattern spinning out of control, the strands going every which way. But they were still there. She should be able to tap into that web, that matrix of magick, at least to buy them some time until it all came apart completely.

But she couldn't.

The ghoul lunged at her. Willow brought her palm up, stiff-armed it in the face, shattering its nose and sending bone shards into its brain. The ghoul went down, dead.

Willow stared at her own hands in astonishment.

Cordelia screamed. Willow looked up to see that Cordy and Xander were having trouble with several of the crewmen from the *Flying Dutchman.* In a few more seconds, they were going to be dead.

She had to figure out what to do about it. Angel had been about to ask her if she could bind these things. She knew that. And Willow knew now that she was going to have to say no. The only way for her to be able to do that would be if—

Behind her, something howled.

Willow freaked, spun to see where it had come from, and then bit her lip in grief and agony. She had known before she turned what she would see, and here it was. Right there before her.

The man she loved.

"Oz, no . . ." she whispered.

The werewolf sniffed the air and looked at her with nothing more than a ravenous hunger in its burning yellow eyes. Then it came for her. It bounded across the courtyard, snapping at the air, all the violence around it driving it even more wild than usual.

Willow did the only thing she could do.

She ran.

And Oz came after her. He had his sights set on her now, his prey, and he wasn't about to let her go. Out of the corner of her eye, Willow saw Angel fighting hand to hand with something much larger than he, some mythological creature with the body of a lion and the head and talons of an eagle. It slashed at him and tried to peck his eyes out.

She glanced back over her shoulder. Oz was snorting, howling, gaining on her.

Past him, she saw Xander and Cordy again. Somehow, Xander had gotten a sword in his hands. His eyes met the fleeing Willow's, and he shouted her name. For a moment, hope rose in her chest. Then it was dashed as another pirate attacked Xander, and he was too busy saving his own life to save hers.

"Great," she whispered.

Willow realized there was nowhere she could go. The courtyard was a square of well-landscaped paths and gardens that was bordered on every side by the Gatehouse. This was the center of the Gatehouse, in a way. But three walls were shimmering, disgorging creatures and things. The fourth wall was nothing but rubble, where Jacques Regnier had fallen. In between was chaos, and she knew that the man they called Il Maestro hadn't even really gotten started yet. Soon the whole world would look like this courtyard.

If Il Maestro had his way.

And he would, too, because very soon . . .

Another skyquake rumbled above, and Willow felt as though she were standing right in front of the amps at the Bronze. The thunderous noise cut through her, and a spike of pain shot through her head. A ball of fire blazed past her face, and though she ducked in time, Willow felt her eyebrows and found them singed.

"Stop it!" she screamed hysterically, panicking now, barely able to keep her feet under her as she ran. "Stopitstopitstopitstopit!"

Willow fled toward the crumbled part of the house, the only place monsters were not coming from. Oz shifted direction, and now he was only a few paces away from dragging her down, ripping out her throat and then her belly and innards with his powerful, grinding jaws . . .

Willow was headed across the courtyard when, suddenly, something occurred to her. She'd thought, only a moment before, that the courtyard was the center of the Gatehouse. Up ahead, nearly hidden in overgrowth, was a marble fountain. It was where the paths from the four doors from the four sides of the house met. The center of the courtyard.

The middle of it all.

Then she got it. Willow ran the few extra steps toward the fountain, putting every ounce of strength into that sprint. She barely made it. When she reached it, she hopped over the low wall and into the icy, stagnant water. Her mind had put it all together almost too quickly; so fast that she didn't have time to examine, only to go by instinct and half-remembered theories.

She turned to face Oz. He leaped for her. Willow dropped down in the stagnant water and he overshot. It would take him two, perhaps three seconds to right himself, and then he would be on her. She didn't even bother to stand from the greenish fountain water.

Willow raised her hands and screamed, *"Masters of Order, I bid thee come, and see thy greatest creation! The center* must *hold!"*

Oz roared and leaped for her, and was instantly repelled by a crackling sphere of energy that formed around her.

"The center must *hold!"* she repeated. And then she began to chant, as best she could, a binding spell she had read in old Latin from Giles's notes on the Gatekeeper.

On his paws again, Oz began to circle, growling dangerously at Willow where she stood in the vile fountain water. But she ignored him. She was safe from him now. *He* was safe, at least for the moment.

Instead, she closed her eyes. Closed her eyes to the horrors that swept across the courtyard. Closed her eyes to the sight of her dearest friends swarmed by monsters, the sight of Angel going down beneath the pummeling fists of a family of angry trolls.

Willow closed her eyes.

She stretched out her hands. In her mind she visualized the skeins of power that had been woven together to create the intricate web of magick that was the Gatehouse. That was the magick of this fountain. It was the center. She could feel it.

Willow Rosenberg was no sorceress, no magician. She wasn't even a witch, not really. What she was, she admitted most readily, was little more than a dabbler, a spellcaster who had attempted some things that ought to have been beyond her, and succeeded with pure strength of will and a little bit of luck.

But she didn't need skill right now. What she needed, more than anything, was that will and focus and intensity that she revealed to others so very infrequently. But it was there. It had always been there. In the moment when she was needed, Willow would always come through.

Like now.

She reached out for the skeins of magick, the strands of spells and rituals and charms and glamours that had been built into this house in the course of centuries—reached out for them, grabbed hold, and *pulled.*

A skyquake shattered the air. Ball lightning burned in abacus rows across the courtyard. Monsters screamed.

And were pulled, physically, metaphysically, psychically, ectoplasmically . . . whatever it took, they were pulled back toward the house. By a little spellcaster with a knack for magick and a strength of will that even she would never underestimate again.

"Willow!" she heard Xander shout. "You did it!"

She opened her eyes. Angel and Cordelia and Xander were running across the overgrown courtyard toward the fountain, where she stood, her feet numb with cold from the chill of the water.

"I don't know *how* you did it," Cordelia said as she approached. "I'm not even one hundred percent sure it was *you* who did it, but Xander thinks so. So . . ."

Cordelia smiled. "Thanks."

Willow shrugged. Looked around nervously. "It isn't much. It won't save the world or anything. And it won't last very long."

"Long enough for us to get out of here," Xander said. "Don't sell yourself short there, Rosenberg. That's your parents' job."

Willow stepped out of the cold, filthy water, and joined her friends. She was about to say something about going out through one of the sides, trying to figure out how to avoid Fulcanelli.

Then she heard the growl.

She'd forgotten about Oz.

He howled even as she turned to face him.

Then he lunged for her throat.

For just a moment, there was peace and calm.

And order.

That was all it took.

Jacques Regnier had been badly burned by Fulcanelli's magick, a horrible spell that caused his mind to shriek in agony even as his body burst into flame and he tumbled back onto the roof of the house that was shattering beneath him. Then he was falling, falling along with timbers.

The house and its keeper were inextricably linked now, because there was no heir. No one else to take up the reins. What happened to Jacques Regnier happened to the Gatehouse. The same pains, the same fire and explosions that wracked his body and mind caused the west wing to collapse in upon itself.

But amid the rubble, Jacques lay in a bubble of crackling green fire. Healing. Aware. Fighting, even at that time, to regain control of the house and everything around him. Fulcanelli had not had time to merge with the Gatehouse. Jacques had been able to control that, at least. The sorcerer was also weakened by the battle. The revelation of his true face, the cracked, leather, hellish face that his eons of intimacy with the black arts had transformed him into was now revealed. His shell was cracked, and his power was leaking out of it.

Somehow, Jacques had been able to tap into all of that. He could sense that Fulcanelli felt exhilarated with his true face showing, but it was a false feeling caused by the flow of power through him . . . out of him. It was a good thing, for Jacques was not entirely prepared for the job that lay before him. He had hoped, somehow, that his grandmother's ghost would remain to aid him. But she was gone, and his father as well.

Still, all the memories, all the lessons, all the power of the entire line of Gatekeepers, the Regnier family, lived within him. It was as though he could consult any of them at any time, so he was not truly alone. But such a consultation would take concentration and focus, and he had time for neither at the moment.

So he kept Fulcanelli at bay. And he healed his body. And he tried, oh so desperately, to keep the house from falling apart completely, to keep the monsters in.

At that, he had failed. They were too powerful, all railing against his power, all struggling simultaneously to be free of their captivity in the house. It was too much, all of it at once.

Or it had been.

Then there had come that single moment of peace and calm and order. Somehow, the Gatehouse's strength had been restored, just for a moment. All the monsters were back in their chambers, each with its own little pocket dimension, magickally bound within the house. It was an enormous puzzle, but it reverted most suddenly back to form.

For an instant.

And that was all he needed.

With a sudden burst of energy that made Jacques Regnier cry out with the pleasure of raw power, green magick spread out from him as though he had wings of flame. And then he flew.

Up, out of the rubble.

Behind him, the house repaired itself as he passed. Timbers righted themselves. A wave of sorcery swept over the house, and Jacques rejoiced with the knowledge that it was *not* his doing. The house was repairing itself, just as he had. It was returning to the pattern, so carefully crafted, that it had become familiar with after all these years.

Jacques soared above the house, flying on wings of magick, feeling the night wind against his face and the power thrumming, burning in his every muscle.

Then he looked down, the euphoria dissipating. Fulcanelli still attacked the house, still stung it with his bleeding magicks. It pained Jacques for the house to be damaged, and he knew that it was time to put a stop to it, once and for all.

Fulcanelli was infuriated. It wasn't supposed to happen like this. The Gatekeeper was dead.

"Dead, do you hear me?" he screamed at the front doors, again and again.

But they remained closed to him.

Hc had been so close. He had been *inside* the house, in the foyer, battling the would-be Gatekeeper that the Harris boy had become. Then the Regnier heir had returned, and the battle had changed. Before Fulcanelli even realized that things had changed appreciably, and before he could prepare, the young Jacques had used magick to drive him out, to thrash him soundly, and to reconstitute heavy oaken doors that were then slammed in his face.

Then the boy had appeared on the roof, attacking him from there as though it were the battlement of some mythic castle. Just like a boy of eleven might do. Which was, in the end, what he was.

Fulcanelli had laughed then. He was just a boy. And he would die. And the future would belong to Il Maestro, and to none other.

With every ounce of power he could summon, every bit of magick crackling through his transformed body, the hard, leathery folds of his face and arms and chest sparking with the sheer energy of it, Fulcanelli had reached deeply into the recesses of his memory, into the vaults of pain and agony he had mastered long ago, and he had thrust that magick at the boy.

And the boy had fallen.

The house had crumbled, at least partially, and the web of magicks that kept the monsters bound had begun to unravel. None of which he had really wanted. But if the Gatekeeper had been vanquished, he knew he would be able to handle some few small disappointments.

For victory belonged to Fulcanelli.

He had rejoiced. And then he had tried to enter the house.

And it would not open to him.

So he had struggled for several long minutes, trying to magickally batter his way in. Still the house had resisted.

And now . . . he heard his name.

"Fulcanelli!"

It was the voice of the boy, and it roared down at him from above. Il Maestro stood on the reconstituted steps in front of the Gatehouse, and he stared up in astonishment at a corner of the house that had now transformed itself into a castle battlement. Upon it stood Jacques Regnier, the boy who was now the Gatekeeper. The boy whom he had killed only minutes earlier.

Fulcanelli had been right about the boy's imagination. The castle battlement. The house had created it to suit the boy's needs, out of the boy's mind. The two were joined, one and the same.

Then Il Maestro knew that somehow, in all his machinations, he had gone wrong. By depriving the boy of his father, by attacking when there was no heir, he had forced a union he could never have expected. The Gatehouse and its keeper had somehow merged in a way that no Gatekeeper before had managed . . . because never before had any Gatekeeper been pushed to it.

This boy had no other choice.

In that moment, Il Maestro knew that he had lost. He knew it, in fact, even before the torrent of green magick swept down from the battlement atop the Gatehouse and blew him off his feet and across the lawn, where he slammed against the heavy iron gate, his body shattered.

He lay on the grass, broken and bleeding.

Dying.

"Ethan!"

Buffy looked up at the sound of Giles's voice. She had been wiping her hands on a paper towel from the roll Giles kept to work on the endless leaks of the Gilesmobile, as he began to back up.

Sure enough, Ethan Rayne was staggering toward them.

From the backseat, Micaela said, "He doesn't look well."

Buffy frowned. "Good."

"No, Buffy," Giles corrected. "Much as I hate to say it, we need Ethan."

Buffy and Giles got out and approached the Brit. Ethan looked at them, eyes bloodshot, barely able to maintain his balance. For a moment, Buffy thought he might be drunk. Then she saw the fear in the man's eyes and noticed how rapidly he was breathing, and she knew that alcohol had nothing to do with his current state.

"What happened?" Giles demanded. "The sphere? What happened?"

"It worked perfectly," Ethan drawled, eyes rolling to white in his head, then coming back to focus again. "Order. Putrid, horrid, repulsive order consumed . . . everything. The . . . demons were destroyed. I left . . . walked out to see what these hands had wrought . . ."

He held up his hands weakly as they began to walk back to the car.

"The Sons of Entropy wanted to make sure I was telling the truth. Sort of like you, dear boy."

There was a long pause, as though Ethan had fallen asleep. His eyelids drooped. Buffy was about to slap him when they opened again. He swayed. Blinked several times.

"What happened?"

"I'm just so bloody good at what I do," Ethan sighed. "But something was wrong. What she was fighting . . . Belphegor . . . too strong . . . and when it broke through, into this world, it sent a wave of chaos across the town, through the sphere.

"It nearly killed me."

"What a shame that would have been," Buffy muttered.

Micaela climbed out of the car. Ethan briefly acknowledged her. She lifted his drooping chin. Buffy saw her then, saw the fear and the passion in her eyes, and she trusted the woman. She was beautiful, her honey-blond hair spilling about her shoulders, her eyes piercing, but Buffy knew now that wasn't what had attracted Giles to her. It was this burning fire.

She was a fighter.

She would stand with them against the devil himself. Buffy was sure of that now.

But it wasn't much of a comfort.

"Ethan, how do we stop it?" Micaela asked.

The two-bit wizard looked at her, a tiny smile played at the corners of his mouth.

"Ethan!" Giles snapped. "If you know how to kill this thing, tell us, or so help me God . . ."

Ethan looked at him blearily, raised his hands, unable to speak. Then he collapsed in Giles's arms.

"Damn it!" the Watcher snapped. "Get him in the car!"

Micaela whipped open one of the rear doors and Buffy helped Giles load Ethan in. She was about to climb in back with him when Micaela let out a short gasp.

"Rupert," she said anxiously.

Buffy looked across the cemetery, back the way they'd come. In the light of the full moon, she could clearly see that a long, thick, gray-mottled tentacle, lined with razor tines, jutted from the door to the sepulchre. And then the entire crypt just seemed to explode.

In the sphere of order that still existed around the town, a crack formed. A ripple that spread chaos and living evil into the control that order had taken. And tainted it. The sphere had held back so many other horrors, demons and monsters had been destroyed or captured by it.

But this was different. This was one of the Lords of Hell.

Belphegor was coming.

"Giles, get us out of here!" Buffy screamed.

Even as she hopped into the backseat, Giles and Micaela slammed the doors to his car, and Giles started it up. For once, the Citroen ran like a dream. The sphere of order was still there, but it was falling apart, cracking like a huge eggshell as Belphegor surged forth.

Giles stomped on the gas and the Citroen shot forward, reaching speeds it hadn't seen in a decade.

"What now?" Buffy shouted. "There isn't a whole lot we can do while we're running away."

"We're not running far," Giles replied. "Just to the library. Now that we know exactly what we're dealing with, I believe we'll be able to find some way to defeat it."

"You believe?" Buffy asked, eyebrows raised.

"We'll find a way, Buffy," Micaela assured her, pushing her hair away from her face. "You'll see. No matter how powerful Belphegor is, there is always going to be something more powerful."

"Great," Buffy said, sighing. "Let's just hope we don't have to fight *that,* too."

Chapter 15

OZ LUNGED FOR WILLOW. SHE SCREAMED AND FELL backward into the fountain. The cold water closed over her head and she collided with something hard. For a moment, she saw a rush of red and black dots, which began to stretch into a dull haze. A hum filled her head and she started to go away somewhere. Understanding that she was about to pass out, she forced herself back up to a sitting position. As she choked on the fetid water, she made herself spit it out and scrambled not to fall over again.

Through her wet hair, she saw Angel in full vamp face, trying to pull Oz away from the fountain. Oz whirled on him and slashed a deep cut in Angel's arm. Angel staggered backward.

Xander swung a fallen tree branch at the werewolf, striking him on the shoulder and yelling, "C'mon, man, back off!"

Oz growled and backhanded Xander across the face, sending him flying.

"Willow, do something!" Cordelia shrieked.

Willow held out her arms and began the binding spell.

"To the old gods, I give all deference and honor," she began. Tears welled and she faltered. If this worked, she was going to bind Oz into the Gatehouse. She had no idea what that would do to him. And if the Gatehouse fell or collapsed into another dimension, what would happen to her boyfriend?

She hesitated. As Oz charged Angel again, Xander sat up on one elbow and cried, "Go, Willow, keep going!"

"Pan, hear my plea," she said. Her voice wavered, but her resolve stayed firm. She had found the depths of her inner strength today, and she knew she could do this.

Then, as Oz was surrounded by a brilliant light, Willow knew perhaps a fraction of the sorrow Buffy must have felt when she had sent Angel to Hell. Because Oz turned and roared at her just as he disappeared, and she swore he understood what she had done.

Where Oz stood, the light dimmed, and then it was just the four of them.

Willow exhaled. She was cold; she stank; and all she wanted to do was take a hot shower, climb into a nice, warm bed, and sleep for the rest of her life.

After they saved Oz.

Oh, yeah, and the world.

At the moment, a pretty long list.

Xander and Angel both reached her at the same time. Each one took a hand and gently helped her out of the fountain. Her ankle hurt worse than before, and she tried to hide it as she stepped forward. But it gave way and she found herself pressed against Xander's chest.

"Will, you did the right thing. Jacques will free him as soon as he can," Xander murmured.

Willow let herself collapse against him for a few moments. They stood in the garden as Willow caught her breath. Then she nodded once, hard, and started to move. But her ankle was still tender, and she had to lean on them for support.

"I'm sorry I'm so stinky," she said.

"You're not really," Xander replied, as he carried her across the courtyard.

"Are you kidding?" Cordelia asked, then glared at Xander. "What?"

Xander glared back. "You know what."

She rolled her eyes. "Oh, the *tact* thing." She cleared her throat and said to Willow, "Well, let's see, you *don't* smell as bad as a landfill." She narrowed her eyes at Xander. "Okay? Effort made. And it doesn't work for me. I just can't do it."

Willow almost smiled, but she was too worried about Oz to manage it. Cordelia looked at her hard, then caught up to them and touched Willow's shoulder.

"But I can say this, Willow. You did the right thing."

Willow sighed. *Great.* Cordelia thought she'd done the right thing. Somehow that didn't make her feel much better.

They trooped into the house. In the same lavish room where they had first talked to Jean-Marc Regnier, there was the little kid who was now Gatekeeper, his back turned to them. Cordelia had never been so happy to see anyone in her life—even Xander, including when she thought he had died on the ghost roads—okay, maybe not quite that much—but she rushed ahead of the others to tell him at the very least that she was glad he hadn't been annihilated.

"Hey, Gate-boy!" she began, excitedly.

He turned around. His eyes were swollen from crying. Bitter, heavy tears streamed down his young face.

Cordelia said, "Oh," and took a step back.

"Forgive me," the boy murmured, wiping his cheeks.

"Hey, Jacques, you okay?" Xander asked.

"What's wrong?" Willow added, in that gentle way she had that usually made Buffy spill whatever it was that was eating her guts that day. Which was usually Angel or some other variation of the boy-girl scene.

"It's just that . . ." Jacques waved his hand. "This is my life from now on. Though I can no longer sense him, I'm certain Fulcanelli shall return, if not today or tomorrow, then in a year or a century. I saw the ghost of my father for but a moment, and now he is gone. As is the spirit of my grandmother, who has been released."

He bowed his head.

"In all the world, I am quite alone."

"Hey, no," Cordelia said, trying to sound cheery. "You've got us. And, well, it's true that if the world doesn't end, we'll have to go back to Sunnydale to finish senior year, but we can always come back for a visit." She smiled brightly. "I can take you shopping and everything. Get you some great, ah, Gatekeeper fashions."

He actually smiled, and Cordelia felt a flash of triumph. *Let 'em keep their tact.* She could win friends and influence people with the truth just fine, thank you.

"You're an exquisite lady," he said, and that flustered her a little. Most eleven-year-olds she knew didn't talk like that. Okay, none. She wondered if maybe she was supposed to curtsy or something, but she just winked at him.

"You're not so bad, either. Maybe I'll wait for you to grow up," she drawled.

"Oh, I won't marry for at least a hundred years," he replied. "It's something in our life pattern, the way the Regniers exist. I don't understand it, but I know that's how it will be."

Cordelia blinked. "Wow. I could be dead by then." A chill ran down her spine. *So* not what she wanted to think about.

Willow said quickly, "Excuse me, but I sort of had to bind my boyfriend into the Gatehouse—"

"And you want him unbound," Jacques finished for her. He closed his eyes. "He still wears wolf fur. It would be dangerous for him and for you."

"Then tell me he's all right." Willow's big brown eyes were wide and hopeful. "Or make him all right."

Jacques touched his temples. "I see him clearly. He's in a room by himself. He doesn't like it, but there's no way he can come to harm.

"You did well, spellcaster."

"Oh, well, I . . ." Willow shrugged.

Cordelia was a little miffed. True, Willow had pretty much saved their butts, but was that any reason for her to insist on being the center of attention?

"And I would like a heart, and Angel here wants to

get back to Kansas," Xander cut in, stepping forward. "But seriously, Jacques, what should we do now, go to Disney World?"

The Gatekeeper looked at Xander, and suddenly Xander extended his arm. Jacques clasped his small hand around Xander's wrist, and Xander did the same. It was like they were in the same club. Which Cordelia supposed they were, or had been. The Gatekeeper Club.

"Thank you," Xander said.

"No, it is I who thank you," Jacques replied.

"Okay, whatever." Cordelia waved her hands. "You guys can do this male-bonding-Gatekeeper thing some other time. Because I'm betting there's something we have to do right now or we'll all die or explode, am I right?"

Jacques walked a ways apart from them. "I need some time alone to become accustomed to my situation. And to put my house in order." He shrugged. "So to speak."

The others chuckled, but Cordelia didn't get what was funny. Nothing about this was funny.

In fact, it was really sad.

Outside the Gatehouse, just beyond the edges of the magickal glamour that hid the house from any passersby, Fulcanelli lay wrapped in a glamour of his own. He wasn't certain if he had successfully hidden his presence from the young Gatekeeper. But since the child hadn't renewed his attack, he guessed that for the time being he was safe.

The ancient sorcerer closed his eyes and willed fresh human skin to grow over his leathery, scarred face. In the new world of his making, such niceties would be unnecessary. That world, however, had yet to be born, thanks to the brat and his supporters. That damned Slayer.

"You must not hate your enemies," Hadrius had said one night, after he had beaten Giacomo senseless. The tall, armored man knelt over Giacomo's pallet by the fire and examined the wounds. "It is a luxury you must deny yourself. Else you'll strike when it will do you no good."

Giacomo made himself look steadily into the eyes of his cruel master even as his fingers wrapped around the dagger he clutched beneath his thin, coarse blanket. He must not give himself away. If Hadrius suspected anything, he would surely put Giacomo to death.

Slowly.

"I hate no one," Giacomo said, but his voice shook.

Hadrius laughed. Then, without taking his gaze from Giacomo's face, he tore the blanket back, exposing the dagger.

Giacomo blanched but did not cry out.

"Well done," Hadrius said approvingly. "The time approaches when I shall truly fear you. But that time is not tonight, boy."

Still smiling, he pulled back his fist and slammed it into Giacomo's face.

Giacomo's head snapped backward and he collapsed on the pallet. In a trice, the dagger was at his own neck, the point piercing the skin. As he gasped with pain, Hadrius ran it down the length of his throat, etching a thin line that bobbled over his Adam's apple, then centered in the hollow between his collar bones.

"There are so many ways to torture one's victims," Hadrius said, his voice almost wistful. "I shall endeav-

or to show them all to you, before you succeed in assassinating me."

Confused, Giacomo swallowed hard, and the sharp point pushed more deeply into his skin. He heard the tear of flesh, and the roar of fear that threatened to overwhelm all his senses as he shut his eyes.

"Coward," Hadrius said with disdain.

The point went in still further. Giacomo's forehead beaded with sweat and he gritted his teeth together.

"Fool," Hadrius jeered, and pushed again.

"Stop!" Giacomo cried, grabbing at the dagger. He was surprised when Hadrius yielded it to him.

"Never show your belly, or men will kick you like a dog," the man said, rising from the pallet. "Buona notte, mio filio."

My son. So it was true.

Giacomo shook. He bit his lips so hard they bled. Tears streamed down his cheeks. As he wiped them away, something deep inside him, which may at one time have been his heart, grew hard and cold and proud. The son of Hadrius would be stronger than Hadrius ever dreamed of being. He would be crueler and more heartless.

It was the only way to win his father's respect.

And the only way to survive.

Later that same night, Giacomo crept through the keep, feet muffled in fur wraps, in search of the castle wise woman. His wounds were weeping and his forehead was blazing, though each icy breath created a mist. He was sick deep down into his soul; he needed a poultice or he would die a humiliatingly natural death.

Staggering, he nearly knocked over a full coat of armor standing beside an arched wooden doorway, which was always locked shut. Tonight, however, it was ajar, and moans issued from it.

Giacomo halted, listening. Who lay on the rack? Whose flesh sizzled beneath a heated blade? He remembered Hadrius' spoken desire to present to him all forms of torture.

Stealthily, with a repellent fascination, he tiptoed to the crack of light issuing from the opened door and peered with one eye inside.

He was stunned by what he saw: the beautiful daughter of the wise woman, who could not be more than fifteen, lay locked in rapturous delight with Hadrius. And the fearsome lord of the keep, the dread, dark shadow whom all feared, appeared to be nothing more than a naked middle-aged man, pleasuring himself with a slip of a maid.

Now would be the time to do it, to strike him down and end the torment and the humiliation.

"Cara, bella cara," *Hadrius murmured to the girl.* "Ti amo, bella."

He stroked her hair and her face with gentle fingers; she rippled with pleasure and cried out for more.

Then Hadrius turned toward the doorway and spread wide his mouth. His teeth flashed in the light. It was more than a grin, it was a leer. It was the mouth of a beast.

As Giacomo watched in shock, he sank his teeth into the chest of the girl. She screamed and struggled. He grabbed her wrists in one hand and burrowed down more deeply.

His head arched back. Something ripped from her chest, red and beating.

Giacomo turned and vomited. He ran.

* * *

He thought he would never sleep again, but dawn had begun to creep across the stone floor when Hadrius kicked at the pallet. Giacomo bolted awake, his eyes huge, and raised the dagger menacingly.

"Good." His hands full with a brass platter, Hadrius smiled approvingly. Then he blinked at the dagger and it grew white-hot. As Giacomo cried out and dropped it, it sludged across the foot of his pallet, a puddle of molten metal.

"Now. Let us break the fast together," the sorcerer said with a smile.

He sat on Giacomo's pallet and showed him what was on the platter: the main course was the size and shape of a human heart, surrounded by smaller ones. Giacomo felt his bile rise, but this time he forced his stomach not to revolt.

"Better," Hadrius said. "Now." From his sleeve he withdrew a golden fork, as it was the custom of the day to carry one's own cutlery on one's person.

He handed the fork to Giacomo.

"If you do not eat, I will kill you," he said. "If you do not enjoy, I will beat you senseless."

"Father," Giacomo blurted. It was the first time he had given Hadrius that title.

Hadrius' face hardened. "Never think to trade on my affections. I have none. I do not love you and I never shall. The best you can hope for from me is my pride in you. And even in that, I shall be most sparing."

Giacomo looked down at the heart. There were pieces missing from it.

But at least the girl had had one.

He was certain, from this moment on, that if he touched the left side of his chest, there would be no pulse.

Forcing himself to calmness, he took the fork from his father and stabbed the heart. Hadrius produced a jeweled stiletto, and Giacomo accepted that as well.

He cut a bite. Put it between his lips.

"It's rather like venison, is it not? Gamey. The flesh of nobles is more refined," Hadrius told him easily, stretching. "Dawn is nearly here. What a day it will be, boy. We'll have to do something glorious today."

Giacomo chewed. For an instant he wasn't certain if he would be able to swallow, but then he remembered that he had no heart.

The morsel went down with surprising ease.

Hadrius sat and watched while Giacomo ate the entire thing. When Giacomo had consumed the last bite, he realized he was extremely full. Uncomfortably so. A human heart made for a prodigious meal.

The pleased look on his father's face made the sinful food lie heavy on his stomach. Giacomo knew the man was intent upon making him into a monster, knew he was many steps closer this morning.

"So." Hadrius rubbed his hands together and took the platter back. Also the fork, with which he speared one of the tinier hearts and popped it into his mouth. He chewed with relish. "Dress, and we'll be off on a fine adventure."

Giacomo inclined his head, quite aware of the jeweled stiletto in his hand.

Hadrius began to leave the chill room. Then he snapped his fingers and whirled on his heel.

"Your mother," he said, as if suddenly recalling something. "You thought your so-called father and his paramour betrayed her." He cocked his head and stabbed another small heart. "But now you know better, don't you."

He popped the heart into his mouth.

Giacomo stared at him. Nothing registered. Everything inside him, every nerve, every thought, went numb.

"Perhaps you didn't hear me. I was the one who sent the soldiers for your mother. I as much as lit the fire at the hem of that fine nightdress."

Still Giacomo gaped. Unbidden, the memory of his mother burning and writhing filled his brain and shot down his spine. Rage ignited within him. It roared as the flames. It shot through him, used him, moved him.

Shrieking, he flew at Hadrius, the stiletto aimed straight for the bastard's belly.

By an unseen hand, he was thrown the length of the room. He slammed hard against the wall and crashed to the floor. His withered arm burst into flame. He threw back his head and screamed in agony.

"Thus she died. Feeling that. Feeling it all over her body. And I did that to her."

Giacomo kept screaming. Then he forced himself to shriek, "Why?"

At once the flames were doused, but the pain throbbed up and down his blackened limb. Hadrius stared at him, chewing thoughtfully.

"Why?" Giacomo asked again, assuming the obvious: that Hadrius had tired of her, or that she had betrayed him in some way.

"In hopes that I might have this chat with you one day," Hadrius replied simply. "Only for that, Giacomo. Only as a lesson for you. For the sake of your destiny, of what you must become. Think of that. She meant that little to me."

Giacomo drew back his lips. Hatred filled every fiber of his being. As soon as he could move . . .

"Uh-uh-uh." Hadrius wagged his finger at him. "Have you learned nothing? Never hate your enemies. Never."

His arm burst into flame again.

Hadrius turned back on his heel and left.

Giacomo's screams echoed beyond the castle walls and into the forest, where the few peasants who dared to enter there crossed themselves and whispered to both the Virgin and the old gods to save them.

They were not saved.

And neither was Giacomo.

And now, dressed in the guise of a modern-day peasant—a homeless man he was called in these times—Fulcanelli gathered up the scars and wrinkles that once again lined his face and staggered down the street. As the dawn rose, he stumbled toward Boston, knowing that to fight another day, he must rest and recuperate. The young Gatekeeper had let him go, foolishly allowed him to survive. It was a mistake the boy would live to regret only for a short while.

With a smile, he lurched forward, laughing silently to himself when one of Boston's denizens muttered at him, "Get a job."

There and then, he created within the man an embolism. As the man clutched his chest and groaned, Fulcanelli laughed silently to himself.

He was fully employed, thank you so for your concern.

Busily ending the world, so that such idiots as the freshly dead man would serve a useful purpose.

As the Gilesmobile wobbled on the broken street toward the library, the sky cracked open and fire rained down. Then a horde of misshapen figures covered with hair lumbered in front of the car, not even noticing when Giles stepped too late on the brake and rammed one of them. It fell over, rolled, got to its feet, and lumbered on.

"Okay, Ethan," Buffy said. "Enough with Cousin It, It, and their other brother Darryl. What's going on?"

"I don't understand," Ethan muttered. "The sphere of order appears to be collapsing."

Buffy turned around to look at him just in time to see him grin.

"This is amusing why?" she demanded angrily.

He flashed her a guilty look, like a little boy trying to charm his way out of trouble. When she didn't soften, he shrugged and said, "I believe this is simply proof that all systems tend towards entropy."

Buffy stared at him.

"Disorder is the natural way of things," he added.

"Tell that to my mom next time she wants me to clean my room," Buffy told him. "And see how long you live."

Ethan brightened. "Oh, I do so love the sparring bits. Let's see, how shall I riposte?"

"You'll cast another spell, is what you'll do," Giles said. He looked at Buffy. "I'm afraid he's right. Order's breaking down. We're going to have to work fast. We can't tolerate any added distractions. Belphegor must be destroyed, but we're going to have a hell of a time doing that if we have to fight various and sundry escapees from the Otherworld and, frankly, Hell itself."

"Yeah, that would be a major drag," Buffy drawled.

Giles gave her a Giles look. "What I mean is, they

would simply serve as a distraction from our main purpose."

"What Ripper's trying to say," Ethan drawled, "is that it would be a bit awkward for you to be dismembered by, say, a family of Rumanian *verdulak* rather than enjoying the sublime opportunity of fighting the big cheese himself."

Buffy shook her head. "Wake me up when you English people start speaking English."

Giles said, "What he meant was—"

"Yeah, okay, thanks." Over her shoulder, she said to Ethan, "Okay, I give. What are *verdulak?*"

Ethan tsk-tsked. "Really, Miss Thing. They're a type of vampire."

"I knew that," she said.

She looked out the window at the Milky Way–style barrage of ball lightning arcing across the sky. The heavy rain, the pieces of street shooting up like titanic plates or teutonic plates or whatever that whole continental thing was about. If the world got through this, the authorities in Sunnydale would have a heck of a time explaining all this away. But the funny thing was, they would manage it. And everyone would believe them.

Pleasantville. Love it or leave it.

Just then the hedges in front of the school assumed animal shapes—mostly lions and tigers, some bears—and began to move menacingly toward the road.

"The cosmos has been reading old Stephen King novels," Buffy said.

"Good Lord." Giles nearly lost control of the car. Nothing new there.

"Please hurry," Ethan said. "Obviously, my spell

has been completely and totally overruled, and someone's adding new ingredients. Moving hedgerows are not a sign of disorder. Chaotic though they may be." He sounded both pleased and insulted. Kind of like Cordelia whenever Xander spoke to her.

Just then, something shot out of the street directly in front of them and aimed straight for the windshield. It was an enormous reptilian creature with flappy, leathery wings tipped with claws.

Buffy grabbed the steering wheel from Giles and headed straight for the curb. The creature reared its head in frustration and trotted after them, trumpeting in a high, shrill voice.

"You know what I'm thinking?" Ethan said loudly.

"That this would make a great ride at Universal Studios?" Buffy replied. She said to Giles, "Okay, drive some more," and turned around.

"Please, Ethan, tell me what you're thinking. Especially if it involves stopping the insanity."

"I'm thinking I *do* know how to stop it." He smiled broadly. "But I have to confirm a few things. With the books."

"Step on it, Giles," Buffy said.

And the night Giacomo Fulcanelli killed Hadrius, his father?

It was a winter's night, cold and bleak, the stars merciless in a punctured sky.

Of late, Hadrius had grown somewhat forgetful. Giacomo was taken aback by the deterioration in the man. Rather than seize the advantage and thrust a dagger through his heart, he waited to see what was going on with the old devil. It could be a trick. Hadrius was forever testing him . . . and punishing him when he disappointed.

But tonight, as Giacomo tossed on his pallet and listened to the man murmuring spells to himself down the hall, the wind whistled plans to him, urging him to patricide. The killing of one's father.

The murder, if you will, of part of oneself.

Giacomo listened.

He rose from his bed barehanded and tiptoed through the drafty keep.

Years before, the wise woman, whose daughter Hadrius had so viciously butchered, had killed herself on a night just like this. Now it seemed to Giacomo that her ghost glided alongside him, begging him for vengeance.

But Giacomo had learned his lessons well. He did not hate Hadrius. Nowhere inside his bones lived the wish to pay Hadrius for his cruelty. He observed only that it was necessary to kill his father if he had any hope of inheriting his role as the most fearsome conjurer of the black arts in this plane. Simple ambition, a clear direction, a need—those were the things that sped him along the hall. And against such clarity of thought—without accompanying emotion—Hadrius had no defense.

Giacomo simply came up behind him, put his hands around the old man's neck, and squeezed the life out of him.

His father put up surprisingly little struggle, and when his head plunged into the boiling cauldron of noxious liquid, no dark shadow rose out of him, as Giacomo had expected to see. The man simply died.

Giacomo was almost disappointed.

It was not until centuries later that he remembered how to hate again. And that was when Richard Regnier threatened his position at the court of Francis I, in the sixteenth century at Fontainebleau.

But that was another story. Now, as the day began, he found himself at the entrance to what was so charmingly called a residential hotel—a storage facility for the indigent.

Never mind the niceties; he waved his hand at the desk clerk, who handed him a key. Then he stumbled inside, into a barren room with a bed and a small table. He lay on the bed, closed his eyes, and willed himself to be made whole.

The world awaited.

It cried.

It begged.

Despite his pain, he smiled.

AS GILES PRESSED THE GAS PEDAL TO THE FLOOR—NO guarantee there that the car would actually go any faster—the section of road that had disgorged the flying reptile blew up in a hail of blacktop and concrete so hot that it was molten. Gobs of it pelted the hood of the car, burning holes right through the metal. So far, the engine still worked.

"Giles!" Buffy shouted, "Reverse. Reverse!"

"You know my car hates reverse," he retorted, but made the gearshift scream anyway.

They began to back up.

"Um," Ethan said, "also not a good idea."

Buffy turned to look just as Micaela let out a scream.

The dead were on the march.

Rotting corpses, some in their moldy Sunday best, staggered mindlessly toward the Gilesmobile. Eyes missing, still they stared. Their jaws clacked together like some kind of demonic windup toys. Among them, ex-folks in a worse state of decay—cleaned skeletons missing limbs or skulls—dragged themselves along.

Surrounding the zombie army, hideous, bruise-colored demons with scarlet wraparound eyes and enormous, fang-infested mouths rode black, fire-breathing horses that glided over the road. Whips snapped over their heads and lashed at the cadavers that lurched and staggered.

"Let's go sideways," Ethan suggested, and Buffy was sure he was about to whip up a nifty spell to do just that when something tall and gelatinous shot up from the ground to their right. Like a large beach ball, it rolled slowly toward them. It glowed a sickly green, and where it touched the road, the blacktop melted.

On the other side of the car, a stream of Otherworld creatures appeared on the horizon and rushed the car in a frenzied panic. Trolls, unicorns, sprites, a man in Victorian clothes, and Buffy's old friends, the panther guys, swarmed from what had to be an enormous breach just out of sight. The first rank slammed into the side of the car as if they didn't understand that it was solid. The car was rocked wildly from side to side, everyone inside thrown around like dolls.

As Ethan shouted in fear and Micaela started a binding spell, someone—or something—managed to yank the left-hand passenger door open. As Buffy tried to scramble over the seats, an enormous figure made of green leaves and green vines pulled Ethan out of the car.

Then he disappeared into the mob.

"No," Buffy cried, not so much because she cared about the sorcerer, but because he was the only one among them who had the slightest idea how to kill Belphegor. "Give him back, you guys!"

Okay, time for a Slayer assessment of the sitch: Ethan was nowhere to be seen, and the creatures kept coming. On the other side, the gelatinous thingie lumbered toward them. Hell itself looked to be opening up in front of the car, and the dead were massing at the rear.

Pushed by the throng, a green ghoul dove in after Micaela, but between her spell and the stake in Buffy's hand, at least Micaela managed to stay inside the car. But for how long?

"Look," Giles said, pointing. "That's the cause of their panic."

In the distance, behind the hundreds of Otherworld inhabitants, a row of the same bruise-colored demons that were herding the dead had fanned out on horseback and were forcing the creatures forward. Though many of the Otherworld beings were running away from them out of animal instinct, others clearly knew what the score was: demons everything, and everybody else, goose eggs.

Buffy said, "I've gotta get Ethan."

"No," Micaela blurted, reaching out for her. "They'll kill you."

Giles pushed up his glasses and dodged another flying lizard-thing as it rammed the windshield. Its left wing broke the glass at the same time that it spit some kind of acid at Giles, who expertly dodged it. The spray shot through the car and took out half the back window.

"She has a point," Giles said. "About the killing bit."

As he spoke, the gelatinous creature collided with the passenger's side of the car, and the Gilesmobile began to melt.

Then the first column of the army of the mortally challenged made contact with the rear bumper and began to push it toward the fiery chasm that yawned directly ahead of them.

At the same moment, the driver's door was ripped from its hinges, and something very tall, dark green and brown and covered with scales and gills and spikes wrapped around Giles's head and arm.

"Giles!" Buffy shouted, her hands glomming on to his other arm. But the pain from the spikes made her jerk back in surprise; before she could realize what was happening, much less do anything about it, Giles was whisked out of the car.

She flew after him. Her heart was pounding as she punch-kicked a troll that leaped into her path, then rammed her fist into the face of a small, fleshy creature that seemed to be all eyes. With that one, she wasn't sure where it came from—Hell or the Otherworld—and come to think about it, the line between demon and Otherworldly monster was sort of disappearing for her.

On the other hand, some of the monsters from the Otherworld looked downright terrified of the demons. So, okay, no picnic for the boys from limbo, either.

"Out of my way!" she bellowed at the dozens of things that blocked her path. "Slayer coming through! Giles. *Giles!*"

Part of her realized that she was doing it again: she was allowing herself to be distracted from what was necessary by trying to save someone she loved. Her first priority had to be Ethan. The world was counting on her to stop Belphegor. Millions—billions of lives—depended on her, and yet, here she was, willing to throw it away for one man.

But he wasn't just a man.

He was Giles.

And it didn't matter. She was out of the car now, and she was committed. The right side of the Gilesmobile was little more than a pile of oozy spare parts and the hair-gel monster was still rolling; Buffy had no idea if Micaela had survived. Sad to say—Giles's new flame or not—the daughter of Il Maestro was low on her list of priorities. She knew Ethan should be at the top of it, but even as she threw a fierce roundhouse kick into the face of a tree-woman, still she searched for her Watcher.

The tree-woman staggered backward, but each time Buffy succeeded in pushing back one attacker, a dozen more took its place. She knew it was only a matter of time.

She was going to die, and the world was going to end.

"I'm sorry," she breathed, thinking of Willow, Oz, and Xander in Boston. Her mother, at Angel's house. Giles.

And, as always, Angel.

Angel, who had been to Hell and back, and might return there this very day.

"So very sorry . . ."

Buffy's head whipped up. The words were hers, but the voice was not.

She couldn't help the intake of breath, the moment of sheer panic that froze her to the burning ground. The demons and monsters had all drawn back, terrified of what was coming.

Rising from the cavern that had once been the road, covered with steam and blood, Belphegor towered over her.

"Sssslayer," it greeted her. Its tentacles slithered toward her. Its seven mouths opened and something streamed out, something thick and black and reeking. She covered her mouth to keep herself from throwing up.

"At last."

"Yeah, it's about time," she said, choking back her intense desire to retch. "Time for you to do that whole 'whence you came' bit. Time for me to abandon my ladylike pretensions and kick your demon ass!"

"How I have longed for this. So much so that I'm almost sorry it will be over soon."

"That's what they all say." She flashed a sharp, brittle smile as she hunkered down into position for battle. She had no weapons. No backup. But hope, she had plenty of.

"And you know what?" she flung at it. "They're still longing. 'Cause with me, see, it's never over. That's my destiny, right? My responsibility."

"To the last, a hero."

"Let's cut the chitchat, all right? It's really cheapening the moment." She doubled her fists and took a deep breath.

If this was it—if she was going to die—she wanted to do as much damage as possible before she went down.

"If it was in me to spare you, I would," Belphegor told her.

Buffy lifted her chin. "What a demon. You're all heart."

"Not at all," Belphegor responded.
"I have no heart."

Angel saw the beams of sunlight across the wall of the Gatekeeper's parlor and said, "I need to go deeper into the house."

He was tired, and the dawn was making him sluggish. He wished that weren't so; he agreed with Jacques that Il Maestro would probably make an unscheduled reappearance, and Angel wanted to be in fighting trim when he did. But at the moment, he needed to rest. He figured he would be more useful if he acknowledged that fact and took care of himself, but it still frustrated him that it was necessary.

"Go," Jacques said with a wave of his hand, as if he were giving Angel his permission.

"If you run into Oz," Willow began, and then she brightened. "Hey, morning," she said eagerly. "No more werewolf."

Jacques inclined his head. "You're right. I can release him."

He closed his eyes and murmured to himself, gesturing briefly with his fingers. Then he smiled and looked at Willow.

"He will be joining us in a few minutes."

"Oz?" Willow called out. She looked at the Gatekeeper. "Which way?"

"Angel will escort you." Jacques looked at Angel. "Down the hall and to the right."

"Thank you!" Willow sang out, racing out of the room.

Angel flashed a crooked smile at the young Gatekeeper.

"Love," he drawled.

The Gatekeeper looked hard at Angel. "Indeed," he replied, as though a boy of his age could even begin to understand all the meanings encompassed by that one word.

Jacques turned away, and Angel walked out of the room. Angel followed his directions and came across Willow, who was wrapped in Oz's arms and planting little happy kisses all over his face. Oz, who was wearing a bathrobe of sorts, wore an expression of pure delight as he returned Willow's kisses.

Not for the first time, Angel wondered how Buffy was. The others didn't talk about it, either, but he knew they were all worried sick for her. And not just because she was the Slayer; no, not because if she fell, the world would fall. It was because they loved her.

Because he loved her . . .

A door to a dark, quiet room hung open. By the scent of werewolf, Angel realized this was where Willow had bound Oz. He had been safe in here. Angel would be safe, too.

He shut the door and crossed into the dark room. Against the wall, he found a soft mattress on the floor, which Oz had not touched. Gratefully, Angel sank down and closed his eyes.

As he drowsed, he saw in his mind's eye a shadow drift across the wall. Which didn't make sense; the room was too dark. Yet the silhouette of a woman wafted through the blackness in slow motion like a cloud . . .

Or like a dream.

And though Angel knew this dream was a gift the Gatekeeper was giving him, it seemed so real that in the dream, he held his arms open to Buffy, and she wrapped herself around him. Her heart pounded against his chest; her breath was warm on his neck. He would never forget what Buffy smelled like, a sweet, spicy fragrance that was sometimes a hint of lavender and sometimes a whisper of vanilla. He would always remember how slender she was, yet how powerful.

Her kisses . . .

Angel drifted in sleep, and smiled, and sighed.

Buffy.

If the gods heard the prayers of vampires, they would keep her safe.

It was a long shot.

At the last, Fulcanelli sent himself deep into the Pit, and stood now before another demon, one that was the peer of Belphegor. It was red, and very evil; it wore horns and was known to men as the Devil. But it was more than a simple symbol, a figurehead. It was one of the most powerful demons in Hell.

The Fatal One stroked its sore-encrusted face and laughed heartily.

"So, you have lost control of my brother, and you wish to go against him?" it asked. *"And you wish to squander my armies to do it?"*

"Exactly," Il Maestro said boldy.

"And you propose to do this how?"

Fulcanelli realized he had been shortsighted to depend on mortal followers. True, some of the Sons of Entropy had been first-rate sorcerers, but there was nothing like minions of Hell to really get the job done.

"First I'll kill the Gatekeeper," he assured his new sponsor. "Then I'll overrun the ghost roads and take Belphegor down in Sunnydale, where he has gone to kill the Slayer."

"Ah, yes, the Slayer." The demon leaned forward from his throne of bones and skins and flexed its jagged fingernails as it folded its hands. *"Any chance you will deliver her to me?"*

Fulcanelli hesitated. "Is that your price?"

The demon smiled evilly. *"I am not that foolish. The power of a Slayer is a temptation indeed, but I have lived this long without it. Still, if you gave her to me, I would look upon you most kindly. In this world, and the next, and the next."*

It smiled broadly at Fulcanelli. *"I don't suppose it would surprise you to know that there are worse places than Hell, and that I have friends who rule them. Friends who could prove very helpful to you."*

"Prove it," Fulcanelli said.

Blinking, the demon threw back its head and burst into laughter. *"Your tone with my brother was very different. With me, you speak as an equal."*

Though he was fearful, Fulcanelli had learned over the centuries to hide his feelings very well. A legacy from his father. Now he managed a careless shrug. He had learned an important lesson in his dealings with Belphegor: not to show quite so much deference. The most powerful demons took and took, and they did not stand on ceremony; they did not give you respect unless you demanded it.

"I have given up the charade of courtesy," Fulcanelli said. "My previous ally, Belphe—"

The demon raised his hand. *"Please, do not speak his name. You know it is a source of power."*

The sorcerer shrugged. In time, he would learn this demon's name as well.

"As you wish," he said.

"That's better."

The demon clapped his hands. *"I will join with you, mortal man. I will give you warriors to battle the Gatekeeper. But if you waste them . . ."* He imitated Fulcanelli's shrug. *"I, too, will give up the charade of courtesy."*

For one second, Fulcanelli wavered. One only. Then he said, "It is always good to know where one stands. We have a bargain, then."

"Indeed," the demon answered.

Cordelia wished they had something good to read at the Gatehouse. A guy who was going to live hundreds of years in one place, you'd think he'd subscribe to a few magazines—at the very least, *Entertainment Weekly* or *TV Guide*. Or maybe *Better Sorcerers and Gardens*.

She smiled at her own joke—hey, Buffy and the others weren't the only ones with a sense of humor; hers just got overlooked because they kept focusing on the tact thing—and rearranged herself on the burgundy velvet loveseat. Everyone was dozing except Jacques, who kept vigil at the window. He was certain that Il Maestro would be back, and with reinforcements.

Cordelia had a feeling he was right. When one hung with the Slayer and her crowd long enough, lots of weird bad stuff seemed more normal than no bad stuff at all.

And sure enough, just as she was about to fall asleep dreaming that Jacques had pay-per-view, he tensed at the window and murmured, *"I call upon all gods, ancient and newborn. I summon my guardian spirits. Across the cosmos, I alert my forefathers."*

"Um, so . . ." Cordelia began, then uneasily got up

from the loveseat and walked over to Jacques. "What . . . ?"

She looked out the window.

That was when she lost it, completely and totally.

Cordelia had wigged many times in the past three years. When she and Buffy had almost been sacrificed to the reptile god, Machida, of that snooty fraternity, she had wigged. When she thought Springheel Jack was going to toast both her and Xander, she had wigged. In fact, the first time she had found out Buffy was the Slayer, she had wigged.

But now, as she stared down at the lawn of the Gatehouse, she felt every single part of her body go numb. Her eyes rolled back in her head and she sank to the floor, only slightly aware that she narrowly avoided cracking her head on the leg of Jacques's overstuffed chair.

Then she went down to a place where it was dark and there was nothing to think about, and she decided to stay there for a while.

Demons straight from Hell were massing on the Gatehouse. A slathering, bestial band of unspeakably hideous and malformed creatures rushed the wrought-iron gates as Jacques attempted to magickally repel them. Jacques sent forth every ounce of his energy, blood vessels bursting from the strain. Sweat poured down his face; he stank with fear and concentration.

He did not know if these were Belphegor's minions, or those of some other demon.

He did know that it was possible they were too strong for him.

"Father," he whispered, feeling horribly alone and

inadequate. He closed his eyes and, without words, called for help once more.

None came.

At that moment, the Gatehouse was assaulted by every form of magick ever known to Jacques: crackling tendrils of energy, the gale force of a hurricane and the shock wave of an earthquake. As he fought the attack, he struggled to keep the Gatehouse intact.

As before, he could only succeed at one task.

The Gatehouse flickered in and out of existence. He heard Fulcanelli's voice inside his head, accompanied by the laughter of the lost and the damned: *"So it ends, boy. I shall make you nothing more than a curiosity of the Otherworld, before I destroy you. And I* shall *destroy you."*

"Father," Jacques called again, doubling his fists.

The Gatehouse flickered.

With a roar of triumph, Fulcanelli's troops charged the gates and pushed them down.

As the room lightened, then disappeared altogether, Angel shouted in surprise and pain. The sun burned his leg and arm, making them smoke. He rolled out of the path of the rays to a dark corner, only to discover that the corner had flickered out of existence.

He got up and ran into the corridor, but that was flickering, too.

He was in trouble. Very bad trouble.

Then Oz, Willow, and Xander raced toward him. Their faces were gray.

"Angel, we're wading in the deep stuff," Xander said. "There are major bad guys outside and they want in."

"I think they're succeeding," Angel said.

Around them, the corridor faded and the sun hit Angel. He shouted and went down. Xander leaped on top of him, yelling, "Cover him up!"

The corridor became solid again. Xander slid off him, saying, "Don't write that in your diary," and helped him to a standing position.

Willow looked around. "This is really bad. *Really* bad."

"It's been bad before," Angel said.

Xander nodded. "Except on Tuesdays, when they serve burritos." He raised his hand. "All in favor of checking out what Jacques is up to?"

It was unanimous.

They dashed into the room where the Gatekeeper stood, a revived Cordelia shrieking at his side. Energy ricocheted around the room, and though Jacques was trying to return fire, he was outgunned.

Angel knew Jacques wasn't going to win this one.

Nevertheless, he joined the boy at the window and gestured the others over.

"We go together," he said.

Xander nodded. Willow and Oz held hands. Cordelia whispered, "Oh, my God," and moved to Xander's side.

Angel looked at them all for a moment. Then he said what he hoped would comfort them most.

"Buffy would be very proud of you."

"And your parents, too," Oz whispered to Willow.

Then the Gatehouse jittered like a neon sign about to go out, and Angel steeled himself for the pain, with one last thought of Buffy.

* * *

Just as Buffy prepared herself for Belphegor's attack, a decomposing body launched itself at her. She moved to slam it out of her way, then blinked as the body bounced off some kind of shield surrounding her.

"It won't hold long," said a voice beside her. It was Micaela, who had bravely climbed out of the car and joined her. "It's a spell of protection."

"And it will do no good against me," Belphegor informed her.

"Yeah, well, you can't have everything," Buffy said.

Then, as she watched, Micaela raised her hands and Giles and Ethan rose limply above the heads of the mob of creatures and monsters. Both of them were covered with blood and their clothes were practically torn from their bodies. But Ethan, at least, appeared to be alive, as Micaela magickally lowered them to the ground just behind Buffy.

Ethan gestured toward Belphegor, but then his eyes closed and his head fell forward on his chest. Buffy shouted, "Ethan, wake up!" and gave him a hard kick.

There was no response.

Then, as clearly as if he were standing next to her talking, Buffy heard Ethan's voice:

"Born from the bowels of the Old Ones;
The Lord of the Vile Flesh;
His heart a whisper of shadow;
He watches the world of man with human eyes;
The eyes of man, the darkest passage;
The path he must follow, the world which he covets;
Belphegor, scion of worlds old and new;

Wanderer in Darkness, shying from infernal flame;
Yet the dawn of man shall not burn his eyes;
Yet the sword of man shall not cut him down;
For man's only weapon must be himself."

Buffy looked at Micaela. "What's going on? Who's talking?"

Micaela gestured to Ethan. "His subconscious. To you. And you only," she said pointedly. "Don't speak aloud."

"But—"

"Sssslayer," Belphegor whispered. *"I hunger."*

Buffy couldn't help the tremor of fear that went through her. She had no weapons, and no idea how to kill this thing. But she had to. There was no other way this could come down.

She had to.

But she was losing it. Everything inside her screamed at her to run. This was death staring her in the face.

Her death, and the death of everything.

For an instant, she saw her mother's eyes and her mother's smile. Remembered so many things—the first time she'd met Willow; the time when, under Amy's spell, she had come on to Xander; Angel's first kiss.

My life is passing before my eyes, she thought desperately. *I'm giving up.*

Belphegor swiped at her with two of its tentacles. She leaped back, her fear threatening to overpower her. Make her numb. Make her clumsy.

"Micaela!" she shouted. "There's got to be more."

But Micaela was chanting a protective spell to

shield Giles and Ethan—a spell that might hold back some of the others, but wouldn't affect Belphegor in the least. She had no words to spare for Buffy.

Then suddenly, Buffy saw the words written down, in what she had to assume was Ethan's handwriting.

But why should she trust him? For all she knew, Ethan had cut a deal with Belphegor. He was still alive, wasn't he?

"Ethan, damn it," she muttered to herself. "Wake up and tell me what to do," she said.

He remained as he was. But it wasn't really Ethan she wanted advice from. It was Giles. And maybe her mother, too. The two people whose expectations she had railed against so often . . . now she wanted nothing more than their counsel.

With a sickening expulsion of air, Belphegor came at her with all it possessed—mouths, whipping tentacles—and Buffy's Slayer reflexes came into play. She dodged and kicked and hit and she would have bitten him if she'd thought it would help.

A wind whipped up. The sky went black and lightning pierced the road around them. Dozens of Otherworld creatures and zombies shot into flame. They ran screaming.

Belphegor was clearing an arena for their combat.

Surrounded by flames erupting several stories high, Buffy leaped forward and grabbed a sword from a trapped man who was half-horse, half-goat, soon to be neither because he was on fire. She had to run him through to make him let go of the sword, and she was a little sorry for that. Then a woman with snakes for hair rushed her, and Buffy cut off her head. The walking dead came, and Belphegor burned them at the same time that Buffy fought them away. For a few bizarre moments, they acted together, toward the same goal.

Then they faced off again. Buffy's chest was heaving. Her legs were so tired they were shaking. But she kept her chin up and her voice steady as she flung at it, "Okay, you big, ugly thing. No more time to waste. Let's do it."

"Excellent," Belphegor said, with deep and obvious satisfaction.

The windstorm rose around her, fanning the flames of the fire. Cinders singed her and her hair began to smoke. Her arms blistered and the sword was growing white-hot. If she didn't defeat the demon soon, she would probably burn to death.

She didn't care what happened to her if she could save the world. Not in this fierce, surreal moment when she faced the one thing even the Gatekeepers feared. This was no minor demon, the likes of which she'd fought and killed dozens of times. This was one of the Lords of Hell, one of the most powerful creations of the inferno. In its path, the Slayer was so very small. This kind of evil was supposed to be confronted by a host of angels, or whatever.

But Sunnydale didn't have any angels.

It only had Buffy.

Again, unbidden, Ethan's words snapped into focus. She shook her head, but the words were etched into her eyelids.

He watches the world of man with human eyes;
The eyes of man, the darkest passage;
The path he must follow, the world which he
covets;
Belphegor, scion of worlds old and new;

Wanderer in Darkness, shying from infernal flame;
Yet the dawn of man shall not burn his eyes;
Yet the sword of man shall not cut him down;
For man's only weapon must be himself.

Man's only weapon . . .

Buffy took a deep breath and threw down the sword.

From somewhere beyond the circle, Micaela shouted, "What on earth are you doing?"

"The sword won't do any good," Buffy said. "I'm the weapon."

At that, Belphegor withdrew just a little, retreated maybe one or two inches. Buffy felt a flicker of triumph. What was the rest of the incantation? *He watches the world of man with human eyes; The eyes of man, the darkest passage . . .*

But what did that mean exactly? She had to fight him herself, that seemed clear. Her own hands, that was all. But what good were her bare hands, no matter how hard she hit, against *that?* Unless the references to human flesh, man's weapon . . . maybe the weapon wasn't only her strength, but its weakness.

But Belphegor did not watch the world with human eyes. Its eyes were crescent-shaped and lizardlike. Red. Not human at all.

Forcing herself to stand upright in the wild wind, Buffy frowned. Her hair streamed behind her. She didn't understand. She was going to fail because she didn't understand.

"Ethan!" she shouted. "Giles!"

Belphegor raised its tentacles and they whipped out at her. One of them slapped her in the face and she tumbled to the blacktop. She heard her nose break and felt the crunch of bone, the immediate torrent of blood down her cheeks.

The tentacles lashed at her, ripping out chunks of flesh along her back and the backs of her arms. She tried to get up, but the weight was too great. The pain was unimaginable. She couldn't groan, couldn't breathe. Couldn't think.

It traveled toward her. She felt its nearness, smelled its rotten odor. She couldn't help but vomit.

Then the tentacles rose for another onslaught, and the Slayer rolled out of the way and onto her back.

That was when Belphegor leaned over her. And looked at her with its demonic eyes.

And also with the single, massive eye in the center of its forehead, which began to open slowly. The thickness she had assumed was a scar was its eyelid.

It was a human eye. Overly large, true, but not at all like the others.

Belphegor said, *"This was too easy, Slayer. You disappoint me."*

Grunting, Buffy managed a flip to her feet. She whirled around and jumped as hard and high as she could. Extending both arms, she took a breath. Her right hand hit Belphegor's third eye. For a moment it pressed against the membrane, and then pierced it. Belphegor shrieked and tried to jerk away.

Yes, Buffy thought.

Keeping hold, her fingers shoved through the layers, hitting the fluid beyond, and the horned curve of the socket.

Black liquid sprayed her in a torrent. She hung, her fingers grabbing around the socket, and shot her other hand through the ruins of the eye.

Then, with both hands, she pulled outward, yanking the bits and pieces from Belphegor's forehead.

It screamed with fury and threw her to the ground. Its tentacles flapped wildly. It bent over her with its mouths slashing and cutting.

Buffy fought back with every ounce of her strength, with every fiber of her being. She kicked, she punched, and now she bit.

She hit, and hit, and hit.

She kept hitting, even with the wind died down and the fires banked, and the wail of ambulances keened in the distance.

Until Micaela, beside her on the ruined section of roadbed, touched her shoulder and said, "Buffy, it's dead."

In Boston, the great sorcerer Giacomo Fulcanelli, sometimes known as Il Maestro, shrieked in rage and horror and agony as his barely human, centuries-old body burst into flame and withered in an instant.

Tied so long to the demon Belphegor, his soul had been claimed at last.

At the windows of the Gatehouse, Willow stared, wide-eyed, as Fulcanelli burned. The Gatehouse solidified once more. An instant later, the demons simply disappeared, leaving only the beauty of a spring dawn on Beacon Hill.

With Oz at her side, she began to cry.

Buffy and Micaela stood over the still forms of Giles and Ethan Rayne and watched as the hole at the center of Belphegor's head became a kind of abyss, a dark void that grew and grew. The demons screeched and wailed as they were dragged toward it, into that portal to Hell.

"The eyes of man," Buffy croaked weakly. "The darkest passage."

By ripping out that eye, she had opened a passage into Hell. But its horrible vortex did not affect her, nor anything else of the human world. Even as the last of the demons was pulled through, the police sirens still a short distance away, the creatures of the Otherworld began to scream as well.

One by one, in rapid succession, they disappeared into nothingness.

Buffy glanced at Micaela. "So, I guess the Gatekeeper got things under control."

The burgeoning sorceress smiled. "Or something like that."

The sun would not rise for several hours, but to Buffy, it felt like dawn had already arrived.

GILES'S EYES FLUTTERED OPEN. HE COULD HEAR BIRD-song outside the open window, and a light breeze blew across his face. It was quite pleasant, actually. Until his vision came into focus, and he realized that he was, once again, in hospital.

"Oh, this is just too bloody much," he murmured, and tried to sit up a bit, only to be defeated by a sudden bolt of pain, and an overall weakness that made him despair.

Then, into that despair, a ray of light.

A soft smile on her face, her honey-blond hair flowing over her shoulders, Micaela Tomasi moved to the edge of his bed and reached, so tenderly, for his hand.

"Rupert," she breathed.

Giles offered a pained half smile in return. He hoped she understood that it was the best he could manage at the moment.

"You look well," he observed.

And it was an understatement. She looked simply smashing. But rather than the velvet she had donned the night they'd met, today she had chosen more casual attire: blue jeans and a scarlet silk shirt.

"Whereas I," he continued, "probably look rather catastrophic."

She chuckled at that. "You look a damn sight better than you did when they brought you in here."

Giles considered that a moment, and then realized she meant that his healing had been helped along by a spot of magick.

"I guess I should thank you for that," he said, truly touched.

"Well, me . . . and Ethan," she said.

He blinked. "I see. That's a bit of a surprise. And Ethan's gone now, is he?"

"Long gone," Micaela replied, grinning now. "In fact, when he was done here, Buffy couldn't get rid of him fast enough."

"Ah yes, Buffy. Tell me, how did she defeat Belphegor, after all?"

"I'm sure she'll explain it to you, Rupert. As for me, I . . ."

Her words trailed off, and then Micaela's smile began to crack. Then it disappeared entirely, and tears began to well up in her eyes. Giles started to speak, to ask her what was wrong, but she shushed him, and bent over to press her lips lightly, lovingly, against his, before he could protest.

Not that he had any intention of protesting.

The kiss was long and tender, and when Micaela broke away, Giles took a deep breath. There were so many questions involved in his . . . attraction to Micaela. She had been so badly used by Fulcanelli for so long, and she had acquitted herself well, no doubt. But she had betrayed the Council, and him personally, and he was afraid that no matter what else, there would always be a lingering taint between them because of those actions.

"I know what you're thinking," Micaela said quickly. "And you should stop."

Giles raised his eyebrows and looked at her guiltily. "I'm sorry?"

"I'm going back, Rupert," she said quickly, turning to look out the window, avoiding his gaze. "I'm going back to London to present myself to the Watchers' Council. I'll tell them everything, and then I'm going to ask them what it would take for them to begin to trust me again."

She turned to face him, her features grimly determined.

"It's what I must do. I've done a great deal of wrong, and I intend to begin making up for it."

Giles swallowed. There were so many things he wanted to say, but they were things that Micaela already knew. Instead, he merely reached out for her.

She came to him, and he held her hands in his.

"You already have, Micaela, you already have," he said.

"I won't forget you," she said quickly.

"I won't let you," he scolded.

Less than ten minutes after Micaela left, Buffy swept into the room with her mother, both of them loaded down with flowers. Buffy trailed multicolored balloons as well.

"Hey, look who's awake!" Buffy said happily.

Joyce put a hand on her daughter's shoulder and greeted Giles warmly.

"Flowers from, well, everyone!" Buffy exclaimed. "And the balloon bouquet, from Xander and Cordy."

"Balloon bouquet?" Giles replied. "What an insidious concept."

"That's just what I said," Buffy nodded. "But I didn't know what it meant either."

Giles didn't have the energy to engage in the usual Buffy banter, but he was extremely pleased to see her in any case. She looked like, well, Buffy. And that's all Giles had prayed for.

"I'm so glad you're all right," he told her.

"We all are," Joyce confirmed. "This has been almost an entire month of hell, like nothing else you guys have run into. I know that Buffy has a . . . well, a duty to the world, but I hope she never has to go through anything like this again."

Giles felt it then, that moment of tension between himself and Joyce Summers, between her expectations and hopes for Buffy's future, and Giles's terrible knowledge of the girl's duty and destiny.

But all he said was, "So do I."

Buffy glanced back and forth between Giles and her mom. But before she could break up the staring contest, the two smiled at one another again, and all was right with the world.

"So, Buffy, how *did* you defeat Belphegor?" Giles asked.

Buffy opened her mouth to respond, and then glanced at her mother. "Y'know," she said, "maybe that's a story for another time. Mom's getting over a stomach bug and, well, it was pretty vomitrocious."

"Wonderful," Joyce said, rolling her eyes.

"But all is back to normal, eh? In Sunnydale, and at the Gatehouse?"

"Yeah," Buffy said, mind wandering. "The Gatehouse."

"Buffy? What is it?" Giles prodded.

She shrugged. "Nothing, I guess. Just thinking about Jacques. It really sucks for him. I mean, he's just a kid, and now he has all this responsibility just dumped on him. It isn't like he had a choice, right? I mean, he's a Regnier, so there you go, bam! Gatekeeper. And if he tries to blow it off, the whole world's in jeopardy."

Joyce pulled her daughter into a tight embrace and kissed Buffy's hair.

"Sounds a lot like someone else I know," she said softly. "And you're right, honey. It does suck. I'd do anything to make it all go away for you. But I can't. I'm just your mother."

Buffy smiled wanly at that, pulled back, and gave her mom a kiss on the cheek.

"Yup," Buffy said. "I guess we all have our destinies. Yours is to worry like hell, and then be there to tell me it's gonna be all right when I get home."

Joyce smiled back. "You know what? I can do that."

"But all is back to normal, eh? In Buffy's case, and at the Gatehouse."

"Yeah," Buffy said, mind wandering. "The Gatehouse."

"Buffy? What is it?" Giles prodded.

She shrugged. "Nothing, I guess. Just thinking about the Gatehouse. It really sucks for Bauer. I mean, he's just a kid . . . and now he has all this responsibility just dumped on him. It isn't like he had a choice, right? I mean, life's a Slayer, somewhere you're, Aunt Gatekeeper. And if he tries to blow it off, the whole world's in jeopardy."

Joyce pulled her daughter into a tight embrace and kissed Buffy's hair.

"Sounds a lot like someone else I know," she said softly. "And you're right, honey, it does suck. I'd do anything to make it all go away for you. But I can't. I'm just your mother."

Buffy smiled warily at that, pulled back, and gave her mom a kiss on the cheek.

"Yup," Buffy said. "I guess we all have our destinies. Yours is to worry like that and then be there to tell me it's gonna be all right when I get home."

Joyce smiled back. "You know what I can do that."

About the Authors

CHRISTOPHER GOLDEN is a novelist, journalist, and comic book writer. His novels include the vampire epics *Of Saints and Shadows, Angel Souls & Devil Hearts,* and *Of Masques and Martyrs;* the recent hardcover *X-Men: Codename Wolverine,* the upcoming *Strangewood,* and six *Buffy* novels written with Nancy Holder. His latest project is a series of young adult mysteries for Pocket, the first of which, *Body Bags,* is on sale now. Golden's comic book work includes *The Punisher,* as well as *Punisher/Wolverine, The Crow,* and *Spider-Man Unlimited,* and a number of *Buffy* comic book projects.

The editor of the Bram Stoker Award–winning book of criticism *CUT!: Horror Writers on Horror Film,* he has written articles for *The Boston Herald, Disney Adventures,* and *Billboard,* among others, and was a regular columnist for the worldwide service BPI Entertainment News Wire. He is one of the authors of the recently released book *The Watcher's Guide,* the official companion to *Buffy the Vampire Slayer.*

Golden was born and raised in Massachusetts, where he still lives with his family. He graduated from Tufts University. Please visit him at www.christophergolden.com.

NANCY HOLDER has written three dozen books and over 200 short stories. She has worked on nine *Buffy* projects, including six novels and *The Watcher's Guide* with Christopher Golden (with assistance from Keith R.A. DeCandido), as well as *The Angel Chronicles,* volumes 1 and 3, and *The Evil That Men Do. Gambler's Star: Legacies and Lies,* the second book in her science-fiction trilogy for Avon Books, is available now. She also writes novels based on the TV show *Sabrina the Teenage Witch,* for Archway/Minstrel.

Holder is a former editor with FTL Games, as well as the author of comic books and TV commercials in Japan. She has also taught writing. Recent short story appearances include "Little Dedo" in *In the Shadow of the Gargoyle,* and "Appetite," in *Hot Blood X.*

She has received four Bram Stoker Awards, one for her novel *Dead in the Water* and three for short stories. She also received a sales award from Amazon.com for *The Angel Chronicles. Volume 1.* She has been published in over two dozen languages and is a former trustee of the Horror Writers Association.

Holder lives in Southern California with her husband and daughter. A former ballet dancer, she graduated from the University of California at San Diego.

Golden and Holder started working together when Holder sold an essay to Golden's *CUT! Horror Writers on Horror Films.* They write together via the Internet, and to date have collaborated on seven books as well as short fiction, including "Hiding," for *The Ultimate Hulk,* and "Ate," which appeared in *Vampire Magazine* in the U.S. and Canada, and *Vampire Dark* in France.